Outstanding praise for Lori Handeland and

Blue Moon

"*Blue Moon* is fantastic—one of the best books I've read in a long, long time. Anyone who reads paranormal will love this book and anyone who loves suspense should love it as well. It's an edge-of-the-seat read."

—Christine Feehan, author of *Dark Melody*

"Chilling and sizzling by turns! Lori Handeland has the kind of talent that comes along only once in a blue moon. Her sophisticated, edgy voice sets her apart from the crowd, making her an author to watch, and *Blue Moon* a novel not to be missed."

—Maggie Shayne, author of *Edge of Twilight*

"Presenting an interesting and modern twist on the werewolf legend, Lori Handeland's *Blue Moon* is an intriguing mixture of suspense, clever humor, and sensual tension that never lets up. Vivid secondary characters in a rural, small-town setting create an effective backdrop for paranormal events. Will Cadotte is a tender and sexy hero who might literally be worth dying for. But the real revelation in the book is Handeland's protagonist, police officer Jessie McQuade, a less-than-perfect heroine who is at once self-deprecating, tough, witty, pragmatic and vulnerable. She draws you into the story and holds you there until the very end."

—Susan Krinard, author of *To Catch a Wolf*

"Scary sexy fun. A book this clever only comes along once in a Blue Moon."

—Rachel Gibson, author of *Daisy's Back in Town*

Blue Moon

Lori Handeland

St. Martin's Paperbacks

BLUE MOON

Copyright © 2004 by Lori Handeland.
Excerpt from *Hunter's Moon* copyright © 2004 by Lori Handeland.

ISBN: 0-312-94939-1
EAN: 80312-94939-6

Printed in the United States of America

St. Martin's Paperbacks edition / October 2004

St. Martin's Paperbacks are published by St. Martin's Press, 175 Fifth Avenue, New York, NY 10010.

10 9 8 7 6 5 4

For my husband, Michael:
Who has always believed

Chapter 1

The summer I discovered the world was not black-and-white—the way I liked it—but a host of annoying shades of gray was the summer a lot more changed than my vision.

However, on the night the truth began I was still just another small-town cop—bored, cranky, waiting, even wishing, for something to happen. I learned never to be so open-ended in my wishes again.

The car radio crackled. "Three Adam One, what's your ten-twenty?"

"I'm watching the corn grow on the east side of town."

I waited for the imminent spatter of profanity from the dispatcher on duty. I wasn't disappointed.

"You'd think it was a goddamned full moon. I swear those things bring out every nut cake in three counties."

My lips twitched. Zelda Hupmen was seventy-five if she was a day. A hard-drinking, chain-smoking throwback to the good times when such a lifestyle was commonplace and the fact it would kill you still a mystery.

Obviously Zelda had yet to hear the scientific findings, since she was going to outlive everyone by smoking unfiltered Camels and drinking Jim Beam for breakfast.

"Maybe the crazies are just gearing up for the blue moon we've got coming."

"What in living hell is a blue moon?"

The reason Zee was still working third shift after countless years on the force? Her charming vocabulary.

"Two full moons in one month makes a blue moon on the second course. Very rare. Very powerful. If you're into that stuff."

Living in the north woods of Wisconsin, elbow to elbow with what was left of the Ojibwe nation, I'd heard enough woo-woo legends to last a lifetime.

They always pissed me off. I lived in a modern world where legends had no place except in the history books. To do my job, I needed facts. In Miniwa, depending on who you talked to, facts and fiction blurred together too close for my comfort.

Zee's snort of derision turned into a long, hacking cough. I waited, ever patient, for her to regain her breath.

"Powerful my ass. Now get yours out to Highway One-ninety-nine. We got trouble, girl."

"What kind of trouble?" I flicked on the red lights, considered the siren.

"Got me. Cell call—lots of screaming, lots of static. Brad's on his way."

I had planned to inquire about the second officer on duty, but, as usual, Zee answered questions before they could even be asked. Sometimes she was spookier than anything I heard or saw on the job.

"It'll take him a while," she continued. "He was at the other end of the lake, so you'll be first on the scene. Let me know what happens."

Since I'd never found screaming to be good news, I stopped *considering* the siren and sped my wailing vehicle in the direction of Highway 199.

The Miniwa PD consisted of myself, the sheriff, and

six other officers, plus Zee and an endless array of young dispatchers—until summer, when the force swelled to twenty because of the tourists.

I hated summer. Rich fools from Southern cities traveled the two-lane highway to the north to sit on their butt next to a lake and fry their skin the shade of fuchsia agony. Their kids shrieked, their dogs ran wild, they drove their boats too fast and their minds too slow, but they came into town and spent their easy money in the bars, restaurants, and junk shops.

As annoying as the tourist trade was for a cop, the three months of torture kept Miniwa on the map. According to my calendar, we had just entered week three of hell.

I came over a hill and slammed on my brakes. A gas-sucking, lane-hogging luxury SUV was parked crosswise on the dotted yellow line. A single headlight blazed; the other was a gaping black hole.

Why the owner hadn't pulled the vehicle onto the shoulder I had no idea. But then, I'd always suspected the majority of the population were too stupid to live.

I inched my squad car off the road, positioning my lights on the vehicle. Leaving the red dome flashing, I turned off the siren. The resulting hush was as deafening as the shrill wail had been.

The clip of my boots on the asphalt made a lonely, ghostly sound. If my headlights hadn't illuminated the hazy outline of a person in the driver's seat, I'd have believed I was alone, so deep was the silence, so complete the stillness of the night.

"Hello?" I called.

No response. Not a hint of movement.

I hurried around the front of the car, taking in the pieces of the grille and one headlight splayed across the pavement. For a car that cost upward of $40,000 it sure broke into pieces easily enough.

That's what I liked about the department's custom-issue Ford Crown Victoria. The thing was built like a tank, and it drove like one, too. Other cities might have switched over to SUVs, but Miniwa stuck with the tried and true.

Sure, four-wheel drive was nice, but sandbags in the trunk and chains on the tires worked just as well. Besides, nothing had an engine like my CV. I could catch damn near anyone driving that thing, and she didn't roll if I took a tight curve.

"Miniwa PD," I called as I skirted the fender of the SUV.

My gaze flicked over the droplets of blood that shone black beneath the silver moonlight. They trailed off toward the far side of the road. I took a minute to check the ditch for any sign of a wounded animal or human being, but there was nothing.

Returning to the car, I yanked open the door and blinked to find a woman behind the wheel. In my experience men drove these cars—or soccer moms. I saw no soccer balls, no kids, no wedding ring. *Hmm.*

"Are you all right?"

She had a bump on her forehead and her eyes were glassy. Very young and very blond—the fairy princess type—she was too petite to be driving a vehicle of this size, but—I gave a mental shrug—it was a free country.

The airbag hadn't deployed, which meant the car was a piece of shit or she hadn't been going very fast when she'd hit . . . whatever it was she'd hit.

I voted on the latter, since she wasn't lying on the pavement shredded from the windshield. The bump indicated she hadn't been wearing her seat belt. Shame on her. A ticketing offense in this state, but a little hard to prove after the fact.

"Ma'am," I tried again when she continued to stare at me without answering. "Are you all right? What's your name?"

She raised her hand to her head. There was blood dripping down her arm. I frowned. No broken glass, except on the front of the car, which appeared to be more plastic than anything else. How had she cut herself?

I grabbed the flashlight from my belt and trained it on her arm. Something had taken a bite-sized chunk out of the skin between her thumb and her wrist.

"What did you hit, ma'am?"

"Karen." Her eyes were wide, pupils dilated; she was shocky. "Karen Larson."

Right answer, wrong question. The distant wail of a siren sliced through the cool night air, and I permitted myself a sigh of relief. Help was on the way.

Since the nearest hospital was a forty-minute drive, Miniwa made do with a small general practice clinic for everything but life-threatening crises. Even so, the clinic was on the other end of town, a good twenty minutes over dark, deserted roads. Brad could transport Miss Larson while I finished up here.

But first things first. I needed to move her vehicle out of the road before someone, if not Brad, plowed into us. Thank God Highway 199 at 3:00 A.M. was not a hotbed of traffic, or there'd be more glass and blood on the pavement.

"Ma'am? Miss Larson, we need to move. Slide over."

She did as I ordered, like a child, and I quickly parked her car near mine. Planning to retrieve my first-aid kit and do some minor cleaning and repairs—perhaps bandage her up just enough to keep the blood off the seats— I paused, half in and half out of the car, when she answered my third question as late as the second.

"Wolf. I hit a wolf."

A litany of Zee's favorites ran through my head. The wolves were becoming a problem. They followed the food, and with the deer herds increasing in alarming numbers despite the generosity of the Department of Natural Resources with hunting licenses, the wolves had multiplied along with their prey. The wolves were not typically aggressive; however, if they were wounded or rabid, *typical* did not apply.

"Did it bite you, ma'am?"

I knew the answer, but I had to ask. For the record.

She nodded. "I-I thought it was a dog."

"Damn big dog," I muttered.

"Yes. Damn big," she repeated. "It ran right in front of my car. I couldn't stop. Black like the night. Chasing, chasing—" She frowned, then moaned as if the effort of the thought was too much for her poor head.

"How did you get bitten?"

"I thought it was dead."

A good rule to remember when dealing with wild animals and soap opera villains? They usually aren't dead—even when everyone thinks that they are.

"Ma'am, I'm just going to check your license and registration, okay?"

She nodded in the same zoned-out manner she'd had all along. I didn't smell alcohol, but even so, she'd be checked for that and drugs at the clinic.

I quickly rifled her wallet. Yep, Karen Larson. The registration in the glove compartment proved she owned the car. All my ducks were in a row, just the way I liked them.

Brad arrived at last. Young, eager, he was one of the summer cops, which meant he wasn't from here. Who knows what he did during the other nine months of the year. From the looks of him he lifted weights and worked on his tan beneath an artificial sun. Having dealt with Brad before, I was of the opinion he'd fried his brain along with his skin. But he was competent enough to take Miss Larson to the clinic.

I met him halfway between his car and hers. "We've got a wolf bite." I had no time for chitchat. Not that I would have bothered even if I did. "Get her to the clinic. I'm going to see if I can find the wolf."

He laughed. "Right, Jessie. You're gonna catch a wolf, in the middle of the night, in these woods. And it'll be the particular wolf you're searching for."

That's why Brad was a summer cop and I was an all-through-the-year cop. I had a brain and I wasn't afraid to use it.

"Call me silly," I pointed at the blood, plastic, and fiberglass on the pavement, "but that's gonna leave a mark. If I find a wolf with a fender-sized dent, I'll just arrest him. Who knows, we might be able to avoid rabies shots for our victim."

Brad blinked. "Oh."

"Yeah. 'Oh.' Can you call Zee, tell her what happened, have her inform the DNR?"

"Why?"

I resisted the urge to thump him upside the head. Maybe I'd shake some sense loose, but I doubted it. "Standard procedure when dealing with wolves is to call the hunting and fishing police."

"Do we have to?"

Though I shared his sentiments—no one around here had much use for the Department of Natural Resources—rules were rules.

The wolf had been an endangered species in Wisconsin until 1999, when the classification was changed to threatened. Recently they had increased in number to the point where they were delisted. Which meant problems—like rabies—could be handled under certain conditions by certain people. If I had to shoot a wolf tonight, I wanted to do so with my butt already covered.

"Yes," I snapped. "We have to. Have Zee get someone else out here to secure, then measure this scene." I patted the walkie-talkie on my belt. "I'll be in touch."

"But— Uh, I was thinking . . . Maybe, um, I should, uh, you know . . ." His uncertain gaze flicked toward the trees, then back to me.

"I know. And you shouldn't."

Think. Ever. My mind mocked, but I had learned a few things in my twenty-six years, and one of them was to keep my smart-ass mind's comments to myself. Mostly.

"I've lived here all my life, Brad. I'm the best hunter on the force."

A fact that did not endear me to many of the guys I worked with. I couldn't recall the last time I hadn't taken top prize in the Big Buck contests run by the taverns every fall. Still Brad appeared uneasy at letting me wander off alone into the darkness.

"Relax," I soothed. "I know these woods. You don't."

Without waiting for further argument, I went in after the wolf.

Chapter 2

I'd learned to follow a blood trail before I grew breasts.

Not from my father. No. He disappeared right about the time I uttered the word *Da-da*. I should have kept my mouth shut. But that was nothing new.

My mother was, make that is, a true girlie-girl. She never knew what to make of a daughter who preferred to play with boys, shoot guns, and get dirty. She still doesn't.

I was a wild child. Not her fault, though she blames herself. I don't think I turned out too bad. I'm a cop, not a delinquent. That has to be good for something.

Except my mother's approval. I gave up on that a long time ago.

I don't hear much from her these days. If she couldn't have the perfect daughter, she'd hoped for perfect grandchildren—as if she'd get them from me. Marriage and family aren't high on my list of priorities.

Oh, wait—they aren't on the list at all.

I had no doubt Miss Larson's wolf was long gone; still I couldn't just give up without trying. It wasn't in me.

Following a blood trail through the dark was a neat trick, one I'd picked up from my best friend in the sixth grade, Craig Simmons, who'd learned it from his best friend in the fifth grade, George Standwater.

The Indian kids didn't mix much with the white kids, and vice versa, despite any smiley-faced propaganda to the contrary. Once in a while a few became friends, but it never lasted long. The adults, on both sides, took care of that.

I'll never forget how awful Craig felt when his parents told him he couldn't see George anymore. Kind of how I felt, I'm sure, when Craig decided he'd rather play with girls in the Biblical sense and he no longer had any need for a friend-girl like Jessie McQuade.

With a near audible whoosh, the forest closed in around me, leaving the civilized world of cars, electric lights, and roads behind. Beneath the canopy of the evergreens and birch trees I could barely see the stars. That's how a lot of losers got lost.

I'd learned in my years on the force that quite a few more people disappeared than the public ever heard about. Miniwa was no exception. Folks walked into the woods on a regular basis and never came out.

Not me. I had my flashlight, my gun, and my compass. I could stay out here for days and find my way home, too, even without the antiquated walkie-talkie.

The machine chose that moment to crackle, so I shut if off. All I needed was to get close to the wolf and have Zee cuss a blue streak through the receiver. I'd have one chance, if that, and I wasn't going to blow it.

I wished momentarily for a rifle. With a pistol I'd have to get awfully close, but we didn't keep long-range firearms in the squad cars. They were all locked up safe and tight back at the station—where they were of no use to me at all.

The blood trail veered right, then left, then right again. Nearing three-quarter size, the moon was blaring bright. The kind of night most animals kept to the forest, spooked into hiding by the shiny disc in the sky. Except for the wolves. They seemed to like it.

Tonight, I liked it, too. Because the silver sheen bounced off a glistening splotch on the ground here, a leaf there. That the blood was still wet gave me hope my quarry might not be too far ahead. The wolf could even be dead, which would solve a whole lot of problems.

Still, I kept my gun handy. I knew better than to follow a wounded wild animal without protection.

The breeze ruffled the short length of my hair and I paused, lifted my face to the night, then cursed. I was upwind. If the wolf wasn't dead, he knew I was coming.

A howl split the night, rising on the breeze, sifting through the darkness, and fleeing toward the moon. Not the soulful sound of a lonely animal searching for a mate, but the furious, aggressive wail of a dominant male, which caused the back of my neck to tingle.

He knew I was coming, and he was ready.

My adrenaline kicked in. I wanted to move faster. Get there. Fight, not flee. Finish this. But I had to follow the blood, and that hadn't gotten any easier.

Then, suddenly, the trail was gone. I backtracked. Located the blood again. Moved forward, found nothing.

My wolf seemed to have disappeared into thin air. Uneasy, I glanced up at the swaying silhouettes of the trees. A laugh escaped, the sound more nervous than amused. What kind of wolf could climb a tree? Not one that I wanted to meet.

A movement ahead had me scurrying forward, damn the blood trail. I burst through the brush and into a clearing, nearly stumbled, and fell at the sight of a shiny log cabin that hadn't been there a few weeks ago. Had it sprouted from the dirt?

My curiosity about the new house vanished when my gaze lit on a swaying, shivering bush at the far side of the clearing. The windows of the cabin were dark. If I was lucky, the occupants were asleep or, even better, not in residence. I didn't want to scare anyone with gunshots outside their new home at 4:00 A.M., but I wasn't going to let my quarry get away, either.

Gun drawn, I advanced.

A single, glistening drop of blood on a leaf made me cock my pistol. The bush stilled.

I was so tense my body ached with it. I couldn't just shoot without knowing what was there. But what if the wolf leaped out, jaws slashing before I could fire?

Decisions, decisions. I hated them. Give me a nice, sure, clean shot any day. Black-and-white. Right and wrong. Good versus evil.

"Hey!" I shouted, hoping the wolf would run the other way and I could blast him.

No such luck. The bush began to shake again, and a shadow lifted, lengthened, grew broader, and took the shape of a man.

A very handsome, well-proportioned, naked man.

"What the—?"

From far to the north came the cry of a wolf, silencing my question, reminding me I needed to move on.

Ignoring the naked man—which wasn't easy, he was quite spectacular and I hadn't seen one in a long, long time—I searched the ground and the trees for the blood trail. However, it was well and truly gone this time.

"Damn it!" I holstered my weapon.

"Problem?"

His voice was deep, almost soothing, flowing like water over smooth stones. He was taller than me by a good five inches, which made him six-three in bare feet. The moon shone silver across his golden skin, which appeared to be the same hue all over. He obviously had no qualms about going bare-assed beneath the sun as well as the moon.

He stared at me calmly, as if he didn't know, or maybe just didn't care, that he'd forgotten his clothes when he'd stepped outside.

Well, if he could be nonchalant, so could I. "Did a wolf run through here?"

He crossed his arms over his chest. His biceps flexed; so did the muscles in his stomach. I couldn't help myself. I stared. Ridges and dips in all the right places. He'd been working out.

"Seen enough?" he murmured.

With no small amount of difficulty, I raised my gaze to his face. I refused to be embarrassed. He was the one standing naked in the night.

"Why? Is there more?"

His teeth flashed against the darker shade of his face. His eyes were black, his hair, too, and nearly as short as my own. A golden feather swung from one ear.

Interesting. Most Native American jewelry was silver.

If he were white, he'd take a lot of heat for that earring in a place like Miniwa. This might be a new millennium, but in small Midwestern towns earrings were for faggots, just as tattoos were for motorcycle gangs. Unless you were an Indian; then folks just ignored you. However, I doubted a man who looked like he did was ignored by the *entire* population.

"You're after a wolf?"

He stepped from behind the bush, giving me a much clearer view of a whole lot more. My cheeks heated. For all my bravado and smart-mouthed comments, I'd never had much use for men beyond friendship. Probably because they'd never had much use for me.

Still, a girl has needs, or so I discovered beneath the shiny, silver moon.

"You wanna put on some clothes before we chat?" I aimed for a bored, woman-of-the-world tone. I got a breathless, sexy rasp. To cover my embarrassment I snapped, "What are you doing out here?"

"I'm not *out* anywhere. This is my place, my land. And I don't have to explain anything. You're trespassing."

"Hot pursuit. Exigent circumstances," I mumbled. "Just seems odd to be out in the dark in the buff."

"Why have a cabin in the woods if you can't walk around naked whenever the urge strikes you?"

"Oh, I don't know. Maybe poison ivy in all the wrong places?"

I thought he laughed, but when I glanced at him, he'd turned away. I lost my train of thought again at the sight of his back. The muscles rippled as he moved. Was it hot out here?

"You're chasing a wolf, alone, through the woods in the middle of the night, Officer . . . ?"

Suddenly he was right in front of me. Had I been so entranced with my fantasies that I hadn't noticed him slip in close? Obviously.

A slim, dark finger reached out; the white moon of a nail brushed the nameplate perched on my left breast. " 'McQuade,' " he read, then lifted his eyes to mine.

I had to tilt my head back, not a common occurrence for me. I could usually stare guys straight in the eye, and I was rarely this close to them. They were never naked.

He smelled like the forest—green trees, brown earth, and . . . something wild, something free. I felt as if I were falling into his dark, endless eyes. His cheekbones were sharp, his lips full, his skin perfect. The man was prettier than I was.

I took a giant step back. Just because I was in a woodland clearing with a gorgeous, naked Indian man didn't mean I had to swoon like the heroine of a historical romance novel. I wasn't the type.

"I'm doing my job," I said, as much to answer him as remind myself. "A wolf bit a woman out on the highway. I need to find the thing."

Something flickered in his eyes and was gone so quickly I wasn't sure if I'd seen anything beyond the shift of the moon through the trees.

"I doubt you'll succeed." He turned away again, and this time my gaze caught on a nasty bruise along his hip.

"Ouch," I murmured.

"What?"

"I—uh—" I waved my hand vaguely at his ass. "What happened?"

He twisted, glanced down, frowned, then raised his eyes to mine. "I'm not sure. I must have been clumsy."

As he strolled toward the cabin, I watched him move. Funny, he didn't appear clumsy at all.

He plucked a pair of cutoffs from the porch and yanked them on without benefit of underwear. Why I found that incredibly erotic, I have no idea. But there it was.

Not bothering with a shirt, either, he returned. I found myself entranced by his chest. Smooth, strong, no hair to mar the perfection, would he taste as good as he smelled?

I rubbed my eyes to make the image go away. I needed to get laid and fast. When my pulse leaped in response to the thought, my cheeks heated again.

Down, girl, I admonished my panting libido. *You're in the minors; he's a major leaguer.*

Still, I could dream, couldn't I?

"Uh . . . Um. Could you help me pick up the trail?"

Nice, Jessie. Why don't you stutter and drool while you're at it?

Thankfully, he didn't seem to notice my red face and awkward tongue.

"Me?" He ran his fingers through his short hair, frowned, and shook his head, almost as if the cut was new, unfamiliar. His earring danced in the moonlight.

"The blood disappears beyond that bush where you—" I frowned. "You're sure you didn't see him?"

He gave an impatient sigh. "I'm sure."

"Then maybe you could help me pick up the trail again?"

"Why would you think that I know how to track a wolf? Just because I'm Ojibwe?"

"You are?"

He rolled his eyes. "Come on, Officer, you aren't blind and you've been looking."

"You've been showing. I'm also not stupid."

His lips twitched. He nearly smiled before he caught himself. "Even if I knew jack about tracking in the dark, I wouldn't help you find that wolf. You'll kill him."

I shrugged. "He bit a woman. She's going to need rabies shots if I don't find him."

"You won't find him."

Annoyance flashed through me. "You psychic or something?"

"Something."

Whatever that meant.

Chapter 3

As it turned out, he was right. I didn't find that wolf or any other.

The woods were strangely empty that night. I chalked it up to the brightness of the moon and my less than graceful manner of crashing through the underbrush. But later I wondered.

Hell, later I wondered a lot of things.

Like who was that unmasked man? He'd learned my name but never offered his. And I'd had little opportunity to ask.

I'd stepped from the clearing, searching once more for a trace of the trail, and when I glanced back he'd disappeared as suddenly as he'd appeared. Logically I knew he had gone inside—rude as that was without a good-bye—still, I never heard the creak of a porch board or the click of the door.

I moved on, but when the sun came up and I was still empty-handed, I returned to the scene of the accident. Someone had towed Miss Larson's oversize vehicle away, leaving the glass, plastic, and blood behind. Peachy.

I rousted Zee on the radio.

"Damn, girl. Where have you been? I was gonna send out the cavalry pretty soon."

"I'm fine. Didn't Brad tell you where I was?"

"Off in the woods, alone in the night. You nuts?"

"I had a big gun."

"Someday, Jessie, you are gonna meet someone smarter and meaner than you."

"Someday," I agreed.

"I take it you didn't find what you were lookin' for."

The stranger's face, and everything else, flashed through my mind. I'd found something better, but I wasn't going to tell Zee that. As she informed anyone who would listen, she was old; she wasn't dead. She'd want more details about the man than I could comfortably give.

"The wolf is gone," I answered. "Why wasn't this scene secured like I asked?"

"Things got a little busy here. Domestic dispute, bar fight."

"The usual."

"Damn straight. I didn't have anyone free to secure anything but their own ass. What difference does it make anyway? You don't have a major crime scene being contaminated. It's an accident plain and simple."

I'd learned early on that nothing was plain or simple. My gaze swept over the glass and skid marks. Not even this.

"Have you talked to Brad about the victim?" I asked.

"Yeah. He stayed with her until she left, but—"

"Left?"

"You don't have to shout."

"How could she leave? She was bitten by a wild animal. She needs rabies shots."

"Only if she'll take them. And she wouldn't."

"Why not?"

"The clinic didn't have the serum. They could get it

from Clearwater, but it would have taken several hours. She refused."

"That makes no sense."

"Since when does anything make sense?"

Zee had a point. I tried to raise Brad on the radio and got no response. I dialed his cell phone, but he didn't answer. A glance at my watch revealed the shift had changed ten minutes ago. Brad was nothing if not prompt. My opinions on that would have done Zee proud.

The sun was up; I was tired. Working third shift had made me a vampire of sorts, unable to sleep when everyone else did, unable to stay awake when the world was alive.

Despite my exhaustion, and the fact that overtime was a no-no, I vowed to hunt down Brad later and find out what he'd learned from Miss Larson. Right now I'd head to the clinic and talk to the doctor. See if I could find Miss Larson and have a word with her—if she wasn't foaming at the mouth yet.

But first . . . I glanced from my squad car to the glass and plastic still on the pavement. First I got to clean up the mess.

I sketched the scene, measured the skid marks, then swept the remains of the accident into a transparent bag and carried my prize to the side of the road. Holding it up, I jiggled the sack. Something caught my eye.

I reached inside and withdrew a thin rawhide strip. I'd seen them used as necklaces, usually on men, sometimes teenage girls. If there'd been a jewel or a charm threaded onto this one, it could be anywhere.

I jiggled the bag again but saw nothing else unusual. So I walked the center line and found what I was searching for several feet ahead of where the SUV had skidded to a stop.

Leaning down, I picked up a carved onyx figure of a wolf, what the Ojibwe referred to as a totem. As I stared at it the image wavered and shifted. Cool air shot down my sweaty back, making me shiver. I shook my head. For a moment, the wolf's face had appeared almost human. I definitely needed some sleep.

Had the totem been here last night? Or for weeks, perhaps months? What did it mean? To whom did the icon belong? Did it even matter?

I shrugged and dropped the evidence into the bag. I had enough questions to keep me busy most of the morning. Any more could wait for tonight.

My visit to the Miniwa Clinic was not very enlightening. The on-call doctor was young, earnest, and as exhausted as I was. He'd been on duty for forty-eight hours. I was glad I hadn't been brought in bleeding at hour number forty-seven.

"I cleaned the wound, though the officer who brought the victim in had done a decent job of it."

I made a mental note that Brad had been listening in first-aid class. Good boy.

The doctor rested his forehead on one palm and closed his eyes. When he swayed, I grabbed his arm, afraid he was going to tumble face-first onto the floor. "Doc? Hey! You okay?"

"Sorry. It's been a long night—or three."

I made sympathetic noises. Why the medical community insisted on pushing physicians to their physical, emotional, and mental limits was beyond me. Did they believe the doctors who survived the training could then survive anything? Probably.

"Miss Larson," I reminded him.

"Oh, yeah. I treated her like a dog bite victim. Four stitches, antibiotic. Minor really."

"Why did she leave?"

"She had to work."

"Is she a brain surgeon?"

Confusion flickered over his pale face. "I'm sorry?"

"Her work couldn't wait? What if the wolf was rabid?"

"The chances of that are slim, Officer. Rabid animals tend more toward bats or the rodent family—mice, squirrels." He paused, considered a moment, continued. "Or stray cats. Nasty things. You definitely need rabies shots if you get bit by a stray cat."

I didn't plan on getting bit by any stray cats, since it would be an ice-cold day in Miami before I touched one. However, information is always welcome.

The doctor shook his head. "It's highly unlikely that a wolf is carrying rabies."

"Doesn't mean she's in the clear."

"No. But she has the right to refuse treatment."

"And if she starts gnawing on a co-worker, does she have the right to sue you?"

He winced at the word *sue,* an occupational hazard, I'm sure. "You're like a dog with a bone on this."

Dog? Bone?

I waited for him to snicker, but he was either too tired to get his own joke or he was amusement-challenged. Maybe a little bit of both.

"I like all my ends neat and tidy," I continued. "Call me anal. Everyone else does."

His lips never twitched. Definitely amusement-challenged.

"You can follow up." He scribbled on a notepad. "Here's her address and place of business."

Karen Larson's home was located just off Highway 199.

Huh. That huge car had screamed tourist. Getting out of her vehicle to check on an injured wolf shouted moron. If she wasn't a temporary resident, she was at least very new. Until folks had lived here for a winter they always thought they needed huge tires to roll over the huge snowdrifts.

Her address explained her presence on the highway. It did not, however, explain why she was driving home alone at 3.00 A.M. on a weeknight. Maybe I was nosy, but little details like that bugged me. Perhaps that was why I'd become a cop. It gave me license to snoop.

I glanced at the doctor's chicken scratch again. Miss Larson was a teacher at Treetop Elementary.

Though some schools finished before Memorial Day weekend, others, like ours, continued classes nearly all the way through June. This was a direct result of the state lawmakers and their brilliant idea that schools should begin after Labor Day in order to make the most out of the tourist season. None of them ever seemed to understand that this only cut several weeks off the other end of summer.

Since Miss Larson had been so all-fired concerned about work—I glanced at my watch—and she should be there by now, I headed in that direction, too.

My decision was a sound one. By the time I reached Treetop Elementary, there was a whole lot of screaming going on.

I was the first officer on the scene. Probably because everyone was more interested in getting out of the building than dialing 911, although sirens in the distance assured me someone *had* phoned in an emergency.

I wasn't on duty, but what the hell? People running, children screaming, call me silly, but the situation called for a cop.

I parked my squad car at the curb, radioed in my

location, then got out and pushed against the tide of bodies leaving the building. Once inside, I searched for someone in charge. As no one was volunteering, I snagged the arm of the nearest adult. At my touch she shrieked, causing several of the children around her to burst into tears.

Their behavior made me edgy. Had the nightmare of a school shooting reached the north woods? Though I didn't hear any gunfire, that didn't mean there hadn't been any.

"What happened?" I demanded, none too nicely.

"I-I don't know. Down there." She jabbed her free hand back the way she'd come. "Screaming. Crying. Shouting. They said evacuate calmly. Then everyone ran."

Which didn't sound good. Typical, but not good.

I released her, and she ushered the few stragglers onto the lawn.

The school had gone eerily silent. I should probably wait for backup, but if there was a gunman inside I didn't plan to let the little bastard do any more damage than he'd already done.

Honestly, if every child who'd ever been teased or tormented grabbed a weapon, none of us would have survived our school years. What was going on in the world that made kids believe it was all right to solve their troubles with a gun? But then again, who was I to throw stones?

I drew my service revolver and headed down the deserted hallway.

The lack of gunfire and the sudden absence of screaming made it difficult for me to locate the source of the problem. I wouldn't have, except for a slight, nearly undetectable whimper that drifted from a room ahead and to my left.

A sign on the wall outside the door read, MISS LAR-SON. THIRD GRADE.

"Shit," I muttered. "I hate being right."

Having my school shooting scenario go up in smoke should have made me happy. Instead, what I found when I opened the classroom door made me sick.

Karen Larson wasn't well. The fairy princess aura had vanished, the air of fragility, too. Her hair hung across her face in sweaty hanks, only partially obscuring her eyes.

Too bad. Because her eyes reminded me of a man I'd testified against once in an insanity trial. He'd gone to Happy Hill for the rest of his days. But what bothered me more than her appearance was the little boy in her grasp.

He was probably eight years old and not small by any means. Yet she held him aloft with one hand; his Nikes dangled a foot above the floor. His body was limp, though I could see his chest rise and fall with a steady breath.

Unconscious. Good. From the appearance of Miss Larson, life was going to get unpleasant.

"Put him down." I didn't shout, but I didn't whisper, either. Calm but firm worked best in almost any situation.

Miss Larson glanced up. Her mouth was flecked with pink foam. It wasn't a good look for her.

Out of the corner of my eye, I glimpsed another body nearby. Larger. Not a child, but a man. Maybe the janitor, or the principal. He wasn't moving, even to breathe, and there was blood spattered all around. I understood why Miss Larson's foam was pink. *Uck.*

I cocked my gun. My window for playing nice had closed.

"Put him down!" My voice was louder and less calm than before. "Do it, Karen."

She cocked her head like a dog who had recognized its name somewhere in the jumble of human words. I shivered. This was just too weird.

Things got weirder when she growled at me. Seriously. She did. Flecks of foam flew from her mouth, and there were bloodstains on her teeth.

I inched forward and she snarled, tugged the limp boy closer, nuzzled his hair, licked his neck. What happened next I'm not certain.

I would swear to this day that she smiled at me with perfect clarity. As if she were fine, this had all been a mistake. I would also vow, though never out loud, that in the next instant a feral mask descended over her face; the spirit of an animal lived in her eyes.

She lifted her head, reared back as if to tear out the throat of the child in her arms, and a gunshot thundered through the room.

I'll never be able to prove if I imagined the change in Karen Larson or if it was real, because her head snapped back as a bullet took out her brain.

Thank God the kid was unconscious. Considering the mess, I wish I had been.

Chapter 4

Before you get the wrong impression, I didn't shoot her.

I spun around, coming face-to-face with my boss, Sheriff Clyde Johnston.

"Were you gonna shoot that pistol or whistle Dixie?" he grumbled.

If Clyde wasn't three-quarters Indian, he'd be a good old boy to rival them all. As it was, his belly stretched his sheriff's shirt to bursting, the chew in his mouth garbled his speech, and the size of his gun made me remember old jokes about large weapons and small male equipment. His habit of parroting lines from Clint Eastwood movies in normal conversation frayed the patience of better men than me.

His Clint fixation also explained why we carried .44 Magnums in Miniwa when a lot of other departments had moved into the world of semiautomatic weapons. But I agreed with Clyde that revolvers were more reliable than the newfangled automatics, which required a higher quality of ammunition and had a habit of misfiring. When dealing with guns, I vote for reliability over speed any day.

My ears ringing from the volume of the blast, I ran across the room and picked up the little boy. He was still unconscious. A quick glance at the other body, principal from the cut of the suit, revealed he was as dead as Karen Larson, though not from the same cause. Her head sported a large hole. The principal's neck did.

"Guess .44 Magnum *is* the most powerful handgun in the world," Clyde observed. "Nearly blew her head clean off."

This was a bit much, even for me. I headed for the door with the kid and left Clyde to clean up after himself for a change. He took one glance at my face and didn't stop me.

The EMTs were in the hall. I handed the boy to the nearest one. "This is the only known injury. The others are fatalities."

The woman gave a quick, capable nod as she checked him over. "What's his name?"

"Don't know. He was unconscious when I got here. He might not even be hurt. That's not his blood or—" I broke off. No need to detail what else wasn't his.

"Right," she said. "We'll take it from here."

They whisked him off to points unknown, and though I didn't want to, I returned to the crime scene.

Clyde had everything under control. He might look like a fool, but he wasn't. That's how he'd stayed sheriff of Miniwa for thirty years. The Indians trusted him, and the white folks held him up as their token native. That he was smart as a shiny new shoe and had never allowed a crime to go unpunished on his watch didn't hurt, either.

He hovered near the scene, intent on preserving it until the techs and the medical examiner arrived. Miniwa being such a small community, we shared both with Clearwater, across the lake, and several other tiny towns.

As I entered the room, Clyde glanced up, then quirked a dark, bushy brow. "Tell me, Jessie, how is it I find little ol' you in the middle of this great big mess?"

Only a man the size of Clyde would consider me little. I'd be fond of him for that alone, if I were capable of it.

"I was following up on a case."

He frowned. "Which case?"

Since he'd just come on duty and I'd just gone off, Clyde wouldn't have seen my report yet, even if I *had* filed one.

"Minor traffic accident. Miss Larson hit a wolf."

"Who?"

I waved my hand in the direction of body number two.

"Oh. So?"

Quickly I filled him in on the details. Wham, bam, down goes the wolf. Nip the hand, chase through the night, no sign of the animal. Then Miss Larson nixing the rabies shots and her subsequent need for them. I left out the naked Indian part. Clyde wouldn't be interested.

"Huh," he muttered. "Papers are gonna have a field day."

I groaned. Small towns had little to do but gossip. The incidents of the past twelve hours were going to turn into a major media event and quite possibly a serious problem. There'd be gunmen in the woods searching for a rabid wolf—DNR orders be damned. We'd have panic-stricken citizens shooting stray dogs and maybe even stray people.

"Exactly." Clyde spit a brown stream into a nearby garbage can. Hadn't anyone informed him of the horrors of tongue cancer? "Maybe you oughta just keep the wolf story to yourself, hmm?"

"But—"

"No buts. You know what'll happen. Once we take care of the wolf, we'll tell the truth. Where's the harm in that?"

True. However—

"I'll have to talk to Brad and Zee," I said. "But they shouldn't be a problem."

Clyde grunted. "Good. Do that."

"There's also a doctor at the clinic—"

"I'll talk to him."

"Okay." I stood there, uncertain. I wanted to ask Clyde a question, but I wasn't sure how.

"You gotta be draggin', Jessie. Go home. Sleep. I can handle this."

"Not much left to handle," I muttered, eyes on the bodies.

I felt his sharp glare. "You got somethin' else to say? Say it."

He knew as well as I did that I couldn't leave until reinforcements arrived. Clyde had just shot a civilian. There were procedures to follow, not the least of which was taking his gun and giving my statement as a witness. I really shouldn't have left him in the room alone, but what choice did I have with an unconscious child in my arms?

Clyde was a good cop. He'd already bagged his gun. The pistol lay on one of the desks, an obscene reminder of too many other guns in schools.

"Jessie?" Clyde prompted.

I continued to hesitate. Clyde had been sheriff since before I was born; who was I to question his methods? Still I couldn't go home and sleep without asking. My curiosity wouldn't let me.

"Did you have to hit her in the head, Clyde? I mean—" I shrugged, spread my hands. "Wouldn't the leg have worked just as well?"

"I've seen perps keep comin' with bullets in their leg, gut, chest, back. But I've never seen any get up after I put one between their eyes."

"But—"

"She was stark ravin' loony. She'd already killed one man and she had a kid in her hands. You wanna argue head or leg with that boy's mama?"

"No, sir."

"I didn't think you would."

Clyde stared at me for a moment, as if taking my measure. Before he could say anything else, the crime scene techs and two of our officers arrived and got to work. I gave my statement and was released.

The medical examiner had not yet arrived to pronounce the victims. Nothing new there. Dr. Prescott Bozeman was a fuckup if ever there was one.

I glanced at Clyde and received a sharp nod. "We know where to find you if we need you, Jessie McQuade."

All the way home I wondered why his words sounded like a threat when I knew that they weren't.

I managed to sleep a few hours, but something in my subconscious kept pricking at me.

A jumble of memories tumbled through my dreams, conversations, medical jargon, a swinging golden earring, and a wolf totem.

I awoke with the midafternoon sun shining hot across my bed. I'd forgotten to pull the heavy curtains I'd purchased so I could sleep in the daytime and work all night. I had to have been exhausted to forget, equally exhausted to sleep through the brightest part of the day.

But now I was awake, and a question kept pounding in my head like the ache pounding behind my eyes.

What was wrong with this picture?

I crawled into the kitchen, turned on the coffeemaker,

shoved my mug onto the hot plate until it was full, then slammed the carafe into place.

The totem bothered me. If it had been on the road before Karen hit the wolf, it should have been dust. If she'd been wearing it, then why had I found the thing so far from the car?

The only other explanation was the wolf had been wearing the necklace, and I had a hard time buying that.

I yanked out the notes I'd made while I waited for the doctor to speak to me. There it was in blue and white. Karen had said the wolf was chasing . . . something.

I figured a rabbit, but they didn't wear necklaces, either.

Though I was sure the totem would turn out to be nothing important, still its presence at the crime scene disturbed me. I decided to discover what the thing meant and who might have been wearing it.

I poured more coffee and took the cup into the shower with me. One of the joys of living alone—I could pretty much do anything I wanted, whenever I wanted, and no one would say a word.

Not that anyone ever had. My mother disapproved of me, sure. I'd known that even before she skipped off to a real city before I turned nineteen. But she would never have been so crass as to nag or bitch, which made me wonder why my dad had skipped ahead of her. As I'd concluded on those other occasions when I'd wondered, it had to be me he'd been leaving behind.

I had my hair full of shampoo when another jolt of brilliance hit me. Not only was the totem an annoying loose end, but there was something about Miss Larson's rabies that wasn't quite right.

After rinsing my hair none too thoroughly, I wrapped myself in a towel and dripped from the bathroom into the living room, where I tapped a few commands into my computer. Rabies information poured onto the screen like water into a storm sewer.

"Aha!" I exclaimed, and hit the print button.

Rabies had an incubation period in humans from one to three months. If a person was bitten near the brain, or an area that contained a lot of nerve endings such as the hand—*bingo*—symptoms would be accelerated. But I doubted that meant from a few months to a few hours.

If not rabies, then what had turned Miss Larson into a mad killer? I'm not saying that being a teacher is conducive to sanity, but eating the principal is taking things a bit too far.

I needed to have a talk with the medical examiner.

"He isn't in."

I'd taken a chance and shown up at the medical examiner's office without calling first. I should have known better.

We had our share of death in Miniwa; however, the deaths were usually quite easily explained. People wandered off up here more than they did other places. If their bodies were ever recovered, an exception and not a rule, they were not in stellar condition.

The last murder had been ten years past, an open-and-shut case of two men, a woman, and a gun. No mystery there. The guy with the gun had done it, leaving very little in the way of medical examination. Which was lucky, because Prescott Bozeman wasn't much of an examiner.

I stood in his outer office, scowling at his perfectly made up and exquisitely dressed secretary. "It's three-thirty on a weekday," I said. "Where is he?"

"Not in."

I ground my teeth. Bozeman had gotten away with

being lazy in Miniwa because there wasn't a whole hell-uva lot to do. But you'd think that when he did have something, he'd do it.

You'd think.

"Did he even make it to the scene this morning?"

"He was unavailable."

I resisted the urge to smack myself in the forehead. I'd only make my headache worse.

"Who pronounced the victims?"

"I couldn't say."

"Could you say when Bozeman might get around to doing his job?"

Her lips pursed. She didn't like me. Fancy that.

Her eyes wandered from my shorn hair, which was neither blond nor brown but somewhere in between, a color a woman like her could never leave alone, past my gray MINIWA PD T-shirt, to my well-loved and much-worn jeans, which made her pert nose wrinkle.

But it was my expensive running shoes that confounded her. Why would a woman like me, who obviously cared nothing for my appearance or my clothes, spend over a hundred dollars on shoes?

Because happy feet made a happy person. I'd learned that the hard way in cop school.

I took in her three-inch spike heels and sneered. Lucky she sat on her ass all day or she might be a cripple before she was thirty. If not from the angle of those nosebleeders, then from falling off of them one too many times.

I'm tall enough not to bother with high heels, not that I would even if I were an itty-bitty woman like this one. But I could tell, even before she sneered right back at me, that she had classic short person's complex. Being tall was a crime and she was the judge, jury, and executioner. Guess what that made me?

"As you'd know if you'd bothered to check, Officer—"

The way she said "Officer" was reminiscent of the way I said "scum-sucking leech," not that I said it so often, but you get the drift.

"Dr. Bozeman is not in on Tuesdays."

"But—"

"Ever."

"There's been an incident."

"I'm well aware of that."

"He couldn't come in today and take off tomorrow?"

"Unlike yours, Officer, Dr. Bozeman's clients aren't going to run away if he isn't looking. They'll still be here when he is."

Small towns. Gotta love 'em. Or else go crazy living in 'em.

When I exited the office, after leaving my name, various numbers, and a request for Bozeman's final report, I slammed the door. Childish, I know. So slap me.

The next item on my agenda was finding a Native American totem expert. This proved a bit more difficult than I'd thought, considering I lived in a county that boasted a nearly fifty-fifty ratio of Indians to everyone else. But I couldn't exactly walk into the Coffee Pot on Center Street and ask the resident counter warmer where I could find such an expert.

Zee, usually the authority on everything, knew nothing. Like most residents, she wasn't a big supporter of the Indians. They had their lives, she had hers, and never the two should meet. This was the opinion of a lot of the old folks, on both sides of the fence, and too many young ones as well.

I could drive out to the reservation and ask around, but my best bet was Miniwa University. Situated on the largest acreage at the far side of Clearwater Lake, the college had once been a boarding school back in the days when the government had taken Indian children away from their parents and tried to raise them white.

Every time I saw the school, I cringed. What *had* they been thinking?

They hadn't been. Eventually someone had seen the idea for what it was—stupid—and all the children were sent back to where they'd come from. The buildings had slowly reverted to their original use. Learning.

Miniwa was primarily a liberal arts university. However, many of the local Indian scholars, and quite a few from other tribes, became visiting lecturers for a semester or two.

I was confident that someone would know someone who knew something about the totem in my pocket.

I was right. Within five minutes I was directed to the office of William Cadotte, visiting professor from Minnesota and, conveniently, an expert on Native American totems.

I'd heard the name. Cadotte was also an activist, a purveyor of the old ways, to many a troublemaker. Clyde had him on our handy-dandy watch list, though for what I wasn't quite sure.

I followed the directions to a corner office. *William Cadotte* had been scrawled on a piece of paper and taped to the wall. The door was ajar. I glanced inside.

The place was the size of a storage closet, the chairs piled with books. Tiny bits of wood, metal, and stone were scattered across the surface of the desk. With no window, the room smelled stale; the lighting was murky.

A shuffle from the shadows made me straighten and step back. He was inside. I tapped a knuckle against the door.

I expected Dr. Cadotte to be elderly, with a lined,

brown face, heavily veined hands, and a waist-length iron gray ponytail. No such luck.

The door swung open. I didn't recognize him at first. But then, he was wearing clothes.

Chapter 5

He raised a brow. "Miss me?"

I pushed past him into the room, but he was alone. "What did you do with Dr. Cadotte?"

His earring swayed when he tilted his head. "Do?"

He was also wearing glasses. No wonder I hadn't recognized him. Not that the small, round wire frames could detract from the sheer beauty of his face or the intensity of his eyes, but they made him appear . . . older, wiser, scholarly. And sexier than he'd been while standing naked in the moonlight.

I scowled at the unusual direction of my thoughts. Well, unusual for me anyway. I rarely thought about the sexual nature of anyone, specifically a stranger. Though I could be excused in this case, since I'd seen more of this man than almost any other of my acquaintance.

I recovered my sanity enough to hear what he'd said. "Are you Dr. Cadotte?"

"No."

My glance around the area was rhetorical. No one could hide in this joke of an office. I raised a brow.

"I'm William Cadotte, but I'm not a doctor. Yet. There's that pesky matter of a thesis, which I haven't been able to finish." He moved into the room. "Can I help you?"

His voice captured me again as it had last night. Not loud, yet still powerful, the ebb and flow just different enough to make me listen more closely to everything he said.

I'm not sure if he meant to crowd me or not, but the place was small and he was big. His heat brushed my face. Or perhaps I was just blushing again—something I seemed to do a lot of around him.

"No," I blurted. "I mean yes. Hell."

I was blabbering like a teenager. How could he seem taller, broader, more intimidating with his clothes on?

"Which is it? Yes, no, or hell?"

I could smell him, that same scent from last night— wind, trees, a certain wildness. He stared at me intently, as if I fascinated him, and that couldn't be true. A man who looked like he did would not stare at a woman like Jessie McQuade unless he—

My thoughts tumbled into an abyss. Unless he what? There was no reason for him to stare. None. So why was he?

"I wanted to talk to William Cadotte. I didn't know he was you."

"I see." He pulled off his glasses and slipped them into the pocket of his blue work shirt, then patted the pocket gently. "Or actually I don't see very well up close without these. Age and too many books."

I made a noncommittal murmur. He didn't appear much older than me. However, appearances were deceiving. Like a host of other things.

"What did you want to talk about? I assume you don't plan to arrest me for indecent exposure, since you didn't know who I was."

"If you don't mind, I'd like to forget all about that."

"Would you?"

No.

"Yes."

He gave a knowing smirk, which I did my best to ignore.

"Did you catch your wolf?"

" 'Fraid not."

His eyes said, *I told you so,* but to his credit he didn't voice the words.

"Did your bite victim get her shots?"

"Nope. She's a little too dead for them to help."

His mouth opened, shut. He tried to run his fingers through his hair, found nothing there to run them through, and let his hand drop back to his side.

"Isn't that a bit quick, even for rabies?"

I shrugged but didn't elaborate. Clyde wanted to keep things quiet, and I'd already said enough.

"What can I do for you?" He glanced at my T-shirt. "Are you here as an officer or a private citizen?"

His gaze lingered on my breasts, something that happened to me a lot. Guys might not be interested in me, but since I'd hit a 38 D cup in the eighth grade—much to my dismay and mortification—they *had* been interested in what I stored inside my T-shirt.

"I'm on my own time, following up with the case." His eyes met mine; they didn't stray south again. "I have a question, and I was told you were the expert."

"In what? I have several and varied interests."

His lips twitched. I ignored the implication. I'd never been any good at flirting. What a surprise.

Instead, I dug the totem out of my pocket, then held out my hand, palm up. The tiny wolf lay in the center.

Before I could ask a single question he snatched the stone and hurried around the side of his desk, turning on the lamp as he went.

"Hey! That's evidence, Slick."

His answer was a grunt. He tilted the lamp so the

glare was square on the totem, squinted, muttered, and pulled out his glasses.

"What is it?"

"Shh!"

So much for the charming flirt. Cadotte now ignored me as he peered at the carved wolf, mumbled, and scribbled notes on a scrap of paper he'd torn randomly from what looked to be a student essay.

I settled into the only chair not piled with books and waited. As I waited, I also watched. I couldn't help myself.

He wasn't dressed like any professor I'd ever had. But then I'd gone to technical school in Madison. While the city had a reputation—at least in Wisconsin—for being a hotbed of anarchy, my police science instructors had been nothing if not staid. None of them would ever have worn a faded cotton shirt and even more faded jeans. An earring was out of the question.

Of course the sight of his jeans only made me wonder if he was wearing anything beneath them. Just because he hadn't bothered with underwear under his cutoffs didn't mean he didn't wear it to work. I considered what it would be like to sit in his class, listen to him lecture, knowing he was naked inside the denim. I shifted in my chair and forced my thoughts away from last night.

Perhaps fifteen minutes passed before he glanced up, blinked as if he'd forgotten I was there, tried to rub his eyes, smacked his knuckles into his glasses, and removed them.

Why did I find his absentminded professor behavior so appealing?

"Well?" I demanded.

"Where did you get this?"

"I thought I was asking the questions?"

"I can't answer yours until you answer a few of mine."

"Fine. Center line of Highway One-ninety-nine."

He frowned. "I don't understand."

"You and me both. The accident last night—"

"With the wolf?" His gaze was as sharp as his voice.

"That's the one."

His eyes shifted from keen to distracted in the space of an instant. Figuring he was deep in thought, I let him stay there as long as I could. Of course that wasn't very long. I never said I was patient.

"Professor Cadotte?"

My voice brought him back from wherever it was that he'd gone. "Mmm?"

"Can you tell me what this is? Who might have dropped the thing? Any clues as to why it was lying in the middle of the highway?"

"Yes. Maybe. And none at all."

Well, that was what I got for asking too many non-specific questions. I tried again. "What is it?"

"Totem. Or *dodaim* in Ojibwe."

"That much I knew. But it's different from the ones I've seen in town."

"The figures they sell two for a dollar at the T-shirt shop?" I nodded and he made a face. "A waste of bad plastic. What you have here is an Ojibwe wolf clan totem. Whoever lost this is probably frantic to get it back."

"Why?"

"Family protection, spiritual power, magic."

"Woo-woo," I muttered. I *hated* woo-woo.

His glance was quick and probing. "You say that as if you don't believe."

"In magic stones and wolf spirits? You got it."

"I suppose you only believe in what you can see, hear, and touch."

"What else is there?"

"What we know is true but can't prove."

"Bullshit?"

"Faith, Officer."

I gave a snort so unladylike my mother would have fainted if she'd heard it. William Cadotte merely smiled. For some reason he found me amusing. Like a pet or a child, maybe an imbecile.

"Faith is for fools who don't know their own mind," I snapped.

As a kid I'd spent countless hours praying for my daddy to come home. He hadn't. I'd spent equal time praying to be like everyone else. I wasn't. So I'd given up praying long ago.

"I'd rather be a fool," he said quietly, "than believe in nothing at all."

I did believe in something—facts—but I found no reason to tell him that. Living in the middle of woo-woo land had taught me quite quickly that arguing with someone who believed the unbelievable was like smacking your head against a brick wall. Maybe someday you'd move the brick, but you were more likely to be dead first. I changed the subject.

"Any idea who might belong to that totem?"

He turned away and I frowned. Up until now he'd looked me in the eye when he spoke to me. Why the sudden change? Unless he couldn't lie to my face.

"Professor? You said you might know."

"I'm familiar with a few of the wolf clan in the area."

"How's that?"

"Because I'm one, too."

"It's a fraternity or something?"

"No."

He faced me again, and any amusement I might have seen once was gone. Had I offended him? I wasn't sure how, but then, I rarely understood how I'd pissed some-one off. Queen of the social gaffe? Me?

"In Ojibwe tradition each person belongs to a clan, the descent of which comes through the father. Legend has it that we are the ancestors of the animal our clan is named for. So even if you were of the Lac du Flambeau band and I was Grand Portage, which I am, if we were wolf clan, we were blood. We couldn't marry."

"Double damn," I said dryly.

His lips quirked. Maybe I hadn't offended him after all.

"In other words, your people believed that wolf clan members descended from the wolves—"

"And bear clan from the bear, crane from the crane. Exactly."

"Interesting." And weird.

"It's a legend. Not too many of us keep up with to-temic clan lore these days."

"Except for you."

He shrugged. "It's my job, even if I didn't believe we should keep the old ways alive."

"Do you know who might belong to this totem?"

"Maybe."

He picked up the tiny black herald, rolled the stone between his fingers. The thought of him using those fin-gers on me in much the same way made me forget for an instant what I was doing here.

"This isn't a common wolf clan totem," he continued, and I yanked my mind from fantasy to reality. "I'd like to keep this to study some more. I've never seen one like it."

"What's so different?"

"The wolf is . . . odd, and there are markings that dis-turb me. Something is not quite right."

Disturb? Odd? Not right?

"What are you getting at?"

"Ever heard of a manitou?"

"What?" His quick change in topic left me floundering to catch up. "You mean a spirit?"

"Kind of. *Manitou* means 'mystery,' 'godlike,' 'essence.' An all-encompassing spirit. Legend has it that Kitchi-Manitou, the great mystery, created all."

The great mystery. Despite my skepticism of all things woo-woo, I liked that. *The great mystery* was a good phrase for God and everything in that realm.

"Everyone has manitoulike attributes," Cadotte went on. "We each have our special talent. Yours must be sarcasm."

"Ha-ha."

He quirked a brow. "Or maybe something hidden, which I'll uncover later."

"Don't count on it, Slick. What's your special attribute?"

"Besides my great big—" I caught my breath. "Brain?"

The air hissed out through my teeth, making a derisive sound. "Yeah, besides that."

"Maybe you'll give me a chance to show you my special talent sometime."

"I repeat, don't count on it."

He smiled. "Getting back to my story. Most of the manitous are helpful. They're guardians over us poor humans."

"And the ones that aren't helpful?"

"Two. Both are man-hunting manitous. *Weendigos*, or the Great Cannibals, and the *Matchi-auwishuk*."

"Translation?"

His smile faded. "The Evil Ones."

Even though I believed none of this, the hair on my forearms tingled.

"I don't like the sound of either one," I admitted. "But what do they have to do with our totem?"

"The markings on this wolf remind me of certain drawings I've studied of Matchi-auwishuk."

"What does that mean?"

"I'm not sure."

"Swell." Silence fell between us.

"Why are you so interested in this?" he asked.

Good question. The totem could be anyone's, dropped at the scene of the accident for any number of reasons. It might not have anything to do with Miss Larson at all.

But I found it a tad too coincidental to discover a wolf clan totem at the scene of an accident involving a wolf. That, combined with the information on manitous and evil ones, as well as the violent death of the victim within twenty-four hours . . .

Well, call me silly, but my nerve endings were doing the tango.

I might not believe in woo-woo, or anything I couldn't verify by fact, but I'd had enough hunches turn out true that I'd learned long ago not to ignore the steady hum in my head that said something was rotten in Miniwa.

Chapter 6

Cadotte's voice broke into my thoughts. "You aren't going to tell me, are you?"

"Tell you what?"

"Why you're so interested in a stray wolf totem."

"I'm curious."

"Funny, but you don't seem the curious type."

"You're wrong." I stood. "Number one on the 'what you need to be a good cop' list is curiosity. Otherwise we wouldn't keep asking all those annoying questions."

"Hmm." He got up and strode around his desk, coming too close, crowding me again.

I liked my personal circle of space, and he was invading it. But to back off would mean I was nervous, that he affected me. I was and he did, but why let him know? Perhaps one of my other attributes was bullheaded stubbornness.

Nah.

"So, should I call you?"

I gaped. "C-call me?"

There went my tough girl image.

"If I find out anything about the totem."

Of course. The totem. Not me. Never me.

Poof went my silly female fantasy.

"Yeah. Sure." I dug out a card with my various phone numbers.

He stared at it, then lifted his eyes to mine. He was still too close. I was still not backing away.

"Jessie?" he murmured. "Short for Jessica?"

"As if."

Jessica was the name of a pink-cheeked, blond-haired, petite ballerina girl.

He laughed. "I can keep this?" He flicked a finger at the totem, which remained on his desk.

I hesitated. Though I hadn't logged the thing into evidence yet, I should. Whether it meant anything or not, who could say? Maybe William Cadotte.

"For now." I grabbed a plain piece of paper, scribbled on it, then stabbed my finger at the bottom. "Sign this."

He picked up a pen and signed before asking, "What is it?"

A lawyer he wasn't. "That's evidence. You just signed for it, but I'll need the thing back."

"All right."

Silence again. Time to say good-bye. I wasn't sure how.

"I'll be in touch. Jessie."

The way he said my name made me recall the sheen of his skin in the moonlight. The way his muscles had rippled, the way his earring had swayed.

When was the last time I'd had sex? Far too long, from the direction of my thoughts. Far too long, since I couldn't quite recall. Not the when, nor the why, I could barely recall the who.

I needed to remember that Cadotte was an expert consultant, nothing more, before I made a bigger fool of myself than I already had.

I got a grip and pulled out what company manners I had. "Thanks for your time, Professor."

He took the hand I offered. My mind went all girlie again. I wanted to know what those dark, long fingers could do; I wanted to feel those large, rough palms against my skin. I wanted to see everything I'd seen last night. Touch it, taste it, too.

"My friends call me Will." He released my hand.

Friends. Right. I was an idiot.

"I won't," I replied, then escaped.

Yes, my mother would be mortified at my behavior. This time I would have agreed with her. There was no cause for rudeness, beyond my own sense of inadequacy and a tiny kernel of fear that lodged hard and cool beneath my breastbone.

William Cadotte scared the hell out of me, and I didn't like it one bit. So I lashed out.

The need had been born in me long ago to hurt before I could be hurt, reject before I could be rejected, walk away before I could be walked away from. I couldn't change who I was inside, or out for that matter, suddenly become well adjusted, pretty, and proud of it. Don't psychoanalyze me; I've been doing it myself for years.

I'd had friends, but I never let any get too close. I was always waiting for them to turn on me as everyone else had. I'd been in love once, right out of high school. The relationship had ended badly. Probably because I'd been expecting it to.

I knew who I was. A good cop. A decent person. But a loner. I wasn't scared of much, because I had so little to lose. Which was just the way I liked it.

I'd been telling myself this for years, believing it, too. So why did I suddenly feel lonely and sad in the middle of the day?

I left the university and returned to the station, hoping

Dr. Bozeman might have left a message, or even the report. I'd have had better luck hoping the sun would rise in the west.

I filed my own report, then logged the evidence and placed it in the evidence room, leaving the paper Cadotte had signed with the rest.

Since my shift didn't start for several hours and I hadn't eaten anything lately, I returned to my apartment, where I made a small pizza, watched sitcoms, and tried not to think of the case for a while.

When it was time for work, I changed into my uniform and returned to the station. I was barely in the door before Zee started shouting. "Hell and tarnation, what were you doing at that school today, girl?"

"Hello, Zee. Nice to see you, too."

"Fuck that. You could have been killed."

"I wasn't. Get over it."

She blinked. I was usually more deferential to her moods—or rather mood: she only had one and it was bad. I knew she meant well. Zee might cuss like a construction worker, but her old-time upbringing made her reserve the F-word for serious concerns. She'd been worried about me.

I softened, leaned over the counter, and got a faceful of smoke for my trouble as Zee finished lighting her next cigarette off the stub of the last one.

"Don't you have somewhere to be?" she asked.

I stared at her. She scowled back, not in the spirit to be mollified—by words, at any rate. I'd bring her a doughnut and coffee in an hour. Nothing said "I'm sorry" like fried dough and caffeine.

"Any messages for me?"

"Did I give you any?"

"Uh, no."

"Unless First and Second Shift screwed up again, what does that mean?"

Zee never referred to the other dispatchers by name. Until they'd worked here as long as she had—and no one ever would, or could—they hadn't earned the right to a name.

"I guess that means I have no messages."

Damn, I'd have to dog Bozeman's every step tomorrow.

"Sometimes you are too bright for your own good, princess." Zee turned her back on me.

I left thinking I'd better bring back two doughnuts and coffee with half-and-half if I wanted to ever get into Zee's good graces again.

The night was uneventful—a nice change from the one before. I remembered that Clyde had asked me to talk to Brad and Zee, which I did.

After eating both the doughnuts and drinking all of the coffee, Zee agreed to the wisdom of keeping her mouth shut about Miniwa's little problem. Brad didn't need bribery, just a threat, which had always been my specialty.

I went home on time for a change, slept until two, and headed for the ME's office. Dr. Bozeman should have had time to examine at least one of his bodies, if not both.

Should have. Would have. If he'd had any bodies.

"What is going on here?" I shouted over the amazing din created by Clyde, Dr. Bozeman, and his itty-bitty secretary.

My boss shoved the other two out of his way. "The bodies are gone."

"What?"

"That's what I said. When Bozeman got here this morning, no bodies. They could have been gone since yesterday for all we know." He rubbed his eyes. "This just makes my day."

"They couldn't get up and run off." I glanced at the secretary. "Right?"

She ignored me. I couldn't say that I blamed her. I returned my attention to Clyde. "What happened?"

"No idea. But we'd better find out." Clyde beckoned me away from the others. "Jessie, you aren't gonna like this, but before you explode, hear me out."

I didn't like it already, but I shrugged, so he continued.

"The DNR is sending someone to kill the wolf."

I blinked, frowned, shook my head. I could not have heard that right.

"But didn't you tell them? I mean, how could anyone from away be better at hunting these forests than—?" I broke off.

"You?"

"Well, yeah. You've always sent me when we had animal trouble before."

"I know, and I'm sorry as hell about it, but I have no choice. You know how the DNR is, especially about their wolves. They're sending a *Jäger-Sucher.*"

"A what?"

"That's hunter-searcher in German." Clyde lifted one broad shoulder. "It's what he calls himself."

"Who?"

"Edward Mandenauer. From what I hear he's the Special Forces of wolf hunters."

"I can't take my rifle and blast this thing into the next county?"

"I wish. But this is out of my hands. The guy's hired and here already." He paused and rubbed the back of his neck as if it ached. "I was hoping you'd go to the office, drive him out to the scene. I won't be able to today."

"You're kidding, right?"

"I rarely kid, Jessie."

How true. Five minutes later I was at the station. First Shift was at the desk. Hell, I didn't even know her name anymore. Had I ever?

I glanced at the tag on her chest, but the word was too long and too Polish to figure out without closer scrutiny and a translator. Her eyebrows lifted in surprise at seeing me in the office two shifts ahead of myself.

"Clyde wants me to meet and greet his super-elite wolf killer. I can't wait to get a load of this geek."

First Shift didn't answer. Instead she stared over my shoulder with a frozen smile. Ah, hell.

I turned. I had to force myself not to gape, but I did blink. The man was still there. He was still the most pathetic excuse for a super-elite wolf killer I'd ever seen. Not that I'd seen very many.

Mandenauer stared at me with eyes so light a blue they were eerie. His white hair had the muted hue of the once blond; his complexion was that of the Aryan brotherhood ventured out in the sun too many times.

He was tall, cadaverous thin, and at least eighty-five. I couldn't imagine this man striking terror into the heart of any beast. But then, a gun did wondrous things for the fear factor.

I decided that the best defense was an offense. I'd pretend I hadn't said anything rude and maybe he'd let me.

"Hello. I'm Officer McQuade." I offered my hand. "Sheriff Johnston sent me. He's . . . unavoidably detained."

Mandenauer continued to stare. He did not shake my hand. The silence became awkward. I lowered my arm and gave in. "I apologize for my rudeness."

He dipped his chin, a courtly, old-world gesture. "No matter, Officer."

Though I'd been likening him to the master race, his accent still surprised me. He was German, Austrian maybe. The accent was one that never went away no matter how many years the speaker spent in the U.S.— just listen to Schwarzenegger.

"What has detained the sheriff?"

"A problem at the ME's office. The case of the disappearing bodies."

He straightened to a height of at least six-four. How did he sneak through the woods without smacking into a tree limb? His gaze became shrewd. "The bodies? Were they bitten?"

"Yeah."

He started for the door. I glanced at First Shift. She appeared as confused as I was. I hurried after him, catching up on the front steps.

"Sir? Mr. Mandenauer. Don't you want me to take you to the last place the wolf was seen?"

"Not yet. Escort me to the office of the medical examiner."

I raised an eyebrow at the order. I didn't mind being a chauffeur—much—but I didn't care for being a slave.

He must have seen mutiny in my eyes, because he touched my arm and murmured, "Please."

For an instant I almost liked him. Until I remembered why he was here. I pulled my arm out of reach.

"Sure. Fine. Whatever," I muttered. "But why are you so interested?"

"Because we may have a bigger problem in your fair town than one mad wolf."

Chapter 7

I didn't like the sound of that. But lately, I hadn't liked the sound of much.

"What kind of problem?"

His gaze scanned the tree line surrounding the town. He held himself as still as a deer who had just heard the footfall of man. A statue poised for flight the instant the scent of danger wafted past a twitching nostril. Except Mandenauer would never be so gauche as to twitch.

I couldn't help myself. Even though I knew a wolf would never come this close to town, I followed his gaze. Despite the summer sunshine, the thickness of the forest meant that light did not penetrate past the first few rows of trees. Anything could be hiding in there, during the day as well as the night.

When I glanced at Mandenauer again, he was watching me. "Rabies spreads like the plague, Officer, which will be quite a problem. Shall we?"

He stepped onto the sidewalk and waited gallantly for me to join him. I stayed right where I was.

"This isn't rabies."

His frown was quickly suppressed behind a stoic mask. "And you would know that how?"

"By researching rabies on the Internet. It isn't hard."

"Of course not. All the knowledge of the universe is now on the Internet."

I suspected he was being sarcastic—I ought to know—however, his face revealed nothing of the sort.

"The medical examiner?" he pressed.

"Follow me."

Together we walked through the unusually deserted streets of Miniwa. It was three o'clock in the afternoon. Where was everybody?

As we passed the Clip and Curl, Tina Wilson stuck out her silky auburn head. "Jessie." She motioned for me to come closer. "What's this I hear about a mad wolf?"

Tina had been two years ahead of me at Miniwa High. She'd been popular, pretty, petite. Since I was none of the above, I was surprised she knew my name.

She owned the Clip and Curl and spent her days making everyone else beautiful—or at least trying. For reasons that should be obvious, I'd never set foot in the place.

"There isn't a mad wolf," I soothed.

What there was I had no idea, but I didn't need to tell her that. We were supposed to be keeping things quiet. Obviously that wasn't going so well. In small towns like Miniwa, a secret was damn near impossible to maintain. But I'd hoped we'd have more than a day of peace.

Tina's gaze shot to Mandenauer. "Who's he?"

Mandenauer bowed. "Madam, I am the hunter-searcher hired by your Department of Natural Resources to kill the wolves."

"Wolves?" she squeaked. "You mean there's more than one?"

"There are plenty of wolves, Tina. You know that.

But they don't come into town. They're more afraid of us than we are of them."

"That's what I always hear after there's an attack or a mauling. Doesn't help Karen Larson though, does it?" Tina snapped, and slammed the door in my face.

I rubbed the back of my neck. I hadn't done a very good job of calming the populace. I started to have an inkling of how ugly things could get.

"Rabid wolves are aggressive," Mandenauer murmured. "They will come into town. They will attack people. They will attack anything."

"I thought we'd established that this wasn't rabies?"

"You established that, Officer, but if we aren't dealing with rabies, then what are we dealing with?"

I had no answer for that.

Mandenauer gave a sharp nod and allowed me to precede him around the corner, down the street, and into the office of the medical examiner. Clyde, Bozeman, and his secretary were still there. When we walked in, every single one of them frowned.

For whatever reason, Clyde no longer had his chew, which explained why he was crankier than usual. "I thought I told you to take him to the scene."

"And he told me to bring him here."

Clyde's eyes narrowed. "Who's your boss, Officer?"

That tore it.

"You know what?" I threw up my hands and headed for the door. "Take it up with Lurch. I've got work to do."

Mandenauer placed his hand on my arm again, the second time he'd done so in less than half an hour. I'm not big on touching. It makes me uncomfortable. Am I supposed to touch back? Let it happen? Move away?

"Stay, Miss McQuade. Please. I have much to ask you."

"Miss?" The itty-bitty secretary snorted.

Well, that just made me want to stay.

"All right." I shrugged and his hand slipped off my arm. "Sure."

Mandenauer's lips twitched. Had that been a smile? Nah, probably just gas.

"Now, Sheriff." He turned to Clyde. "I hear there are no bodies for me to look over."

Clyde frowned. "Why do you need to see them? Go shoot the wolf."

"All in good time. I like to know every little thing about my quarry."

"It's a wolf. What's to know?"

Mandenauer ignored him and turned to Bozeman. "What did you find when you examined the bodies?"

Bozeman colored. "I, uh, well—"

"He didn't." The words escaped my mouth before I could stop them. Honest.

Mandenauer turned. "Did not find anything?"

"Didn't examine them. It was his day off."

Bozeman glared at me behind Mandenauer's back. Nothing I hadn't seen before.

"I see," Mandenauer said, though I could tell that he didn't. Laziness was no doubt as abhorrent to him as it was to the rest of the population raised during the Great Depression. "If the bodies are found, they should be burned without further ado."

"Burned?" Clyde asked at the same time Bozeman said, "What about the autopsy?"

"The autopsy would be useless with the decay that will no doubt have taken place in the summer heat."

Everyone winced at the thought.

"It is best to burn them before the disease spreads."

"Since when does rabies spread through the air?" Clyde demanded.

"Who is talking about rabies?"

Clyde blinked. "Us?"

Mandenauer shook his head and stared at Bozeman with exaggerated disappointment. "Doctor, haven't you told the good sheriff what our dear Officer McQuade already knows?"

The ME spread his hands and shrugged. Everyone looked at me.

"Jessie?" Clyde's voice held a note of warning. "What the hell is he talking about?"

I hadn't had a chance to tell Clyde everything I'd discovered—about rabies and totems and manitous. I'd left the theories out of my report.

"Rabies has an incubation period of one to three months in humans."

"What?" Clyde shouted.

Bozeman flinched. To be honest, so did I.

"What kind of idiot are you?" Thankfully he was talking to Bozeman and not to me. "Here I am thinking we've got rabies on the loose and it can't be, can it? You're a goddamned doctor. You should know this."

"In my defense, Sheriff, rabies isn't a common occurrence in humans these days. And when it does occur, the virus rarely results in death any longer."

"Tell it to Karen Larson," I muttered.

Bozeman's glare was a replica of the first one. The man had no originality.

"What are we dealing with then?" Clyde asked.

"Kind of hard to tell without the *bodies*." I batted my eyelashes at Bozeman and his itty-bitty secretary.

She seemed to have nothing to say at last. In fact, she appeared a bit guilty. I guess I would, too, if dead bodies had gone missing on my watch.

Bozeman shrugged. Clyde made a disgusted sound.

Mandenauer cleared his throat. "I have an idea."

"Let's hear it."

"Rabies."

Everyone in the room gaped. I wondered if Mandenauer had all his eggs in the carton, his beans in a bag, his wheels going round and round.

"Sir—" I began.

He held up one pale, slim hand and I shut my mouth.

"It would be better if there were bodies. For proof. But based on what you've told me, I will make an educated guess on what we have here."

"Educated?" Bozeman sneered. "What kind of education do you have?"

"Shut the hell up, Prescott." Clyde rounded on him and the ME stumbled back, knocking into his secretary and sending her skinny ass flying about two feet. While the two of them got untangled, Clyde and I listened to Mandenauer.

"I do not have the education of the good doctor."

"Lucky for us," I said.

This time Mandenauer smiled. I was sure of it. However, Clyde didn't, so I zipped my lip. Again.

"This is not for public knowledge, you understand. There would be a panic."

"Something I'd like to avoid," Clyde mumbled.

"Therefore, what I am about to say must stay in this room until we have the problem under control."

Mandenauer glanced at each of us in turn, and we nodded.

"There is a new strain of rabies that matches what you seem to have here. The incubation period is hours instead of months. The level of aggression is intense, and the spread of the infection is beyond anything we have ever known."

"I've never heard of this," Bozeman interjected.

"Why am I not surprised?" I murmured; then a sudden chill rode my spine. "Was this genetically engineered?"

Mandenauer turned to me and in his usually distant gaze I saw a spark of interest. "Perhaps."

Clyde cursed. He was spending way too much time with Zee. Weren't we all?

"You're saying that terrorists have infected the wolf population with genetically engineered rabies?"

"Did I say that? I do not think so."

Clyde scrubbed a hand through his short, dark hair. "Then what are you saying?"

"Evil has come to your town."

"How can a virus be evil?" I asked.

Mandenauer glanced at me. "How indeed?"

"Do you always answer a question with a question?"

"Do I?"

Clyde, who must have sensed I was near my boiling point, stepped between the two of us. "What should we do?"

"Exactly what has been done. You have the best hunter there is." Mandenauer slapped his chest with his palms. "I will kill anything that looks at me crosswise. Once all the infected animals are dead, there will be nothing more to worry about."

"Except the people," I muttered.

Mandenauer let his hands fall slowly back to his sides and gazed at me with a curious expression. "What about the people?"

"If someone gets infected, are you going to shoot them, too?"

"No, they will use the rabies vaccine."

"That'll help?"

"It cannot hurt."

In my experience, whenever someone said that, it hurt.

Chapter 8

After Clyde reamed out Bozeman one more time for the road, he beckoned to me. Leaving Mandenauer with a map of the area that the teeny-tiny secretary had found—I really needed to ask her name, or not—I joined him in the ME's office.

He closed the door. "Jessie, you wound me."

"I'm sorry?"

Clyde frowned, uncertain if I was apologizing or asking what in hell I'd done to disappoint him now. Since I'd never been much for apologizing, he chose the latter, and he was right.

"You have information about this case, which is now on the front burner for all of us, and you don't tell me?"

"Clyde, I—"

"What else do you know?"

His black eyes were intense, and his jaw pumped up and down even though he had no tobacco. I resisted the urge to point out that he shouldn't bother with the mouth cancer aid if he could get the same relief with phantom chewing. Clyde wasn't in the mood for my wit.

Quickly I told him everything I knew. When I got to the part about Professor Cadotte, he interrupted. "William Cadotte?"

Hell. I should have left the guy's name out of it.

"Yeah. That's him."

"He's trouble, Jess. Big trouble."

I frowned. When Clyde called me Jess, he was serious. "He seemed harmless enough to me."

Not really. He'd seemed very, very dangerous. To my celibacy.

Clyde paced the room, tense, edgy. He reminded me of a caged animal, and that just wasn't like Clyde.

"He's an egghead. An activist."

"He's Ojibwe, just like you."

"He's *not* like me. I'm Lac du Flambeau. He's Grand Portage. That's as different as the Welsh and the English."

Okay. I knew each band considered themselves separate from the other. I hadn't realized how separate. Or maybe that was just Clyde's point of view.

"I'd think you'd approve of someone who stood up for the Indians."

"There's standing up and stirring up. I just want to live my life. Do my job. Be myself. I don't need some pretty boy smart-mouth getting everyone angry at me on principle."

Cadotte had certainly stirred me up, but I had a hard time believing he would spend time stirring up the community just for the fun of it, and I told Clyde so.

The last part. Not the first.

"Maybe he's changed. But I doubt it. Stay away from him, Jess."

"I'll do my best."

And I would. Cadotte made me nervous in more ways than one, something I did not need when all hell was about to break loose in Miniwa. Then I remembered.

"I will have to see him one more time."

"What for?"

"To get the totem back."

"You gave him the totem?" His shout rattled the windows in Bozeman's office. "Are you nuts?"

I was getting mighty sick of being yelled at. "I was doing my job, Clyde."

"By giving evidence to a convict?"

"Convict?"

"William Cadotte has been arrested more times than he's been laid."

"And how would you know how many times he's been laid?"

"With a face like his, it's no doubt daily."

Since I had to agree, I let that one pass.

"What's he been arrested for?"

"Disturbing the peace. Inciting a riot."

"Nuisance stuff."

"Breaking the law isn't a nuisance."

"You know as well as I do that half the folks above the age of fifty have those charges on their records. It was called *protesting* if I remember my history books correctly."

"Cadotte isn't over fifty."

"I noticed."

His gaze had been intense before, now it went sharp and suspicious. "You'd better watch yourself. Associating with a known troublemaker will not improve your career options."

My heart gave a sharp thud. All I had was my job, and I loved it. Being a cop was what I did, who I was. It was the only thing I'd ever been any good at.

"Are you threatening me, Clyde?"

"No. Just givin' you good advice."

I knew a threat when I heard one, having given enough of my own to know the difference.

"Get that totem back, Officer. Now."

I executed a military salute, then clicked my heels and goose-stepped out of the office. From the expression on Clyde's face, he did not find me funny.

My thoughts turned to the professor, and I sighed, then pulled out my cell phone. Best put an end to any contact with him before I lost my head and my job.

I dialed his office. A machine picked up. "This is William Cadotte. I'm not in right now, but if you'll leave a message I'll call you back as soon as I am. My office hours are Monday through Friday from one to three."

I glanced at my watch. I'd just missed him.

Beeep!

I started at the loud noise. "I . . . um, this is J—I mean Officer McQuade. We met yesterday?"

I must have sounded as stupid as I felt, because Mandenauer lifted his head from his perusal of the map and contemplated me with a lift of his off-white brows.

I turned my back on him and came face-to-face with Clyde, who stood in the doorway to Bozeman's office. Sheesh, could I even finish the call before he was on my case?

"I need the totem right away. Call me."

I hit the *end* button, then tucked the phone back into its pocket on my belt. "Let's go!" I called to Mandenauer. "I'll take you out to the accident site."

"Jessie," Clyde said.

I gave an exaggerated sigh. "Yes."

"I'll check out Karen Larson's place. Then you don't have to."

I gave a sharp nod and escaped the ME's office. Moments later Mandenauer and I were headed down Highway 199 in my patrol car.

I was still a bit steamed over Clyde's telling me to stay away from Cadotte. Not that I'd planned on being near him more than was necessary—I may be sarcastic, but I'm not stupid—however, Clyde's threat only made me want to see Cadotte a few times just for the hell of it. I guess that makes me stubborn, too.

How convenient that Cadotte's cabin was right on the trail I had been ordered—by Clyde—to show our guest.

Mandenauer was quiet on the drive to the scene of the accident. I glanced at him once. He appeared asleep, his head tilted back against the headrest, but his eyes weren't all the way closed. I could see the whites beneath his fluttering eyelids.

Creepy. I'd have been afraid he was dead except I could see his sunken chest rising slow and steady.

That would be all I'd need. To have Clyde's precious *Jäger-Sucher* turn up dead in my car.

I parked the Crown Victoria on the shoulder of the road. The skid marks from Karen's SUV stood out dark against the gray pavement. I glanced at Mandenauer. He was awake.

"Is there anything you would like to tell me about the accident? Anything I should know that will help me to finish this as quickly as I can?"

He stared at me intently, as if he could force me by his will alone to spill some secret I was guarding. But I didn't have any. Except my embarrassing sexual infatuation with the professor. But that wouldn't help Mandenauer kill the wolf—or most likely wolves by now.

"You read my accident report?"

He nodded. "Before you arrived at the station. Cut-and-dried, as you say."

I thought about the totem, Karen's strange behavior at the scene, and her even stranger behavior later.

"Or perhaps not?" he murmured.

I considered what I should tell and what I shouldn't.

It wouldn't help Mandenauer to find the wolf if I told him about the totem. But I'd already been bitched at enough today for not spilling everything I knew, so I gave him the basics.

"This is what your sheriff was angry about?"

I glanced at him quickly. The door to the office had been closed while Clyde and I talked.

"Sheriff Johnston has a very loud voice and I, despite so many years on this earth, have very good ears."

I shrugged. "I don't know what the totem means. It could have been there for weeks and have nothing to do with this accident at all."

"Perhaps." Mandenauer got out of the car. I joined him. "Or perhaps not," he repeated.

"You sure are a decisive son of a gun, aren't you?"

His lips twitched. From what I'd observed of Mandenauer thus far, he was almost snickering. "I like to keep my mind open."

"To what?"

"To all the possibilities that exist. You never know when something you think is irrelevant is in fact quite relevant."

I agreed with him there. Good police work involved observing from every angle and never letting a thing get by unnoticed. Which was why I wasn't allowing the totem issue to slide.

"Now, if you'll walk me through the scene, show me where the wolf went and where you lost him, I will be most grateful."

I pointed to the skid marks from Miss Larson's SUV. "Their length indicates she wasn't going all that fast, but she didn't have much warning. I hit a deer once, and it was as if the thing appeared out of the pavement. One minute the road was clear; the next I had venison on my grille."

"Charming," Mandenauer murmured.

Charming. Yep, that was me.

I pointed toward the woods. "Blood trail led this way."

He followed me off the road. Not a car had gone by while we'd been examining the evidence. Nothing new. Peak traffic for Highway 199 was Friday night and Sunday afternoon. Then it would be bumper-to-bumper from here to Stevens Point. Otherwise two cars every hour was a convention.

I inched down the slight embankment and stepped from the bright sunlight into the cool shadow of the woods. There were places in this forest so deep and dank the sun had never penetrated. I didn't like those places, avoided them if I could, but they were there.

I walked in the general direction of Cadotte's cottage. The blood trail was long gone, covered by dirt or leaves, erased by rain, perhaps eaten by another animal. If I hadn't followed the shiny black splotches through the moonlight myself, I would have a hard time believing today that they'd existed at all.

"You are sure this is the way?" Mandenauer was keeping up without even breathing hard. He was in damn fine shape for an old guy.

"I have a pretty good sense of direction."

To be honest, in the light of day I didn't need my sense of direction or even the blood trail, because there was a footpath leading directly to Cadotte's cabin. In the dark, even with the moon shining so bright, the forest had seemed overgrown and tangled.

But if I'd been thinking clearly—then and now—I'd have realized Cadotte had to get to his house someway. He couldn't drive, since there wasn't a road. He had to park somewhere and walk in.

Just as they had on my previous visit, the trees gave

way to the clearing, and there was the cabin. *Poof.*

Mandenauer's breath caught and he stopped. At least I wasn't the only one who thought Cadotte's cottage seemed to pop up like something out of a fairy tale.

Grimms' Fairy Tales, of course. The north woods were a little too creepy and dark to play a part in stories that featured silver-winged fairies and dancing mice. They leaned more toward little-girl-devouring wolves and cannibalistic witches.

"I lost him over here."

I walked across the clearing and down the path a few feet. Mandenauer followed. He crouched and peered at the ground. Picked up some dirt, smelled it, and let the earth sift back through his fingers. Then he sniffed the wind.

I shrugged. Whatever tripped his trigger.

"I need to speak with the owner of the cabin."

Mandenauer nodded, waved his hand in an imperial dismissal, and moved a little farther into the woods.

I returned to the clearing and climbed the steps to the front door. No one appeared to be home, although why I thought that, since there was no car and never had been, I don't know. I knocked. No one answered, proving my theory.

I shaded my eyes and pressed my nose to the window in the door. A snarling wolf stared back at me.

"Shit!"

I leaped back, heart thundering, breath coming in sharp gasps, palm slapping onto the butt of my gun, any second expecting the animal to crash through the glass and go for my throat.

Nothing happened.

I crept back to the window and glanced inside. The wolf was still there. But the animal wasn't going to come and get me anytime soon, since it was very, very dead.

Or at least it had better be, since it was hanging on the wall opposite the front door.

I don't know why the wolf bothered me so much. I have head-and-shoulder deer mounts on my walls. Why shoot trophy bucks if you aren't going to display them? You certainly can't eat them. They taste like smelly shoes boiled in rancid garbage water.

But in my apartment the racks are used to hold my first-place shooting medals and, on occasion, my air-drying unmentionables. A head-and-shoulders mount of a wolf would be of no use to me at all.

I wondered why Cadotte had one.

I moved to the edge of the porch. "You about ready to go?" I called.

My answer was the distant howl of a wolf.

Too far away to catch, still the sound made me jump off the top step and hurry toward where I'd left the old man.

He wasn't there.

I cursed as I followed the trail. I shouldn't have had to warn him not to wander off. He was a big boy. But the number of people who got lost and died in the woods every year was staggering.

If I lost Clyde's elite wolf hunter my name would be dumbshit for the rest of my life.

I shouted and heard nothing. I thrashed around and found the same. Suddenly I realized that the forest had gone still. Too still. Even the birds were quiet. Something was coming.

The cry of the wolf sounded again—closer this time—and a second wolf answered.

Why were they howling in the daylight? Had Mandenauer gone after them? He didn't have a gun, or at least one that I could see.

The whisper of stirring foliage wended my way. I

glanced up. The tops of the trees were as still as a lake beneath a new moon. Any wind there had been earlier had died. Then what was moving through the bushes?

A twig snapped. I froze. So did whatever was out there. I had my pistol in my hand. I don't know when I pulled it. I was merely glad that I had.

In the dark, in the forest, it's nearly impossible to tell from which direction a sound is coming. I discovered it was just as impossible in the bright light of day. I stood amid the bushes and the trees as the back of my neck prickled. I was being watched.

"Mandenauer?" I shouted. "Get back here, right now!"

That oughta work, my mind mocked. *If he was here, he'd be* here.

My breath rasped; my heart thundered; a trickle of sweat ran between my breasts and skated down my belly. I cocked the gun, and the birds began to chirp again.

A movement at the corner of my vision had me crouching and swinging my weapon in that direction. Mandenauer raised a brow. "My, aren't we jumpy?"

I uncocked the gun, but I didn't put it back into the holster. "Yes, *we* are. Where were you?"

"Out there."

He waved in a vague circular motion. The movement pulled his shirt tightly against his body and I saw the outline of a gun. I should have known.

"Did you hear the wolves?" I asked.

"I'm old; I'm not deaf."

"You didn't go after them, did you?"

He shook his head. "Those are not the animals I seek."

I frowned. "How would you know?"

"I know."

Whatever. I wanted to get out of here. I hated to admit

it, but I'd been well and truly spooked. Birds didn't stop twittering for no reason. And I didn't feel as if I were being watched unless I was.

"Done?" I asked.

"Most certainly."

We headed for the car and if we left more quickly than we'd come, tough. I didn't get spooked often; when I did, it shook me.

"You can put up the pistol, Officer."

I glanced down, surprised I still held my weapon in my hand. I was also surprised to discover I didn't want to put the gun away.

"Where's your rifle?" I asked.

"Locked and loaded and back at the Eagle's Nest."

So Mandenauer was staying at the Eagle's Nest Resort and Spa, *spa* being a relative term in Miniwa. It meant there were towels available by the lake and an ancient sauna that tilted drunkenly toward the water from its perch on a nearby hill.

"A gun doesn't do you much good in the case under your bed." Or hidden beneath his shirt, for that matter.

Mandenauer put a hand on my shoulder and I paused. "The wolf will not attack us in broad daylight."

"Why not?"

He smiled as if I were simpleminded. "It will not. Trust me."

I snorted. I trusted no one—except Zee and sometimes Clyde. I'd learned the hard way that those you trusted the most were the ones who could hurt you the most, too. So my circle of trust was a very small circle.

"You won't trust me?"

I gave him my "do you think I'm stupid?" glare and he nodded. "Good. Trust no one, Jessie. You will live longer that way."

Mandenauer and I were in agreement on a lot more than I would have imagined.

I tightened my fingers on the grip of my pistol and was comforted. Other women might keep relics from their childhood—dolls, stuffed animals, blankets—and pull them out when the going got tough. Me? I preferred a .44 Magnum anytime.

I didn't care how many wolves Mandenauer had killed, how many times those animals had behaved in a predictable manner; I wasn't going to bet my life, or even his, that this one—or twenty—would behave appropriately.

I remembered Karen Larson's eyes. I would remember them in my sleep for years to come. Right before she'd died there'd been a flicker of knowledge. She'd still been in there behind the insanity caused by the virus, and she'd been very, very afraid.

I hated being afraid. Fear smelled of weakness, and the weak did not survive.

Chapter 9

I deposited Mandenauer at the Eagle's Nest. "Let us know if you need anything."

He leaned in through the passenger window and studied me more closely than I liked. "What if I need an assistant?"

My pulse quickened at the thought of hunting the wolf or wolves, but I knew better than to appear eager. That was the quickest way to lose what I wanted.

"Take it up with Clyde." I shifted into reverse and Mandenauer withdrew his head from the window before he lost it.

The sun was setting as I ambled back toward town. We'd been in the woods longer than I'd thought, which was usually the case. Hours ceased to have meaning when you were walking through the forest. Perhaps that was why I spent so much time there.

I glanced at my watch, half-expecting the thing to have stopped when I entered the trees near Cadotte's cottage. Of course it hadn't. Time had marched on even as I had.

My stomach rumbled. I thought about what I might have in my refrigerator at home, and knew it was the usual. Squat.

When I reached the Sportsman's Bar and Grill, I turned off the highway and went inside. A cheeseburger and soda later I went home. Darkness had descended completely while I was eating. I had three hours before my shift started at eleven. I could have savored another cola in the Sportsman, which was what I usually did when I ate there.

But tonight the patrons, as well as the owner, the bartender, and the waitresses, had been full of questions about what was rotten in Miniwa. I'd answered them as best I could without really telling them anything they didn't already know.

They were nervous, though, and they made me nervous. So I left after one long, tall glass.

Now what?

Nights like these brought home to me the pathetic nature of my life. I had no friends but Zee, and I'd see her soon enough. No boyfriend—no kidding. No family but my mother, who was in Arizona. Thank God.

Most days I was fine with how things had turned out. I had the job I'd always wanted in a town I'd always loved. I had a decent apartment and the promise of a better future.

I'd bought 250 acres just outside of Miniwa where I planned to build a home someday. Right now I kept it free of a trophy buck every fall.

If life wasn't perfect, it certainly didn't suck. But there were times I just felt . . . lonely.

I could drive out to my land and do laps in my private pond. Instead of jogging, as many of my counterparts— excluding Clyde—did to keep in shape, I chose to swim. A lot less stress on the knees and a great way to increase upper body strength.

I'm all for equality in the workplace, but you can't argue with nature. Men had more upper body strength.

I didn't like it, but moaning wouldn't change anything. More reps in the pond would.

I pulled the Crown Victoria into my parking space. Since one of the officer benefits was personal use of the company vehicle—to a point—I didn't even own a car. I rarely went anywhere but here.

I stared up at my apartment. Though it was summer, the night wind in northern Wisconsin had a nip to it. Stripping to my Speedo and diving into a lake held little appeal.

That the lake was nestled at the edge of a very dense, dark section of the woods lessened the appeal even more. I wasn't chicken, but I wasn't foolish, either. I could swim at the rec center as I'd been doing all winter—at least until the wolf problem was resolved.

Maybe I'd have that second cola on my rarely visited balcony, sitting on my seldom-used porch furniture. I had a decent view on my side of the building, if I'd ever take a minute to look. The trees shaded the patio and someone had put a flower garden on a small knoll to the east. Perhaps I'd take a minute now.

Once inside I removed my gun, set the weapon on top of my refrigerator, and stashed the bullets in my pocket. A lot of precautions for a woman who lived alone, but who knows when company might come. This way, if someone found the gun they wouldn't have any bullets. If I needed the gun, the bullets were already on me.

I looped the heavy utility belt over the coatrack. My gaze caught on the cell phone still tucked in the holder.

I frowned. Why hadn't Cadotte called? I needed to get that totem back before Clyde blew another brain cell.

I glanced at my message machine, but the light wasn't blinking. I checked the phone on my belt. Sometimes cell service cuts out in the deep woods, and sometimes it doesn't. Why or why not is a mystery. But my battery was fine and there were no messages there, either.

I caught a whiff of myself and headed for the bedroom. Missing bodies and rabid wolves made for a lot of nervous sweat. I stripped to the waist, then took a quick sponge bath and yanked a fresh khaki short-sleeved shirt from my closet.

Buttoning the front, I returned to the kitchen and snagged one of the two colas I had left. I needed to go grocery shopping—my least favorite thing. When you lived alone and cooked rarely, the amount of choices in a grocery store was confusing. I usually came out with stuff I didn't need and more that I didn't know what to do with.

Something clinked against the floor-length sliding doors leading to my patio. I glanced in that direction. Nothing but black night filled the glass. All I could see was myself.

"Probably a really big bug," I murmured. "Or a low-flying dumb bird."

I headed across the small living area, flicked the lock, picked up the metal rod that braced the door, and slid it open. Crickets chirped; the trees rustled; a chilly wind swirled into the room. I'd never noticed how dark this side of the building was.

I cast a quick, longing glance toward my gun, then shook my head. I was not going to sit on my balcony armed. I was supposed to be relaxing. Besides, what was going to get me up here? Even a rabid wolf couldn't jump fifty feet in the air. Could it?

Since I hated being afraid, I made myself step onto the porch. I leaned my forearms along the railing, cradling my soda in my palms.

The only reason I had a chill down my back was the icy remnants of winter on the breeze. As I stared at the forest, something slunk along the edge of the woods. Something low to the ground, something furry with a tail.

"Coyote," I said, and my voice sounded loud in the stillness of the night.

I thought about what I'd said and frowned. Wolves wouldn't tolerate coyotes in their territory. So had I really seen what I thought I had?

I straightened and scanned the tree line again. But the night was too dark. Where was the moon?

Lifting my gaze to the sky, I caught a muted silver glow hanging halfway between the earth and the apex. When had the clouds moved in?

The scuffle of a foot against rocks and dirt pulled my attention from the sky to the ground. A man stood below my balcony.

The soda slipped from my hand. I gasped. He glanced up and snatched the can from the air seconds before it would have smashed into his head.

Soda sloshed across his shirt. His gaze met mine.

"You throw things at everyone, or am I just lucky?" Cadotte asked.

Chapter 10

"Where the hell did you come from?" I snapped.

My heart thundered and my hands shook. He'd scared me, not only by appearing out of nowhere, but by almost getting himself knocked out in my yard.

"Right now, or in general?"

"What?"

"I come from Minnesota originally. I just came out of those woods right now."

"The woods?"

"You know those trees all bunched together?" He jerked a thumb over his shoulder.

A comedian, exactly what I didn't need.

"You shouldn't be out alone at night."

"I think I can handle myself." He lifted the can of soda to his mouth and drained the rest in one long gulp.

I found myself overly fascinated with the muscles flexing and releasing in his throat. The way he'd snatched that soda can out of thin air had been amazing.

"How'd you do that?" I asked.

He crushed the can in one hand. My heart went pitter-pat.

"Do what?"

I flicked a finger at the can. "Your reflexes seem downright superhuman."

"There's a lot about me that's superhuman." He smirked. "Wanna see?"

The man flirted as easily as he breathed. But why was he flirting with me?

"No thanks. What are you doing here?"

"I got your message." He reached into the pocket of his jeans and held up something between his thumb and forefinger. The moon had come out from behind the clouds, and I could see his face but not much else. Still, from the space between his fingers, I deduced he'd brought me the totem.

"Come on up," I offered. "I've got one cola left. We can share."

"Share? You read my mind."

"Relax, Slick, I'm talking soda here."

"Spoilsport."

I went back into the apartment smiling, but I forced myself to stop. It wouldn't do either one of us any good if I encouraged him. He'd end up disappointed; I'd end up hurt.

He was handsome, sexy, intelligent. I was average, socially inept, and ... average. I'd made it through school; he was nearly a doctor. The professor and the cop—it sounded like a bad romance novel.

Those differences aside, I wasn't even going to address the white/red issue, which didn't bother me but might bother him—or at least his family. There were very few pure Ojibwe left. If he was even one of them, I doubted his parents would appreciate him diluting the gene pool.

I snorted and leaned down to snag the last soda from the refrigerator. We hadn't even progressed to first names and I had us diluting the gene pool. I'd better put on some brakes before I went headlong off the cliff.

Shutting the door, I turned, and an involuntary yelp escaped me. Cadotte stood in my living room.

"How—" I glanced at the window, which was still open. The breeze ruffled the curtains. "I mean, what—?"

He leaned against the wall and crossed his arms. Muscles flexed beneath smooth cinnamon skin. "You told me to come up."

"Ever think of using the door?"

"Why, when the window is so much closer?"

"How did you get up here?"

"Rock face. It wasn't hard." He shoved away from the wall. "For anyone who's done any climbing. You keep this locked, right?" He ran a fingertip along the glass.

"Of course."

He'd climbed up the side of the building like Spiderman? I found that hard to believe, yet here he was.

Distracted, I handed him the can and stepped onto the porch. I leaned out over the railing, measured the distance to the ground—too much—then moved over to the wall and peered closely. The apartment building *was* made of stone. There were footholds of a sort, but you couldn't talk me into climbing the thing.

Of course my rock-climbing experience was limited to county fairs and a single day at the academy during training. There aren't a heck of a lot of mountains to climb in Wisconsin. Hell, there aren't any. What we like to call hills are a joke if you've ever been to Colorado, Montana, or even Tennessee.

Cadotte followed me outside. Suddenly the night was no longer cool and the balcony no longer big enough. He stood between me and the door. The only way out was down.

Though tall, he was lithe. Not muscle-bound, but muscular. Could I take him if I had to? I wasn't sure.

The not knowing made my breath come harder and faster.

I inched closer to the door, into his personal space. If he was polite, he'd move away. He stayed right where he was. So did I.

"I told you to call me." I offered my hand, palm up. "I'd have picked up the totem. You didn't need to come out of your way."

He stared at my hand but made no move to put the totem into it. Where had the thing gone, anyway? My gaze lowered to his pockets. The totem was too small to make much of a bulge. I didn't see it. But there were other, more interesting bulges in the vicinity. I stiffened and yanked my eyes up to his.

He was smiling. Damn. He'd noticed. He seemed to notice everything.

He moved closer. I stepped back and cursed myself for the weakness. But I couldn't help it. His skin gave off an intense heat. I could smell him despite the pines and the flowers and the fresh plastic aroma of my chairs. That wild scent I'd noticed last night—not unappealing, but rather arousing.

I hit the railing. I couldn't go any farther. Thankfully Cadotte stopped, still too close, but at least he wasn't touching me. I wasn't sure what I'd do if he put those long-fingered, clever hands on me.

"If I'd let you come to get the totem, then I'd never have seen your place. I doubt you'd have invited me here."

I frowned as a thought I should have had earlier, if I hadn't been thinking about sex, shot through my brain. "How did you know where I live?"

"It's not hard to find out in a town like this."

True enough.

"Besides." He reached out and brushed one of those

enticing fingers back and forth over the short ends of my hair. "I wanted to see you again."

The shudder that rippled through me at his touch halted immediately at his words.

"What for?"

He dropped his arm. I figured he'd step back, finally let me pass, then tell me he had unpaid parking tickets or a bogus warrant hanging over his head—they were always bogus—or some other legal problem that made him want to see me. You know, the usual.

I was preparing my standard "sorry, can't help you" speech when his descending hand cupped my hip. I had no time to say anything, because he yanked my body flush with his—he was a helluva lot stronger than he looked—and kissed me.

Since my mouth had been half-open, ready to speak, his tongue slid right in. He didn't waste time on niceties but went straight for the good stuff. I liked that in a man.

The tip of his tongue did a hard slide up the center of mine, then teased at the end. He pulled me tighter against him, center to center, then rocked his hips forward. I nearly came right then. Deprivation will do that to a girl.

Moaning, I tried to pull back, but not very hard. Especially when he did some fancy move with his other hand and my starched sheriff shirt popped open past my bra.

Suddenly his mouth left mine and he lowered his head to my breasts. That clever tongue dipped into their center, in and out, as he echoed the motion with his hips.

My body was on fire. My mind a complete mess. It wouldn't take much to convince me to do it right here on the Formica table. I didn't think we'd make it inside.

My arms rose of their own accord, fingers tangling in his hair, so soft, so sleek. I ran my palm over his head, petting him, then urging him on. His mouth closed over my nipple, through the bra, and lightly he bit the tip. I arched, pressing my entire body into his, and that one small movement shoved me over the edge.

From far, far away drifted a low, mournful howl. In the middle of the first orgasm I'd had in several years, the sound confused me. Coyote? Wolf? Human?

Cadotte tensed, lifted his head, and stared past my shoulder into the night. The chill wind brushed my bare skin, iced the moisture left by his mouth. His body was still pressed to mine, but I no longer felt warm.

He pulled his gaze from the trees with obvious effort. His face gentled and he buttoned my blouse up to my throat. I certainly wasn't capable of doing it.

He lowered his forehead to mine and whispered, "That."

"Huh?"

Typical me, grace under fire.

"You asked why I wanted to see you." He kissed my eyebrow. Heat flooded through me, chasing away the chill.

Since when had my eyebrow become an erogenous zone? Apparently today.

"For that."

"You wanted to see me for that?" I repeated, not sure what *that* was. A kiss, a dry hump, a thwarted fuck on the balcony?

"Yes. You have a problem with it?"

At the moment I couldn't find a single problem with the world, but I would. Such was my nature. I shook my head, unable to articulate much of anything.

"Good. I've got to go."

He released me and headed for the front door. I must still have been dazed, or I'd have made a smart comment about jumping from the balcony. As it was, I followed him like a puppy, and when he pressed the totem into my hand, then folded my fingers around it, I merely held on tight and watched him leave.

I never thought to ask him what he'd discovered about the markings.

Chapter 11

I should have driven out to my land and plunged my treacherous body into the chilly pond right then. To hell with the wolves. Though I'd been satisfied, embarrassingly so, I still felt empty, even achy. I knew why. I might have come and it had been great, but I hadn't done what I really wanted to.

Cadotte.

Man, was I in trouble.

Perhaps if I'd swum until I felt nothing but limp, I wouldn't have been so distracted all night. However, I doubt anything could have erased his taste from my mouth and his image from my mind.

I know that an hour's worth of pacing did not get rid of the question: Why me? Cadotte certainly hadn't been dazzled by my charm or my appearance. I wasn't wealthy, brilliant, or hot. What was he up to?

The questions swirled in my head as the mortification swirled in my gut. I'd shared an appallingly intimate moment with a stranger. How was I ever going to look Cadotte in the face again?

I wasn't sure I could, but I'd have to. He hadn't given me one speck of the information I'd asked for.

The memory of my moans and gyrations haunted me

all the way to work, which only meant that I had a mood to match Zee's.

The phones were ringing like the church bells on Christmas Eve when I walked into the station. Thankfully Zee triaged better than anyone I'd ever met. She put one call on hold, routed another to the fire department, a third to the clinic, and spoke to the fourth.

I'd never make it as a dispatcher. My crisis management skills were heavily weighted to action rather than reaction.

"Two Adam Four, do you copy?"

"Two Adam Four, I copy and am ten-forty-two."

"My ass you're off duty," Zee muttered, though not over the radio for a change. She glanced at me. "Henry's been to three fights already tonight. He's going to love this."

As everyone in the department knew, Henry—one of our second shift officers—loathed overtime. He had a young wife and no children—yet—though not for lack of trying.

"Ten-seventy-four that," Zee continued. "There's a ten-ten in progress at the Sportsman."

"Another one? *What* are people drinking? Okay, I'm ten-seventy-six to the Sportsman."

"This whole town has gone ape shit," Zee muttered. "You'd think rabid wolves and a school shooting would make people stay home and play nice. Instead, they're out drinking and driving and fighting."

She picked up the call on hold. "Yeah, she's here now." Zee listened. "I'll tell her."

After hanging up, she lit a new cigarette off the stub of her old one and took a deep drag, letting the smoke blow out of her nose on a sigh of contentment. Zee loved her cigarettes nearly as much as she loved me. Or maybe it was the other way around.

"Who's here?" I prompted when she continued to smoke and ignore me.

"Who the hell do you think? You see anyone else hanging around?"

Since I was accustomed to Zee's usual manner of conversation, I didn't even blink at her words or her tone. "Someone's looking for me?"

"Yeah. That spooky old fart the DNR hired. He's on his way. You're supposed to wait for him."

I flicked a finger at the phones. "Don't I have work to do?"

"Hell, yes. But Clyde said you deal with Dr. Death first."

"Peachy."

I glanced around the office. The second shift hadn't come back in yet. The rest of the third shift must have already gone out. Zee and I were the only lucky ones in the place. I hated waiting around with nothing to do. I stuck my hand in my pocket and my fingertips nicked the totem.

"I'll be in the evidence room," I said. I could at least put this back where it belonged and get Clyde off my ass.

As I walked by Zee, she put down her cigarette and sniffed the murky air. "Where you been?" she asked.

"Home. Where else?"

"You smell funny."

How she could tell with cigarette smoke still swirling around her snowy white hair I have no idea. But Zee had always had the nose of a bloodhound. I wondered what she'd be able to smell if her senses hadn't been depleted by nicotine.

I lifted my arm and sniffed underneath. "No, I don't."

"Aftershave," she announced.

I blushed. I couldn't help it.

Strange, though. I hadn't smelled any aftershave on Cadotte. Only that scent that was his alone—earth, air, forest, man.

"What are you up to, girl?"

Since I rarely had reason to blush, my heated cheeks must stand out like the flash of a searchlight on the night of a new moon. Zee glared at me suspiciously.

"Nothing but my job, Zee."

She snorted and I had a hard time not joining her. If my job involved letting William Cadotte put his mouth all over me, the number of applicants for my position would be greater than ravaging mosquitoes on a muggy summer night.

I escaped from the front office before Zee pried more out of me. Not that I was easy—prior evidence to the contrary—but Zee was even more bullheaded than I was. She'd pick at me until I cracked or she got enough information to come to her own conclusion.

I wouldn't really mind if Zee knew. In fact, I'd like to talk to her about what in hell was wrong with me. But Clyde was another story. Since his relationship with Zee was as close as or even closer than mine was, telling her would be the same as telling him. I'd lose my job, or at the least my involvement with this case. When Clyde had told me to stay away from Cadotte, he hadn't just been whistling Dixie.

Sighing, I slipped into the evidence room. I made my way to the shelf where I'd left the bag of junk that comprised the evidence from Karen Larson's accident. It wasn't there.

I didn't panic right away. Just figured I was on the wrong shelf. My mind wasn't exactly focused. I put the totem into my pocket and searched the room. There wasn't a lot there. My evidence certainly wasn't.

I began to feel uneasy. I remembered putting the bag

on the second shelf, along with the signed note from Cadotte. I got down on my knees and crawled around. Nothing.

I needed to report this to Zee and then to Clyde. The evidence room wasn't Fort Knox, but it was secure enough for Miniwa. I'd had to use my key to get in here, and only officers had keys. If we took evidence out of the room for any reason, we made a notation in the evidence log.

The evidence log!

I smacked myself in the forehead and grabbed the book off the desk next to the door. Quickly I spun through the pages, expecting to see a familiar name scrawled in the margin next to my scribbled listing of Karen Larson's evidence.

Not only was there no name; there was no scribble. Hell, there wasn't even a page.

I opened the book as far as the spine would allow. I couldn't see a shred of paper. Either someone was very good at ripping pages out of books, or I was nuts and I'd never recorded anything at all.

I had to go with the first option, even though that made no sense. Who would want a bag of glass and plastic?

Unless . . .

I patted my pocket, felt the hard ridge of the totem against my thigh. Had the culprit been looking for something else entirely?

Cadotte had said that whoever the totem belonged to would be wanting it back. Then why not just ask? Unless the owner had good reason not to be recognized as such. And if it wasn't the owner, then what possible good could the totem do them?

I was more confused than ever. I couldn't prove I'd brought in the evidence. Couldn't prove the evidence had disappeared. Clyde was going to have my head when he found out.

He was already pissed at me for letting Cadotte keep the icon. But it was lucky I had or we'd have lost that, too.

One thing I knew, I wasn't leaving the totem here to disappear along with everything else. For now the stone was safe right where it was.

Chapter 12

I opened the evidence room door and let out a yelp. Mandenauer stood on the threshold, emaciated arm raised to knock.

"Ah, Officer, good evening."

His *good* sounded like *goot,* and he drew out the word *evening* like a bad Dracula imitation. I would have laughed, if I hadn't been close to crying.

I stepped into the hall and slammed the door behind me. There'd already been one too many people in the evidence room in the past twenty-four hours.

"What are you doing here? This area is off-limits to civilians."

"I am not a civilian. The sheriff has given me temporary clearance."

"You have a key?"

"Certainly."

"Have you been in this room?"

He glanced at the door, his gaze flicked over the word *evidence*, and he shook his head. "No need."

I didn't believe him. That was going around.

"What did you want to see me about?"

"Do you have your rifle?"

"Rifle? What the hell for?"

"Tonight we hunt."

I had been heading for the front office to receive my assignment from Zee. I stopped and turned very slowly. "I'm assigned to you?"

"Yes."

"Why? Don't guys like you work alone?"

His lips twitched. "I am not a cowboy."

I looked him over from the tip of his head—white blond hair now covered with a black skullcap—past his camouflage jumpsuit, to the toes of his black commando boots. "No shit."

He ignored me. The man was catching on.

"Get a rifle. Follow me."

"Shouldn't you be following me? I know these woods."

"But I know wolves. Especially wolves like these. I will teach you things you never thought to learn."

There was something cryptic in that statement, but my mind was still fuddled with sex and the mystery of the missing plastic.

"Clyde's okay with this?" I asked.

"It was Clyde's idea."

I frowned. Why hadn't Clyde told me?

I moved down the back hall to the weapons room and Mandenauer followed me. The rifle I'd been assigned for use in tactical situations had never been out of the case. There weren't a helluva lot of tactical situations in Miniwa. Until lately anyway.

For long-range shooting I preferred my own rifle, but since no one had seen fit to tell me of my change in status from Three Adam One to Mandenauer's backup, my rifle was home in the gun safe. I'd have to make do with city-issue.

"What's so special about these wolves, besides what

you already told me?" I pulled out my gun and checked it over. "They're overly aggressive, extremely violent, fearless."

"And smart." I glanced at him and he shrugged. "The virus appears to increase their brainpower."

"You've got to be kidding me."

"I do not kid."

I wasn't surprised. After pulling out a box of ammo, I relocked the gun cabinet. "So we've got super-pissed-off wolves that are also very smart." My gaze met his. "How smart?"

Something flickered in the depths of his eerily light eyes. Not fear but close.

"How smart, Mandenauer? What are we dealing with here?"

He sighed and glanced away. "Human-level intelligence."

I couldn't seem to find my voice, a novelty for me. When I did, all I could manage was, "That's . . . That's . . ."

What I meant to say was "impossible." Mandenauer filled in another word entirely. "Hazardous. I know. I've seen them formulate a plan, work together, and destroy those who try to destroy them. It's—"

"Creepy."

He raised a brow. "I was going to say 'fascinating.' "

"You would," I muttered.

"Shall we go?"

"Shouldn't we have a plan of our own?"

"Oh, I do, Officer. I do."

"What is it?"

"Come with me and you'll see."

I really didn't like the sound of that.

. . .

An hour later, I didn't like the looks of the plan, either. We were deep in the forest, high up in a tree. Not that I hadn't been in trees before; I'd just never liked it much. I preferred to hunt on the ground. Mandenauer had vetoed that idea immediately.

"One thing these wolves cannot do, yet, is fly. The only place we are safe is in the sky."

There was one word in that statement that bugged me quite a bit. I wasn't going to let it pass. "Yet?" I repeated.

Mandenauer had spent the day scouting the woods and found a tree stand big enough for two, which he'd confiscated for our use. Since it was June, no one would care. Hunting season was still three months away.

"The virus evolves," he murmured. "It is very upsetting."

"Upsetting? Do the Centers for Disease Control know about this mutating virus? How about the president?"

"Everyone who needs to know does."

Yeah, right. Perhaps I'd make a little call to the CDC in the morning.

"Don't we need bait?" I asked. "A sheep or something?"

"No. They will come. It is only a matter of time."

The light dawned. "We're the bait."

Mandenauer didn't answer, which was answer enough.

"I don't like this."

"Do you have a better idea, Jessie?"

"We could go searching for them in the daylight, when they're sleeping."

"These animals disappear in the daylight."

"*Poof! Shazam!* They're invisible?"

"Hardly, Officer. But believe me, it is easier to pick

them off one by one in the night than waste days trying to find an animal that isn't there."

Isn't there? The guy didn't make any sense. But he was right about one thing—he knew more than me about these wolves—so I'd let him be the leader. For now.

The moon was headed toward full and shiny bright. The night had a nip. Warm evenings would not come to the north woods for at least a few weeks.

I wanted to ask Mandenauer a hundred things. Where had he seen wolves like these before? Had he been able to wipe them out before they did serious harm? Where was he from? Were there others like him?

But he put his finger to his lips, then pointed to the silver-tinged forest. We had to be quiet. Wolves could hear for miles, and these could probably hear for hundreds of miles.

I settled in to wait, something I was very good at. Though patience might seem against my nature, patience was needed to hunt, and I'd been hunting over half of my life.

I'd gone along at first to be one of the guys. I'd continued to hunt, year after year, because I was good at it—and I'd been good at precious little as a teen. I certainly had no talent for being a girl and therefore none for pleasing my mother. But I could sit in a tree and wait, then wait some more.

An hour passed, then another. Mandenauer was good at waiting, too. He didn't move; he barely breathed. A couple of times I had to fight the urge to reach over and make sure he hadn't died in that tree. Only the intermittent blinking of his eyes signaled he was alive and awake.

Around 1:00 A.M. a solitary howl split the night. It was answered by several more. Our gazes met. We sat up straighter and slid our rifles into position.

I heard them first—a rustle to the right slinking closer, one to the left, another behind, then in front. They were approaching from every direction. Even though I was high in the sky, I was uneasy.

My finger twitched on the trigger. Mandenauer cut a quick glance my way and frowned. He held up his free hand in a staying gesture. I scowled back. I knew what I was doing. I wouldn't fire until I had a clear shot.

When I returned my gaze to the clearing, a black wolf had appeared. He paused, half in and half out of cover, scanning the area in a wary manner.

The thing was huge—much bigger than any wolf I'd ever seen. The average Wisconsin timber wolf runs about 80 pounds. I'd read they could weigh close to 120 in Alaska. This one had to be even larger than that.

None of the other wolves showed themselves, but I could feel them all around us, waiting for the leader's signal.

The wolf took one step forward, and the bushes flipped closed behind him. His entire body shone blue-black beneath the light of the moon. God, he was beautiful.

My finger hesitated on the trigger. How was I supposed to know which wolves had super-rabies and which ones did not? That would have been a good question for Mandenauer.

We weren't supposed to shoot every wolf we saw. Or were we? DNR policy on Chronic Wasting Disease was to kill as many deer as possible. Maybe the DNR had the same rules for super-rabies.

Suddenly the ruff at his neck rose, and a low growl vibrated from his throat. His head snapped upward and his eyes met mine.

"Shit!"

The word burst from my mouth as my finger clenched

on the trigger. The resulting explosion was so loud my
ears rang.

The wolf leaped into the air, twisted, fell. I experienced a momentary pang to have shot something so gorgeous. But at least I knew now how to tell if the animal
was infected.

The wolf's eyes had been human.

Chapter 13

"What the hell was that?" I asked.

"I was going to ask the very same question."

I glanced at Mandenauer. He was staring at me and not the wolf. I looked back. The thing was gone.

I rubbed my eyes. Tried again. Still gone.

"Where is it?"

"The wolf ran off, along with all the others."

"But . . . but . . . I hit it."

"Are you certain?"

The wolf had jerked, jumped, fallen. "Yes, I hit it."

"Apparently, not well enough."

Which wasn't like me. What I hit, I hit very well indeed.

"Why did you shoot, Officer?"

"Didn't you see that thing?" I shuddered, remembering those eyes.

Wolves had light eyes—yellow, greenish, hazel. This one's had been brown—nothing to write home about except for the unusual flash of white and their expression. A calculated hatred and too human intelligence. I never would have thought intelligence could be evident in the eyes, but I was wrong.

"Of course I saw it," Mandenauer answered. "I was

waiting for the others to show themselves before I shot. They were all infected, Officer."

I winced. I'd screwed up and now we had nothing to show for our hours of patience.

"How do you know they were all infected?"

"They were coming in like a Special Forces operation."

"And how would you know that?"

Mandenauer peered down his long, bony nose. "I know."

Special Forces? Him?

"You're losing it, Mandenauer. How could a group of wolves, supervirus or not, use Special Forces tactics? How could they get to us up here?"

"We will never know now that you scared them off before I could adequately gauge what they were planning."

I stifled the urge to apologize. This guy was nuts. Wolves with human intelligence? Even after I'd seen those eyes, I found that hard to swallow.

The amount of planning he was talking about was beyond an animal, enhanced or not. How did they devise their strategy, by drawing pictures in the dirt with their paws?

"I thought wolves rarely attacked people."

"These are more than wolves."

More than wolves? What did that mean? I could ask, but then he'd probably tell me. I needed to talk to Clyde and a few others before I started questioning Mandenauer. I was having serious doubts about his sanity.

After flicking the safety on my rifle, I reached for the rope used to lower weapons to the ground.

"Where are you going?" Mandenauer sat on the floor of the tree stand with his back against one plank wall.

"Back to work?"

"This is your work now."

I glanced at the woods where the wolves had disappeared. "But—"

"Now that they know we are here they may be back. It isn't safe to be on the ground until morning."

"You mean we have to sit up here all night?"

He shrugged and snuggled his shoulders into the corner. "Wake me if they return."

Then he closed his eyes and went to sleep, just like that.

Morning came—eventually. But none of the wolves did.

I observed a lot of wildlife that night, but nothing out of the ordinary. A raccoon or three, an opossum, a doe and two fawns tripped through just before dawn. Mandenauer slept through everything.

When the sun spread bright fingers of light across the floor of the tree stand, I kicked Mandenauer's boot. He came awake in an instant. I could tell by his face he knew where he was. I wouldn't have. The only people I knew who could come out of a deep sleep and function immediately were ex-military. The longer I knew Mandenauer the more interesting he became.

He glanced into the clearing. "Nothing," he stated.

I didn't bother to answer what hadn't been a question.

We lowered our rifles to the ground, then followed them down, returning to town in silence. Mandenauer must have gotten a car from somewhere, since he'd met me at the station, so instead of dropping him at his cabin, I took him back where I had found him.

Zee was already gone and a new fresh face sat in her place. I wondered where they'd gotten this one. She appeared to be all of twelve years old—fine blond hair, huge blue eyes, porcelain pale skin—she would have been pretty except for that nose. Poor thing had a beak like a hawk.

"Morning, Jessie," she chirped.

Someone had neglected to tell her she should never talk to me before breakfast.

Clyde must have been waiting for us, because he barreled out of his office almost as soon as we walked in. "Gonna make my day?"

The youngster murmured, *"Sudden Impact."* Maybe she was smarter than she looked.

"No, sir," I answered. Set to launch into an explanation of how it was all my fault, I was shocked when Mandenauer put a heavy, staying hand on my shoulder.

"This will take time," he said.

Clyde chewed hard and fast on his first chew of the morning. "I went to Miss Larson's house. Nothing unusual there."

"Any indication of why she might have been out on the road at three A.M.?"

"None. I doubt we'll ever know the answer to that. Hell, maybe she just couldn't sleep."

"I hate loose ends," I muttered.

"You, me, and the rest of the free world." Clyde stalked back into his office and slammed the door.

"He is upset."

I glanced at Mandenauer and tamped down on the urge to say, "No shit." The old man was staring at the door to Clyde's office with a contemplative expression.

"He doesn't do well with change. Rabid wolves, citizens eating each other, that's new around here."

"Hmm. Then we'd best obtain some results for the sheriff. I will meet you tonight?"

"Same bat time, same bat channel," I agreed.

Mandenauer appeared confused. His knowledge of classic television trivia was no doubt sorely lacking. But at least he didn't ask me to explain. I was not in the mood.

What I was, was tired and sore from lounging in that tree stand all night. I wanted food and my pillow, but I had one phone call to make before I could go.

Mandenauer headed for the parking lot; I headed for what passed as my office—a desk among all the other desks—but at least no one else was in the room. Then I looked up the number for the Centers for Disease Control in Atlanta.

"This is Officer Jessie McQuade of the Miniwa, Wisconsin, PD," I began. "I . . . Uh, well, you see, we have a tiny problem here."

How did I explain something that sounded like I'd read it in a fantasy novel? One that had a cheesy, cartoonish, snarling, slavering wolf on the cover?

I took a deep breath and told the switchboard operator everything that I knew. To the woman's credit, she didn't collapse into giggles right away. Who knows what she did after she transferred my call to Dr. Hanover.

"Elise Hanover." The voice on the other end of the line was clipped—all business and very busy.

I began my story all over again, but she interrupted me after only a moment. "Yes, yes. I know about the new rabies strain."

"You do?"

"Of course. I'm working on that problem right now."

"You are?"

An impatient sigh drifted several hundred miles. "Officer, what is it you want to know?"

What did I want to know? That Mandenauer wasn't a psycho with a gun? That he hadn't made up this rabies crap so he could go bonkers in our forest and start killing every wolf that he saw? I guess I knew that now. But as long as I had an expert on the line . . .

"Is this a terrorist infiltration?"

Dr. Hanover snorted. "Like I'd tell you if it was?"

Good point.

"Relax," she said. "Everything that goes to hell in our country isn't the result of a terrorist."

"Yeah, tell it to the media."

Silence met my snarl. I waited for the *click* of the phone or the request for my superior's phone number. Instead the doctor chuckled. "You're a woman after my own heart, Officer."

I blinked, uncertain what to say to that. I wasn't used to female friendliness. The two words were mutually exclusive in my book.

I'd spent my childhood with the boys. I liked them— still did. Boys didn't smile in your face and stab you in the back. They kicked your ass; then they were done. I prefer my hostility out in the open where I can see it.

My only girlfriend was Zee, and she wasn't much of a girl. But her hostility was definitely out in the open. Zee was a woman after *my* own heart.

When I sat there like a lump too long, Dr. Hanover filled in the silence. "The virus is a result of nature, Officer. You've heard, I'm sure, that certain infections are becoming resistant to antibiotics because of overuse of medication?"

"Yes. I also know that infections are different from viruses and antibiotics aren't worth dick if you have the flu. Since rabies is basically the flu on acid, what difference does resistance to antibiotics make?"

"None whatsoever. I was using an analogy. The rabies virus is mutating to get around the vaccine."

"I was told if anyone else was bitten we should use the rabies vaccine."

"For humans, that's true. The only help for animals is a bullet."

"Those I got."

"Silver?"

"Excuse me?" I could not have heard her right.

"Silver bullets work best."

It was my turn to snort. "Doctor, have you been watching too many Lon Chaney movies?"

"Who?"

She was either too young to remember the Wolf Man—hell, I was too young, except I liked black-and-white horror movies—or too much of a brainiac to watch movies at all.

"Never mind," I said. "You're kidding me about the silver bullets, right?"

"Sorry, but no. We've discovered the mutated virus reacts negatively to silver."

"Dead is dead in my book. What difference does it make how?"

"You'd be surprised. I've had reports of animals with a nonkill wound dying if a silver bullet was used. What can it hurt? Dead is dead, right?" I heard the amusement in her voice as she threw my own words back at me.

"Where the hell do I get silver bullets? Werewolves 'R' Us?"

"Try the Internet. You can buy anything there."

The phone went dead in my hand.

"Silver bullets." I shook my head. That'd be the day.

I could see myself trying to explain why my rifle was loaded with silver—to Clyde, to Bozeman, to John Q. Public, even to Mandenauer. They'd lock me up and throw away the key.

I'd take my chances with the lead variety, thank you.

My radio crackled. "Jessie?"

The new dispatcher. Why hadn't she just shouted for me? She had to know I was three doors down the hall.

I got up and walked to the front of the building. She

appeared frazzled; the buttons on her switchboard were lit up like a meteor shower. Someone was chattering into her headphones. I could hear them from five feet away.

I glanced into Clyde's office. He was taking a call and, if the wide sweeps of his hands and the scowl on his face were any indication, he was in the middle of an argument.

"Jessie!" The dispatcher beckoned. "I need you to go out on a call."

"I'm off."

"Nuh-uh."

I raised a brow and glanced at her name tag. She wasn't wearing one. Zee must not think the kid would last through the day.

She waved a hand at the switchboard. "We just got slammed. There's a three-car pileup on the highway and a domestic disturbance on Grand. I sent everyone available; then another call came in." She bit her lip. "Clyde said if I disturbed him I should find another job."

I glanced into his office again. He was still arguing. He caught me staring and turned his back. *Odd.*

"Fine." I saw my blueberry bagel and cool soothing sheets slipping away, but there was nothing I could do about it. "Where and what?"

She beamed. "The university. One of the professors' offices was ransacked."

"Whose?" I asked, but I already knew.

Chapter 14

"Cadotte," she said. "William Cadotte."

One thing I did not need today was a face-to-face encounter with the man who'd had his tongue in my mouth last night.

"I'll take the domestic," I offered, which only proved how desperate I was.

Domestic disturbances were the most dangerous calls. You never knew what you were going to run into when love turned to hate. Besides, I'd never been very good at dealing with family squabbles, never having had one of my own.

The dispatcher shook her head, destroying my hopes. "One Adam Three is already there. One Adam One and Two are en route to the accident. Which leaves you."

I gave up. Sometimes fate was a malicious bitch.

Surrendering any delusion that I might get to sleep soon, I grabbed coffee at the Gas n' Go, then snagged a doughnut, too.

The route to the university was becoming familiar, as was the route to Cadotte's cubbyhole of an office. Students, teachers, security milled aimlessly in the hall. There was no sign of the man himself.

The crowd parted for me like the proverbial Red Sea.

However, I wasn't feeling much like Moses. The land of milk and honey was my apartment, and it felt farther away right now than Egypt.

I likened myself to Pharaoh's soldiers. If I went through these people and into the belly of the sea, I was going to drown, but I had to go. Orders were orders and duty just that, as much now as they had been countless centuries before.

I paused on the threshold of the office. Cadotte sat at his desk, his forehead in his hands. Several colleagues hovered around, trying not to disturb the mess.

Cadotte glanced up, almost as if he'd sensed me there. Our gazes met. The air between us sizzled. I was in way over my head with William Cadotte.

"Jessie," he whispered, and stood.

If I hadn't come here before, I might have thought he was just a pig or a spacey egghead who had better things to do than clean. But I had come, and while the place had been full of stuff, the stuff had been in neat piles. Now it was spread to hell and gone in every corner and all across the floor.

"Everyone out," I ordered.

I couldn't stop staring at Cadotte. Though he appeared as exhausted as I was, he was still something to see. His hair stood on end, as if he'd run agitated fingers through the strands over and over again. His glasses were hooked in the pocket of his shirt, so I could see his dark eyes flare hot in an unusually pale face. He was pissed, and I couldn't say that I blamed him.

I'd been burglarized once. I still remembered how it had felt to know some stranger had invaded my place, touched my things, perhaps seen something private. I'd lost money, my CD player, but more important, I'd lost my sense of security for a long, long time.

The door closed and we were alone. "What happened?" I asked.

"I already went over this with Security."

"And I'll get that information. I want you to tell me."

He sat on the edge of the desk and I was reminded of how easily he moved—at home in his skin, confident with his body—he'd be attractive for the way he held himself alone. The handsome face, rippling muscles, and great big . . . brain were all gravy.

"I came in to work early this morning," he began.

I wanted to ask why, but I knew better. When taking a statement it was best to let the person tell you everything without interruptions first. You didn't want them to forget something important because they were distracted. The second time through was the time for questions.

"My door was ajar. I figured the cleaning crew was running late. I walked right in." He gave an annoyed grunt. "Sorry, I touched the doorknob."

I shrugged and made a circular motion with my finger indicating he should keep rolling. People would be amazed to know—despite countless hours of *NYPD Blue*—how many times evidence was fucked long before we got there.

"The place was like this." He spread his hands to indicate the mess. "I called nine-one-one, then Security. Someone was searching for something."

Since he appeared to be done with his story, I asked, "What?"

"Do you still have the totem?"

I started, frowned, forced my hand to stay at my side and not creep to my pocket to check. I could feel the talisman there, sharp against my upper thigh. If Cadotte had been looking, he'd have been able to see it, too, although the small piece of stone could easily be mistaken for a key or any other paraphernalia of the pocket.

"Not on me," I lied. Then, "You think someone was after the totem, so they trashed your office?"

"Nothing was taken. I checked."

"Perhaps you gave a student one too many zeros."

"I don't give zeros."

"Too many Fs then."

"I don't give those, either."

"Well, sign me up, Professor. Sounds like my kind of class."

His lips twitched. I was glad to see him coming out of that frozen, zombielike state. "Who else knows I had the totem?"

Myself. Cadotte. Clyde.

I frowned. The only one of us who didn't know I had the totem now was Clyde. But what possible reason would he have for trashing Cadotte's office? Clyde might not like him but wouldn't risk his job just to be pissy.

Then I remembered the paper Cadotte had signed for the totem and that it was missing. Hell, anyone with access to the evidence room, or the stolen evidence, could have done this. But why?

"Jessie?"

I raised my gaze. "Maybe the person who lost it was searching for it?"

"And they would come to me instead of you, why?"

Hmm, good point.

"Who knows that I had the thing besides you and me?" he repeated.

"Clyde." I shrugged. "And anyone with access to the evidence room."

Quickly I explained about the receipt, the evidence log, and the missing evidence.

Cadotte gave a long, slow blink. "That makes no sense."

I had to agree. "This was probably an unrelated incident."

"Why my office and no one else's? Why take nothing but look at everything?"

My gaze swept the room. There was an awful lot of paper. Books, notes.

"Are you working on something?"

Cadotte had been staring at the ground, fingering his glasses, and scowling. "Huh?"

He glanced up and I started. For a second there his dark, angry eyes had reminded me of the wolf I had seen in the clearing last night.

I rubbed my own eyes, and when I tried again, all I saw in his was curiosity. Why on earth would I remember a rabid wolf when I looked into Cadotte's eyes?

Because I was way too tired to be working, way too deprived to be anywhere near him. I had a hard time thinking beyond how he tasted, how he smelled, how he had appeared naked in the moonlight and fully clothed on my porch with his tongue between my breasts.

Yet ever since I'd walked into this room, he had given no indication that we were any more than acquaintances. Perhaps in his mind we were. He probably brought women to orgasm with his kiss alone all the time.

Since the idea of him touching anyone else as he had touched me made me angry—how crazy was that? I couldn't even bring myself to call him by his first name—I forced myself back to the matter at hand. Despite all evidence to the contrary, I was a cop, not a silly, hormonal teenager.

"Are you working on a paper? A book? A theory? Something a colleague might want to take a peek at? Steal? Screw up?"

He shook his head. "I just finished a book."

"You wrote a book?" Although I *had* asked, that he'd actually written an entire book made me gape.

Cadotte laughed. "I've written several. That's what professors do when they aren't teaching. Publish or perish. Ever hear of it?"

No. I'd never been much of a student—although I liked to read. What else was a girl supposed to do alone, Friday night after Friday night?

"What are all these notes for?" I waved my hand at the fire hazard living in his office.

"Mostly for you."

"Me?"

I might not be the flowers and chocolate type, but crumpled paper and dusty books didn't do a thing for me.

"The totem, Jessie."

Poof went my ideas of romance. Everything came back to that damn piece of rock.

"You never told me what you found out."

"I wanted to." He lifted one inky brow. "But I was distracted."

My face heated at the memory of that distraction. Suddenly he was staring at me with an expression I could only describe as hungry.

He pushed away from the desk and crossed the space between us in one stride. I should have done something to stop him, but I caught the scent of his skin and my body responded, going tight and wet without him touching me at all.

He stopped less than an inch away. I had to tilt my head back to see his eyes. I wasn't used to being so much smaller than a man—one of the reasons there'd been so few men. Not only did they not like me being as tall as them or as strong; I didn't like it, either.

Call me sexist, but I wanted a guy to tower over me. Right now I wanted this one to do a lot more than tower—I wanted him to touch me, teach me, take me.

As if he had heard what I wanted, his eyes narrowed; his nostrils flared. He grabbed my hips and pulled me against him, then crushed his mouth to mine.

He was rough. I didn't mind. Our teeth clicked together; his scraped my lip; then he licked the tiny hurt. I shuddered. I wanted to take his flesh into my mouth and suckle. I wanted to feel him skin to skin.

He spread his hands over my ass and ground us together. He was hard. It felt so good. I was going to come again, right there in his office. While on duty. *Shit.*

I shoved at his chest. He wouldn't let me go. I wasn't afraid. I was the one with the gun, but how could I explain shooting him? It wouldn't be easy.

His mouth was doing amazing things, and I had a difficult time remembering why I wanted him to stop. While I hesitated, he backed me up against the door, then laid his body flush with mine.

My hands were still pressed to his chest, but instead of shoving, as I should be, my treacherous fingers had found their way into the collar of his shirt and stroked the smooth skin of his throat. One thumb slid into the hollow beneath his Adam's apple. I ran my fingernail lightly across his skin. He growled and the sound vibrated from the tip of my thumb to far more interesting places.

Goose bumps erupted, enhancing my sensitivity. I already felt as if the air itself sizzled. Now my skin was on fire.

The door at my back moved—opened an inch, then slammed shut beneath the weight of both my body and his. Someone knocked, the sound right next to my ear.

"Professor?"

I jumped and Cadotte pulled his tongue out of my mouth. His eyes were so close I could see his pupils dilated almost to the rim of the iris. If I'd been any farther away, I wouldn't have been able to distinguish one from the other, so similar were they in color.

His mouth was swollen and wet. His breath puffed along my face, chilling my own damp lips.

"Yes?" he called, in a cool, distant, nearly normal voice. How could he do that when he was still plastered all over me?

He flexed his hips, riding his erection against the zipper in my pants. My eyes crossed and he chuckled, then kissed my forehead.

"Will you be teaching your first class, Professor, or should I dismiss them?"

"I'll be right there."

I must be losing my mind, but having him talk to the department secretary about mundane daily tasks while his body was doing a vertical tango with mine on the other side of the door was the most erotic moment of my life. Pathetic, but true.

Heels clicked in the other direction, sounding sharp and somewhat annoyed. Why hadn't I heard them approach? Stupid question.

Cadotte brushed his knuckles against the underside of my breast. A moan escaped my lips before I could stop myself. "Though I'd like to stay here and kiss you until you beg, I've gotta go."

Beg? Me? Where was my quick and cutting comeback? I couldn't think of a thing to say.

"I need to go, too." I shifted against him. He stayed right where he was. I stared at a place on the far wall and refused to look at him.

"Jessie," he murmured.

Crap. He wasn't going to let me go until we talked

about this. Why did everyone always want to talk about sex, even when they hadn't really had it yet?

Yet? I was going to have sex with William Cadotte?

My eyes met his. He smiled. I sighed.

Yeah. I was.

Chapter 15

"When do you get off?" Cadotte asked.

"Any second now if you don't move," I muttered.

He laughed and stepped away. Without the heat of his body against mine the room felt cool, though I knew it wasn't. Though the day had not yet warmed beyond the fifties, his office was like a furnace. How did he stand it?

"I meant, when do you get off work?"

I scrubbed my fingers through my hair. I was a mess. No sleep, a night in the forest. Hell, I hadn't brushed my teeth since yesterday. Why on earth had he continued to kiss me?"

Cadotte stepped close and rubbed one thumb against my chin. "Quit thinking so much."

"What kind of statement is that for a teacher to make?"

"Just answer the question, Officer."

"I'm already off. You got overtime."

"Above and beyond. I'm flattered."

"You should be."

"I suppose you practically bribed someone else to come here so you wouldn't have to."

I blinked. Close enough. How did he know me so

well when he didn't really know me at all?

Cadotte slipped on his glasses. I wondered again what he'd look like wearing those and nothing else. I really, really liked his glasses.

Picking up a folder, he scowled at the label, then put the folder back down and chose another.

"Would you meet me for dinner tonight? I'll tell you what I found out about the totem."

"Meet you?" I echoed.

"You'd rather I picked you up?"

"No. I mean . . ." I wasn't sure what I meant.

The thought of having dinner with William Cadotte, in public, caused no small amount of unease. For one thing, I didn't date. Dinner with a man would raise all sorts of questions. Dinner with this man would raise even more.

He was Indian; I wasn't. He was pretty, same thing. He was off-limits, according to my boss.

Cadotte could be more trouble than he was worth. I let my gaze wander over him from the tip of his black, shiny hair to the toe of his . . . toe.

He wasn't wearing any shoes. His feet were tanned, smooth, his toes straight, the nails clipped and clean.

Damn. I was even aroused by his feet. Trouble, trouble, trouble.

I still wanted to see him. More than I'd wanted anything for quite a long time.

"Come to my place instead," I blurted.

Cadotte glanced at me over the rims of his glasses. "Why?"

I had quite a few reasons, the most important being we couldn't seem to keep our hands off each other—even in public. I'd think there'd been a spell cast over me, if I believed in such things.

"Because," I said, and left it at that.

He frowned and a flicker of uncertainty passed through his eyes. I'd never seen him uncertain before.

"What?" I asked.

"You don't want to be seen with me?"

"No! It isn't that."

And it wasn't. Not really. I wouldn't mind being seen with him; hell, I'd love it. What woman wouldn't? What I didn't want to face were the questions, the stares, the speculation.

What on earth was a man like him doing with a woman like me? The inevitable answer: I must be an incredible lay.

"What is it then?"

He'd taken off his glasses so he could stare at me through naked, intense, searching eyes. I glanced away.

"I don't want to discuss business in public."

He didn't say anything. I heard the rustle of papers, the thud of a book. "Fine." His voice was cool and brisk. I wanted the heated huskiness back. "I'll come to your place at . . . ?"

"Seven."

"All right. I'll bring my notes. You bring the totem."

"What?" I shot him a startled glance.

He juggled two books and three folders as he walked past me, then shoved his bare feet into the sandals he'd left by the door. "Bring the totem so we can compare the markings to some of the drawings I found."

The totem again. I ran a thumb over the stub in my pocket. For an instant I could have sworn the thing was hot to the touch. But that was no doubt just my skin—still flushed and sensitive from Cadotte's assault.

He opened the door and paused, giving me a chance to study him. I found no hint of deception in his steady gaze. If he'd wanted the totem for himself, he wouldn't have given the thing back.

I let my eyes wander over the ransacked office. Hell, he'd have the perfect alibi right here. Pretend the totem was stolen, then keep it. I'd be the one taking the heat for letting him have the evidence in the first place.

"I'll see you tonight." He jerked his head toward the hall. "I've got a class."

"Sure. Tonight. I'll—um—order a pizza."

He smiled. "Pepperoni and black olives?"

"No way. Sausage, mushroom, and onion."

He tilted his head and his earring swung free, glittering gold like a harvest moon in a midnight sky. "How about half and half?"

I had a feeling I was agreeing to more than a pizza, but what the hell? "Deal," I said, and then he was gone.

I was left alone in his office with a whole bunch of questions.

Cadotte hadn't been the one to trash this place, so who had? Since nothing had been taken and nothing had been ruined, there wasn't much of a crime. I could call in a fingerprint tech, but we'd have to cross-reference everyone who had been in here.

I thought of all the students, all the teachers, all the staff. "Good luck," I muttered.

My radio crackled. "Jessie?"

Clyde's voice made me jump. What was he doing on the radio?

"Yeah?"

"What's going on out there?"

"Nothing much." I filled him in on what had happened.

"Tell me you got that evidence back from Cadotte, and that it's safely tucked away in the evidence room right now."

I tugged the totem from my pocket and twirled the stone round and round in my fingers. Why was everyone so damn concerned with this thing? It was a carved wolf, nothing more, nothing less. Interesting, but not life-changing—no matter what Cadotte believed.

"Jessie!" Clyde snapped. "Where is that totem?"

I didn't like his tone. It made the hairs on the back of my neck tingle. I'd learned over the years to listen to those hairs. They always signaled trouble.

Of course they'd been standing up and dancing since Professor Cadotte had walked into my life. Maybe that was what was wrong with them now, but I didn't think so.

I folded the tiny wolf into my palm. "I got the totem back."

"Good."

Was his sigh of relief just a little too relieved? When had I stopped trusting Clyde? I wasn't quite sure.

"But it isn't in the evidence room."

"Why the hell not?"

Well, he had to find out sometime. Better now, when he was on one side of town and I was on the other. "Because someone's been in there and everything having to do with Karen Larson's accident is gone."

"Everything?"

I took a deep breath, then did something I had never done before. I lied to my boss. "Everything."

I might be sorry later, but I didn't think so. I opened my hand and stared at the strange little wolf—no bigger than my thumbnail—that lay in my palm. Too many people were far too interested in this thing. Until I found out why, maybe it would be better if they all believed the totem had disappeared.

As I listened to Clyde rant and rave, I pawed around on Cadotte's desk until I found what I needed. A piece of twine, probably used to bind books or papers, which fit perfectly through the tiny hole at the top of the wolf.

I still had a hard time believing someone was after this bit of rock. But since the other evidence had disappeared, I was going to make certain this didn't, too. I was going to keep it in the safest place I could think of—on me.

One knot later, I dropped the icon over my head and under my shirt. The totem slid into the hollow between my breasts, and if I didn't know better I'd swear it snuggled in close and went to sleep.

Which is what I did as soon as I got home. I should have gone in and filed a report on Cadotte's office, as well as one on the missing evidence. But since I didn't want to meet Clyde face-to-face right now, I turned off my radio, my cell phone, and my house phone, and dived between the cool, welcoming sheets of my bed.

I slept and I dreamed. Of wolves with human eyes. Of people I knew with the eyes of a wolf—Cadotte, Clyde, Brad, Mandenauer, even Zee.

Someone was chasing me through the forest. I was naked, which explained why I was so afraid. No place to carry my gun.

And whatever was chasing me sounded big, mean, gun-worthy. Branches thrashed; sticks cracked; heavy footsteps pounded in my wake. But more than two feet. Two people? Or perhaps four paws.

My side ached. I'd been breathing through my mouth, fear making me forget all my lessons in endurance. I hated being afraid as much in the dream as I did when I was awake.

I glanced back. Always a mistake. Something big, black, and furry was after me. I knew what it was.

I stumbled over a branch and hit the ground hard. I couldn't breathe. I felt like I was going to die. Then suddenly air returned to my lungs. I gasped greedily.

Something leaped on top of me. I twisted, grabbed

fistfuls of fur. My fingers tangled in rawhide and a wolf totem swung in front of my face, hanging around the animal's neck like a collar.

The big black wolf with human eyes went for my throat, but instead of biting me, he licked my collarbone, then moved lower and lower still. I shuddered, aroused, and began to come.

I awoke with an audible gasp to find myself on the floor, the sheets tangled around my ankles, the twine tight at my neck. I was slick with sweat and on the verge of an orgasm.

"Hell. Shit. Son of a bitch!" I loosened the twine, shoved sweaty hanks of hair from my forehead.

Thankfully I was alone, so no one heard me curse like a dockworker or saw my hands shaking as I went into the bathroom and turned the shower to a temperature somewhere between ice-cold and lukewarm.

I stepped into the tub and stuck my head under the spray, gasping as chilly water cascaded over my heated skin. My mind cleared instantly, but I couldn't stop trembling, even when I turned the water from cold to hot.

The dream had disturbed me far more than any other I'd ever had.

Chapter 16

I'd slept the day away and only had an hour before Cadotte was supposed to show up. The damn twine had
rubbed a raw circle around my neck. A cold compress
plus a liberal application of vitamin E took away the
sting.

To hide the mark, I put on a sleeveless mock turtle-
neck instead of a tank top; then I transferred the totem
to a gold chain my mother had given me for my six-
teenth birthday, which I'd never worn.

I doubted she'd approve of the way I was wearing it
now, but the chain was my present and she wasn't here.
My rationalization for a lot of the things I did that my
mother wouldn't approve of.

I chose shorts instead of jeans. Judging by the heat
of my apartment, we'd enjoyed the first true day of summer while I'd been asleep. I threw open a few windows.
I couldn't see turning on the air-conditioning when the
setting of the sun was only a few hours away.

Besides, I had good legs and, being tall, I had a lot
of them. Swimming toned much better than jogging. I
preferred round, feminine muscle to stringy sinew and
emaciated calves.

I turned my cell phone on long enough to dial a pizza,

then shut it off again. If there were messages pending, they were no doubt from Clyde. I'd have to deal with him later, and later was when I *would* deal with him. Right now I was going to enjoy the evening.

A little pizza, a little Cadotte. If things went well, I might even be in a good mood by the time I went to work. I was hoping sex could erase the memory of that very strange dream. I'd never been into bestiality, so what was the matter with me now?

The stone shifted between my breasts, making me jump. I'd been standing at the floor-length window, staring at the summer sun. I hadn't moved. Why had the totem?

The dream had me spooked, that's all. Dreams were just dreams, despite any woo-woo propaganda to the contrary. They were not truth or predictions, not buried secrets or hidden hopes. They were just images that meant nothing at all. But what images!

Illusions tumbled through my mind of bodies entwined, sweat-slicked skin, heated flesh. These were followed by the tactile memory of soft fur, a smooth tongue. A man and a beast become one—or had that been a woman and a beast?

The doorbell rang and I started. I was rolling the totem between two fingers like a worry bead. The stone was warm. I dropped the icon back down my shirt as if it were on fire.

Woman and beast? That was a bit too kinky for comfort, and my mind shied away from the thought.

Cadotte stood in the hall with a pizza. I was so hungry I wanted to eat them both. What was wrong with me? Nothing that a little pizza and a lot of sex wouldn't solve.

"I met the delivery boy coming up."

"I'll pay you." I opened the door wide, inviting him in.

"Yeah, you will." He crowded me close, kicked the door shut, then kissed me—hard, deep, and wet. Maybe sex, then pizza was a better idea.

He stepped back and tilted his head. "There, all paid up."

"With one kiss?"

"You're a very good kisser."

I was left standing stunned in the hall when he strode into the apartment. I got so few compliments, and I'd never received one on how well I kissed. I had no idea what to say.

I wasn't required to say anything. By the time I reached the sofa, he had his mouth full of food. He'd brought wine. I got him a glass and a corkscrew.

"You don't drink?" He eyed the single glass.

"I have to work in four hours."

"That doesn't answer my question."

"Sure I drink."

I'd rarely met a cop who didn't, unless at one time they'd overindulged and were now on the wagon. Police work, even in a tiny town like Miniwa, was stressful. Cops drank. Period. A lot of them smoked, too. Or did chew, like Clyde. Thankfully I'd been able to manage my stress, so far, with the occasional Bloody Mary and a twilight swim.

"I suppose working third shift makes a beer at the end of your day a lot less than appealing." He opened the wine.

I'd never thought of it that way, but Cadotte was right. When I got off at 7:00 A.M. I didn't want alcohol; I didn't even want coffee. I just wanted my bed. Although if I kept having weird dreams, pretty soon I wouldn't want that.

"Mmm." Cadotte had his mouth full again, so I joined him.

Fifteen minutes later we were done. Cadotte scooted back on the couch, half-full glass of blood-red wine cradled in his long fingers. His thumb stroked the bowl and I lifted my gaze from his hand to his face.

He took a sip. A drop clung to his lip, and his tongue swept out to capture it. His earring glittered in the glare of the setting sun. I wanted to take that earring in my teeth and tug him into the bedroom.

"Shall we get down to business?"

"Mmm-hmm," I murmured, captivated by the way the light turned the golden feather from red to orange and back again.

"Do you have the totem?"

"Huh?"

He smiled and set his glass on the coffee table with a *click*. Cadotte knew the effect he had on women and I found myself wondering: Was he playing me to get to the totem?

Paranoid? Moi?

Definitely.

Nevertheless, I straightened, shook off the sexual inertia, and turned away. "It's gone."

"Gone? What do you mean, gone?"

"Disappeared? Stolen? *Poof?* Take your pick."

I was getting mighty good at lying.

He got so quiet, if I hadn't heard him breathing I might have thought he'd gone over the balcony—this time in the opposite direction.

"Oh well," he said at last. "I guess it's a good thing I sketched it."

Paper crinkled and I spun around. He leaned over the coffee table, smoothing a white rectangle. Then he pulled a bunch of other papers from his back pocket and set them all side by side.

"Y-you aren't upset about the totem?"

He glanced up. He'd put on his glasses. My heart went ba-boom. "Upset? Why should I be? It wasn't mine."

"Wasn't mine, either," I grumbled.

He studied me for a moment. "What happened?"

I didn't think I should tell him about the evidence room fiasco. Clyde would say that was police business, and since I was in enough trouble with Clyde already, I decided to keep my lips zipped on the subject.

"I really can't say."

"You're in trouble?"

I was, so I nodded. Cadotte beckoned, then patted the sofa at his side. "Come here."

My paranoia seemed just that in the face of his lack of concern over the missing totem. Of course, what good did it do him to be upset? The thing was gone—or so he thought.

When I joined him on the couch, our hips bumped. I shifted away. He followed, pressing his jean-clad thigh to mine. When I cast him a quick glance, however, he was staring at the paperwork and not at me. I left my leg right where it was.

"See this?"

I followed his finger to an extremely accurate pencil drawing of the totem, larger than the actual stone; the markings had been enlarged as well. They were much easier to see this way.

"You're good," I said.

"You have no idea."

That surprised a laugh out of me. The sound made me realize how seldom I heard it. Pretty sad. I was twenty-six and already the laughter had died. Perhaps with this man I could get it back.

Cadotte shuffled the stack of papers—printouts from the World Wide Web.

"What would we do without the Internet?" I murmured.

"A lot of work. I can find more there in an hour than I could find in a week at the library. Aha!" He snatched a sheet out of the center of the pile. "Look at this."

Placing the two papers next to each other, he slid them closer to me. The Internet printout showed an ancient, emaciated being with long teeth and even longer fingernails.

"Matchi-auwishuk," he whispered.

The trees rustled outside, and a sudden breeze came through the open balcony doors. As if expecting it, Cadotte put his hands on top of the papers. The breeze stopped as suddenly as it had begun.

Okay. That was weird.

I glanced at him, but he didn't seem disturbed. By the breeze. Instead, he scowled at the drawings.

"I don't remember seeing that." I pointed at the Matchi-auwishuk.

"I used a magnifier to identify some of the smaller markings. It's there. Take my word for it."

I would. Until he left and I scrounged up my own magnifying glass.

"And take my word on this." He shoved another piece of paper at me.

A shiver ran from my neck to the base of my spine. The Matchi-auwishuk had been ugly, but this was downright creepy—given the circumstances.

The figure was half-man, half-wolf.

"What in hell is that?"

"The wolf god."

The drawing was exemplary, the naked man impressive—sleek and muscled—perfection except for the paws growing where his hands and feet should be. A tail sprouted from his backside and ears from the top of his head. Instead of hair he had fur, and a snout blossomed where his mouth and nose had once been.

But those little foibles weren't what made me shrink away from the table, irrationally terrified of touching the picture or having it touch me.

Nope, what bothered me about the drawing were the damn eyes—sly, intelligent, human.

"Where did you find this?"

"There's an old and obscure legend of the Ojibwe. The wolf god can be brought to life during a blue moon if the way is paved by an army of wolf men. And women."

I turned my head so I could see his face. He wasn't laughing—so I did.

"What does that have to do with anything?"

"Jessie, aren't there a few too many coincidences here? The totem, the madness of the wolves, and the blue moon?"

The blue moon. I remembered telling Zee about it the night Karen Larson had been bitten by a wolf. The night I'd found the totem. The night I'd met William Cadotte running around naked in the woods.

"What's a wolf god, and how is it brought to life?"

He shuffled some of the papers, scowled, pushed his glasses up in an absent gesture. "I'm not sure."

"What good are you then?"

"We'll get to that later." He winked. Even in the middle of his delusion, he was propositioning me. Why did I think that was cute?

Cadotte returned his attention to the gibberish he'd

been reading. "All I've determined so far is that a were-wolf army is needed—"

"Whoa!" I jumped to my feet. "*Werewolf* army? Where did that come from?"

"What do you think wolf men and wolf women are?"

"A figment of your imagination?"

"Mine and whoever else has decided they want to be the wolf god."

I rubbed my forehead. "Back up a minute. *Someone* is going to be the wolf god?"

"I guess so. I haven't been able to determine how that happens, exactly, but the making of a werewolf army between the two moons is the beginning."

"Between what two moons?"

"Two full moons in a single month—"

"Makes a blue moon," I finished.

"When the becoming takes place." He glanced at his watch. "That's in five days."

I plopped down on the couch. "You believe this stuff?"

"It really doesn't matter if I do or not."

"Why?"

"Because someone believes, and they're willing to do whatever it takes to make the legend come to life."

Chapter 17

"Maybe we'd better keep all of this between us for the time being," he murmured.

"No problem."

Like I was going to tell Clyde about the wolf god or that Cadotte believed in werewolves. Hell, I wasn't going to tell Clyde anything about Cadotte at all, unless I had to.

"What else do you know?" I asked. As long as he was sharing his delusion, I preferred he share it all.

"The army is begun by the one who will become the wolf god."

"Begun, how?"

"They're werewolves; how do you think?"

I blinked. "So the wolf god is a werewolf, too?"

"Yes. There's a ceremony that involves the totem, the werewolf army, the one who will become the wolf god, and . . ."

"And what?"

"That's all I know. The information I have is incomplete. So I ordered a book."

"A book? There's a book on this stuff?"

"There's a book on everything. Sadly, this one is out of print. But I found a copy."

"Let me guess—on the Internet."

"Of course. Cost me a bundle, but it should explain a few things. When it shows up."

I grunted, staring at the drawings, thinking of the wolf I'd seen last night. The behavior of Karen Larson. The weird things I'd imagined about the totem. If I were a believer, I just might believe.

Then again . . .

"I talked to the CDC this morning. The doctor said there *is* a new strain of rabies."

"Did you think they'd deny it?"

"But—"

"You expected them to say, 'Oh, no, we don't know what that is. Why don't you panic?' Or maybe, 'Sounds like a werewolf to me. Have a good time.' "

"You aren't funny."

"And I thought I was."

He patted my knee. Skin against skin, my body reacted, even though the touch had been anything but sexual.

"I'm sure the CDC is working on something. But I highly doubt it's a vaccine against a new strain of super-rabies."

"You think they lied to me?"

"Of course not. The government never lies to keep the panic at bay."

"You're being sarcastic."

He merely raised an eyebrow and shuffled his papers into a single stack.

Considering Cadotte was an Indian, an activist, and a professor, I couldn't say I was surprised he had a low opinion of the federal government. But conspiracy theories had never been my forte. They appeared to be his.

"Let me ask you this," he continued. "Did the CDC

give you any advice on dealing with these superwolves?"

I thought back to my conversation with Dr. Hanover. There had been one thing.

"Shit." I lifted my gaze to his. "She told me to use silver bullets."

Cadotte started to laugh. He laughed so hard he choked. I pounded him on the back, none too gently.

"Hey!" he protested. "Take it easy."

He picked up his wineglass and tossed back the remainder of the content. "Silver bullets?" He shook his head. "You thought that was a normal thing to recommend?"

"She had a good reason."

"Wanna share it?"

"The mutated virus reacts negatively to silver."

"I'll just bet it does."

I shook my head. I couldn't believe we were having this conversation.

"I wish we had those bodies," I murmured.

"Mighty convenient that they disappeared, wouldn't you say?"

"I suppose you have a theory on that, too."

"Of course."

"Wanna share it?" I mocked.

His lips twitched, and he cast me a glance that puzzled me. Most guys would have been sick of my mouth by now. Cadotte appeared to like it quite a bit.

"They changed."

"You think Karen Larson and her principal are running through the woods howling at the moon?"

"You got a better idea?"

"Yeah, a million of 'em."

"Name one."

"Someone took them."

"Why?"

I tried to come up with a good reason, but I couldn't. I threw up my hands. "How should I know?"

"You have to admit strange things are happening around here."

"That doesn't mean we've got werewolves. Honestly, Cadotte, have you lost your mind?"

He studied me for a moment. "Why are you so dead set against this?"

"Because I haven't lost mine?"

"You should keep your mind open. Isn't that what they tell you in cop school?"

"They tell us to observe only facts. Study what we can document. What we see, hear, touch is what's real. A theory means nothing. A legend even less."

He sighed. "Jessie, I worry over you."

"I can take care of myself."

"Against human bad guys. But if you won't believe in the inhuman ones, you could get really hurt." He moved closer and ran his hand up my thigh. "You could get dead."

I shook my head. I couldn't believe we were even discussing whether werewolves were real and running around in my forest. I couldn't believe he'd slipped his fingers beneath the hem of my shorts and was stroking the soft skin where my thigh met my hip.

"You really believe in werewolves?" I managed.

He leaned close and his breath brushed my hair. "There's more to this world than what we can see, hear, and touch."

"Like what?"

"There are things out there for which there's no explanation."

"I've never heard or seen them."

"You haven't listened; you haven't looked."

True. Maybe I would.

His finger slipped beneath the elastic leg of my panties.

Later. I'd look later.

His nails scraped me, his thumb rode me hard as he slid a finger inside. His mouth swallowed my cries of completion and I tasted red wine on his tongue. His moan made my lips vibrate.

He continued to stroke me, slower, gentler, then more quickly. More quickly still until I was ready to explode again. What was it about this man that made all my usual inhibitions vanish the instant he touched me?

"My turn," he whispered, taking his hand out of my pants and unzipping his own.

I should have been limp, sated, half-asleep; instead the thought of having him inside me at last revved me up so high I couldn't sit still.

I reached for him, clasped him, tugged him forward and back. He put his hand over mine and showed me what he liked. He was hard, smooth, and hot. I wanted him more than I'd wanted anything for a long, long time.

He seemed to feel the same, since he practically tore the button off my shorts. Neither one of us heard the knock on the door. Hell, they could have been knocking for half an hour and I wouldn't have heard them. Then someone shouted my name and started to pound. The door rattled and shook.

Together we cursed and tugged our clothes back where they belonged. I hurried to the door.

"This had better be good," I said as I opened it.

Edward Mandenauer stood in the hall. Some of my neighbors had come out to see what the fuss was about. They stared at him as if he were crazy. Of course they rarely saw an emaciated old man with a rifle in each hand and a bandolier full of bullets slung over each shoulder in our neck of the woods. He resembled Rambo, sixty years after his last war.

"He's with me," I told my neighbors, and shooed them back inside.

When they disappeared, albeit slowly—we didn't get much excitement in our neck of the woods, either—I turned to Mandenauer. "*What* are you doing here?"

"We must hunt, Jessie." He tossed me a rifle. I had no choice but to catch the weapon or eat it.

"It's nine o' clock. I thought we were supposed to meet at eleven."

"We meet now."

I heard Cadotte get to his feet behind me. His movement drew Mandenauer's gaze. The old man's eyes narrowed, and he gave Cadotte the once-over, then turned to me and did the same.

My cheeks heated. It was like being caught in the backseat of a car by your grandfather.

But he wasn't my grandfather. I was over twenty-one *and* I was off duty, for crying out loud.

"I'm busy."

"Someone has been bitten. We must go." He turned and started down the hall.

"Wait!" I called.

This changed everything.

Mandenauer paused. "We must get to the scene. Quickly."

I glanced down. I couldn't go running through the woods in shorts and a shirt with no sleeves. I'd not only be scratched to pieces; I'd be eaten alive by bugs. Distractions like that destroyed a person's concentration. Without my concentration, I could get killed—and Mandenauer along with me.

"Two minutes," I said, and ran for the bedroom.

I took three, but tough. I had to get my rifle out of

the safe. I put the company issue inside, grabbed a box of bullets, and ran.

Cadotte and Mandenauer were staring at each other like two dogs who'd found the same bone. What was the matter with them?

"I've got to go," I told Cadotte. "Sorry."

And I *was* sorry. My life had been rolling along quite nicely when Mandenauer showed up.

Cadotte nodded. "I know. I'll just clean up and let myself out."

I hesitated. I didn't want to leave him alone in my apartment, but his nicely stacked papers were now scattered all over my table—we must have knocked them over while we were otherwise occupied. His shoes were off. Damn, his jeans weren't buttoned. I could see a slice of smooth, dark skin across his belly. My mouth still tasted of him.

I had to get out of here. "Thanks. I—"

"I'll call you," he said.

Mandenauer snorted. I gave him a dirty look and he shrugged. "Your phones are not working. The sheriff tried to call, as did that foulmouthed harpy who says she is your friend."

Hell. I *had* turned off the phones. I wasn't going to have much of an ass left when Clyde got done chewing on it.

Chapter 18

We climbed into my car and I picked up the radio. "Three Adam One is ten-eight on that ten-eleven. I need a location."

"Judas Priest, girl, where have you been?" Zee's voice, already scratchy from a lifetime of cigarettes, had become even rougher with anger.

"At home. Off duty." I glanced at my watch. "Why are you on the radio now anyway?"

"The shit has hit the fan around here. I got rid of the dingbat on second. She couldn't handle it."

I sighed. Dispatchers came and went with regularity in most departments. The job did not pay enough to offset the high level of stress. But in ours, thanks to Zee's vile tongue and perfectionist nature, we went through them quicker than dogs went through dog food.

"Head to Three-one-five Cooper Court."

"Anyone on-scene?"

"Brad. He's been ordered to secure only, then wait for you."

Brad was on early, too. We must really be strapped.

"I assume creepy crawly found you."

I shot a glance at Mandenauer, but he continued to stare through the windshield as if he couldn't hear every word that was said.

"He's right next to me."

"Good. Ask him the details."

Zee clicked off. I replaced the receiver, cleared my throat. "Um . . . she's not—"

"Nice?" He raised a brow.

"For want of a better word."

"Do not worry, Jessie. I have dealt with far worse than Zelda Hupmen in my life."

Considering his life span, I had no doubt he was right. I nodded and moved on. "What happened?"

"A wolf went through the window of a residence."

I frowned. Cooper Court might be at the edge of town, but it was still town. A new subdivision complete with minivans, bicycles, and kids. I hit the lights and the siren.

"Then what?"

"The wolf was injured from the glass and no doubt disoriented. It ran around the house, and when the owner tried to direct it outside, the animal bit him, then left through the hole in the window."

"Obviously this is one of our special wolves."

He shot me a quick, unreadable glance. "Why obviously?"

"Wolves don't come near people. They particularly don't come into town, or dive through windows in the middle of suburbia. The only known wolf attacks on people have been by rabid wolves or wolf-dog hybrids."

I wasn't sure, but I thought his gaze became a bit more interested. "You've been doing research, Officer."

"You'd be amazed at what I've learned," I muttered, thinking about Cadotte and his werewolf army. But I wasn't going to share that little delusion with Mandenauer. Not when he'd finally stopped treating me like some kid who didn't know her job.

I killed the siren several blocks from Cooper Court.

No reason to wake the entire neighborhood. Unfortunately, that had already been done.

As we turned into the small subdivision at the edge of town, an electric halo pressed against the night sky. Every house blazed like a Christmas tree; every yard light blared. People milled about on their lawns, in the street, in various states of dress and undress. I had to slow to a crawl to avoid rolling over a citizen.

"Hell." I shut off the revolving red dome and ignored the questions people shouted as we passed. There would be no keeping this quiet any longer.

Brad had done a good job with the scene. He'd taped off the entire yard and stood in front of the door. A few other summer cops formed a loose circle at the perimeter. My estimation of Brad's intelligence climbed several notches.

The house was like a hundred others in Miniwa—a ranch that resembled a log cabin—except this one sported a great big hole where the front window ought to be. Glass sprinkled across the bushes and sidewalk, catching the lights and shining like icicles on a moonlit night.

But there was no moon—or rather there was, but it was hidden behind thick, smoky clouds. Not a glimpse could be seen; not a star lit the sky.

I pulled into the driveway and we got out of the car, leaving our weapons behind. Though with Mandenauer wearing enough ammo to start a small war, I'm sure we made quite an impression on the nightly news cameraman, whom I saw filming us from the street.

"Jessie, thank God!"

Brad was glad to see me. Things must be worse than I thought.

I pointed to Mandenauer, who muttered, "We've met."

Well, that saved me from being polite. My favorite way to work. "What happened?"

Brad glanced at the street. I followed his gaze. People lined the yellow border tape, practically hanging over it in their eagerness to hear what we were saying. The television camera was trained right on us, and the reporter watched our mouths with an eagle eye. I'd bet my next doughnut she could read lips.

All three of us stepped inside. Considering the fiasco at the medical examiner's office, I was surprised the press hadn't been more avidly on my ass—or at least Clyde's. But without the bodies there wasn't much of a story beyond that. After tonight, there would be.

The low rumble of voices from the living room drew my attention. "Who's that?"

"The victim and his wife."

My estimation of Brad's brains plummeted. "He hasn't been sent to the hospital?"

"He refused."

Mandenauer and I exchanged glances. I raced him to the living room.

Pale and blond, the victim was perhaps six-foot-four, though it was hard to tell since he was sitting down. He must have weighed 240. I didn't see an ounce of fat on him. He could have throttled the wolf with his bare hands. Maybe he'd tried, since his hand had been bitten.

Just like Karen Larson's.

His wife was as small as he was large. Why was it that huge guys always ended up marrying tiny women? I'd think they'd be afraid of breaking them, or maybe that was part of the appeal.

I cleared my throat and they both glanced up. I stifled a curse. The wife was Prescott Bozeman's secretary.

Her eyes narrowed. "You," she spat.

"You, too. How . . . odd."

And it was. Not that the size of the town precluded running into people more often than I liked. But coincidences always bugged the hell out of me.

"Get an ambulance out here, Brad."

"No, I-I'm fine," the man said. He was pale, sweating. If he hadn't been in such good shape, I'd worry that he was going to have a heart attack right in front of us all. He still might.

"He doesn't like doctors." The wife rolled her eyes.

"Mr. . . ." I let my voice trail off hopefully. He didn't answer, and I raised an eyebrow at itty-bitty snot-nosed bitch.

"Gerard," she supplied, though I could tell she didn't want me to know their name. As if I'd start calling her up and asking her to come out and play. "Mel Gerard, and I'm Cherry."

Of course she was.

I managed to keep any snide comments to myself and get on with business. "Mr. Gerard, you'll need to go to the hospital and have a rabies vaccine."

"Vaccine?" His voice raised to a near hysterical pitch on the end of the word. I frowned.

"Big manly man is afraid of shots." Cherry patted Mel on the hand that wasn't wrapped in gauze.

"D-don't want a shot."

He was more coherent than Karen Larson had been when I talked to her. Still, I remembered what Karen had been doing less than five hours after she was bitten. From the size of Mel, he could do a lot more damage. We needed to get him a vaccine and quick.

"He needs the medicine, Cherry."

"No. He'll be all right. Mel's never been sick a day in his life."

"We're dealing with something worse than the flu."

Her face went mulish and I sighed, then threw up my hands. She wasn't going to listen to me.

"It is for the best," Mandenauer murmured, moving in closer, talking low, keeping calm. "He must take the medicine. What can it hurt?"

Mel had lost interest in the conversation. His eyes were half-closed. He leaned on Cherry so heavily she was pressed into the arm of the couch. In the distance, the wail of a siren announced that Brad had done as I asked.

"I suppose that's true," Cherry said quietly. "A little old vaccine can't hurt Mel now."

"Right." I knelt in front of Mel. "I just need to ask him a few quick questions."

"Jessie, we must go," Mandenauer pressed.

"We will."

I knew better than to walk away before interviewing the victim. Look what had happened the last time.

"Now," he snapped. "The animal flees farther and farther into the night."

I glanced over my shoulder. "What kind of wolf hunter are you if you can't find him?"

"It is better if we go immediately."

I sighed. While we'd been arguing, Mel had fallen asleep on his wife's shoulder. From the glare Cherry was giving me, she didn't plan on letting me wake him. I got to my feet.

"Fine. Let's go."

"I did an initial interview." Brad hovered in the doorway.

"You what?" My voice was deceptively calm. What I wanted to do was rip into Brad the way the wolf had ripped into Mel. Brad was a summer cop—muscle and no brain—he wasn't trained to do anything but stand there and follow orders.

Color spread from Brad's collar to the hairline. He cleared his throat, shuffled his feet, fumbled in his pocket for a notebook, and practically threw it in my face.

"He was talking, rambling really, so I wrote it down, asked him a few things."

"You were supposed to secure the scene. That's all."

"So I should ignore a victim's testimony? I'm not quite that stupid."

Sometimes I wondered. But in this case Brad had done the right thing. I hoped. If what he'd written down wasn't gibberish.

"Did you hear any of this?" I asked Cherry.

"She arrived after I did," Brad said.

Cherry shrugged and nodded.

"Jessie."

Mandenauer stood at the window. Something in his voice made me join him. There, behind the crowd that still peered in our direction, stood the big, black wolf. I could swear the thing was staring right at me, and as he did, the totem I'd forgotten shifted and slid across my chest. I gasped.

The sound seemed to break the inertia. As we watched, the wolf melted into the trees.

"Did you see that?" Mandenauer asked.

But I was already heading for the front door.

We nearly ran into the EMTs as we left the house. I paused to tell them what had happened and what needed to happen. I stressed the latter.

"This guy needs that vaccine," I insisted. "Make sure he doesn't go home without it."

They nodded, but I had my doubts. This was still America, last time I checked, and Mel didn't have to accept the vaccine if he didn't want to. I only hoped that

Cherry was as bitchy with him as she had been with me. I had a feeling she would be.

Mandenauer and I retrieved our rifles. He glanced at the crowd, then jerked his head toward the back of the house. "We will take the long way around." He frowned at my gun. "What is that?"

"A Winchester."

"Where is the one I brought to you?"

"At my apartment. I like my own gun. I missed that wolf last night. I won't with this." I raised my rifle.

He contemplated me for a moment, then shook his head. "As you say . . . whatever." He continued around the side of the house.

The forest had spread into the backyard, as forests will. The lack of moonlight, the heavy cover of the branches, contributed to a near complete darkness.

"Here." Mandenauer threw me a bandolier of bullets. Once again, I had to catch them or eat them.

"Could you stop doing that?" I asked.

"What?"

"Throwing things at me." I looped the bandolier over my shoulder. "Besides, I like my own ammo."

I shook the box I'd taken from the safe. Bullets rattled, their number a comforting weight in my palm.

"Mine are better."

I frowned. "Why?"

"They were made for wolves."

"Let me guess." I fingered the shiny bullets in the bandolier. At least they were the right caliber. "Silver?"

I expected him to scoff, if not laugh. Instead, he narrowed his eyes and cocked his head. He opened his mouth to say . . . I'm not sure what . . . and a long, mournful howl split the darkness, so close both of us jumped. Mandenauer headed into the forest. I was right on his heels.

With no moon to light the trail, we were forced to use a flashlight. Flecks of blood on the dirt, a bush, a branch revealed the wolf that had bitten Mel must have been cut by the window glass.

But were the black wolf and the kamikaze one and the same? I had no idea. The thought that we were following one wolf, with another following us, made me twitchy, and I longed for a nice, safe tree stand.

Mandenauer was another story. His step was spry. He was damn near skipping. I could feel the excitement rolling off him like a vapor.

He stopped dead on the trail and I nearly bumped into his back. "What?" I whispered.

Mandenauer stiffened, then slashed his hand across his neck in a violent gesture.

I lifted one hand in surrender. *Okay, okay, I'll shut up.*

I lowered my hand and spread it open and out indicating the question I'd already asked: *What?*

He flicked a long, bony finger to the left, then to the right. The trail split here.

He knelt and so did I. When he turned the light to the right, splatters of blood shone in a black wavering line across the dirt and leaves. He sniffed once, twice, then moved the beam to the left. A large, fresh pile of feces sat in the center of that trail.

Hmm. That appeared to be the wolf equivalent of "Na, na, na, na, na."

Mandenauer's hand tightened on his rifle. He glanced at me and for the first time I saw true emotion in his eyes. He was furious. He jabbed a finger at himself, then pointed down the trail to the left. He pointed me to the trail on the right. I frowned and shook my head.

Separate? That sounded like a really, really bad idea.

He held up two fingers. Pointed again to the divergent trails. Two of them, two of us.

He lifted his rifle. We had the guns.

True. So why wasn't I impressed?

In the end, I went to the right and Mandenauer to the left. Through sign language—every time I tried to whisper, he made that creepy throat-slashing movement—I understood we were to meet in an hour back at the house. If one of us found a wolf, he or she should shoot it. The other would hear the shot and follow the sound.

I was to use his bullets in my gun. What the hell? Silver killed as good as lead. In this case, perhaps even better.

I used the small penlight I kept in the glove compartment and let Mandenauer keep the blaring city-issue flashlight. Even if he moved like he was fifty, he was still eighty, and so were his eyes.

As a result I progressed more slowly than he did, stopping often to ascertain the blood still trailed ahead of me. It wasn't long before any trace of Mandenauer—both sound and sight—disappeared. I was truly alone, and for the first time in my life I didn't like it.

I'd walked these woods at all hours of the day and the night. I'd never felt uneasy, watched, exposed. Tonight I felt all of those things, as well as . . .

A branch broke behind me. I spun around. Nothing was there. Nothing that I could see, anyway.

"You are *not* being stalked."

I'd hoped the sound of my own voice would calm me. Instead, it was louder than a gunshot and only served to make my heart beat even faster. Now that I'd started talking to myself, could complete insanity be far behind? Next thing I knew, I'd be believing in Cadotte's werewolves.

Crunch.

I let my eyes wander over the forest. A shadow cut between two trees—more man-sized than wolf-. I shook my head. Closed my eyes, opened them again. Nothing was there.

I was letting my imagination run away with me, and I had no one to blame but myself if I became too distracted by fairy tales to see a real-live big bad wolf creeping up on me. I tightened my grip on the rifle and continued down the path.

But the thought of Cadotte could not be banished as easily as that. He invaded my mind even though I tried to push him back out. When would I see him again? What would happen when I did?

I gave a mental snort. I knew the answer to the latter, if not the former. We'd end up in bed—sooner rather than later. It was a given.

The shadow flickered again at the corner of my eye. I flashed the light across the shrubbery as an opossum skittered away from the beam.

The breeze picked up, making the trees whisper. No wonder I was seeing shadows. The forest was full of them.

Then I smelled it—a scent I'd become quite familiar with in the past few days. Leaves, wind, wildness. "Will?"

My voice carried in the night. From far down the trail came the howl of a wolf. The hair on the back of my neck rose, causing me to shiver even though the temperature stood at near sixty-five degrees.

Another wolf answered the first—from the left, off where Mandenauer must be by now.

I don't know why I started running. I only know that when the gunshot ended the sorrowful serenade, I tripped and fell to my knees. Thank goodness for safeties on guns. I could have blown my head off being so careless. As it was, my knee hit a rock, and I writhed around on the trail awhile cursing.

If a wolf had truly been after me, now would have been the perfect time to finish me off. Instead, I lay there until the pain receded enough for me to catch my breath. Then I got to my feet and followed the sound of that gunshot.

Chapter 19

I smelled the fire before I saw the flames. Gimping along with my sore knee, I forgot there had been two wolves and only one gunshot. I forgot a lot of things, including my sudden unease in the forest.

I crashed through the underbrush like a cow. Domestic animals rarely bothered to move quietly. Why should they? I'm sure Mandenauer heard me coming long before I arrived.

My trail crossed another. I paused, glancing first one way and then the other. The two paths merged here. Mandenauer and I would have eventually met. Just as the wolves had.

Ahead orange flames glowed brightly against the night. Since it was June and not yet high tide for forest fires, I didn't panic, but I did gimp along faster.

I should have known Mandenauer could light a bonfire that wouldn't burn down the entire forest. The scent of searing fur and flesh hit me as soon as I stepped into the clearing. If you've ever smelled it, you know why I gagged.

"What the hell are you doing?" I shouted when I managed to regain my breath.

He didn't look at me, just continued to stare into the

flames as if hypnotized. At least he'd surrounded the conflagration with rocks and placed the bonfire on dirt, as far away from trees and bushes as was possible in the middle of the freaking forest.

I limped to his side and tried again. "Have you lost what's left of your mind?"

He laughed. The sound was rusty. I'm sure Mandenauer didn't laugh much, if ever. Why he'd choose now was beyond me. This situation was anything but funny.

"Strange you should ask that, since my mind, along with my soul, was lost a very long time ago."

I frowned. "Feeling a little sorry for ourselves, are we?"

The remnants of his smile deepened. "You amuse me, Jessie McQuade."

"Yeah, I live to please."

I contemplated the fire. In the depths I saw the outline of a wolf. What else would he be burning? Though the fur was gone, the size was wrong to be the huge black beast that had been taunting us. I squinted against the leaping flames. It appeared the wolf had been tossed on a pile of . . . something. Hard to tell what, but probably leaves. They made good kindling.

"You want to tell me why you're burning this wolf?"

"I told you at the office of the medical examiner. It is safer to burn them."

That's right. He had.

"Flames and trees do not mix, mister."

"I am careful. I have done this a thousand times before."

A thousand? Right. Maybe his mind was more lost than even he was willing to admit.

"You couldn't wait? Burn it somewhere safer? Don't you think the DNR would like to check this out? Even the CDC?"

"I am sure they would." He took several steps to the left and stomped on a stray ember with his boot. Then he raised his gaze to mine. "But it is too late now, is it not?"

"I'd say so, thanks to you."

He turned away, but not before I could swear I saw him smile again.

Which made me wonder . . . a whole bunch of things.

Was Mandenauer crazier than he appeared? Could he be a holdover from the wolf hunters who had nearly eradicated the species by the mid-1900s?

Back then the wolf had been considered evil—out to kill every domestic animal it found. Ranchers hated them—still do—and hired wolf hunters to take care of the problem. However, the true culprits were often coyotes or feral dogs, as well as wolves.

I'd seen pictures, read stories, about the atrocities committed upon the wolf population. They had sickened me. I'm not saying wolves aren't varmints, that they don't kill stock and even a pet or two. But shoot the damn things; don't mutilate them. Sometimes the inhumanity of men made me want to become a complete recluse rather than remain a civil servant.

I'd met a few wolf hunters and they were as creepy as Mandenauer. They continued to kill wolves whenever they could—despite any laws to the contrary—as if in doing so they recaptured a bit of their youth.

But Mandenauer had been hired by the DNR, which, contrary to popular belief, was far from stupid. They would have checked him out thoroughly and made certain he was the kind of man who would follow their anal ordinances to the letter.

The CDC agreed a new strain of rabies was spreading. I had seen some of these wolves, and they weren't acting like wolves. Of course they could be werewolves, as Cadotte would have me believe.

I kicked the dirt. Hell, I was starting to see a conspiracy behind every tree.

Something sparkled in the dirt I'd stirred up. I glanced at Mandenauer, but he was busy with his wolf pyre. I winced as I bent my sore knee to scoop the bright and shiny item into my hand.

A single key. No key ring. No markings to indicate it belonged to a car. Most likely a house key, but how had it gotten here? I shrugged and slipped the thing into my pocket.

A chorus of yips started nearby and I jumped, then spun toward them, rifle raised, my hand halfway to the safety before I recognized the nature of the calls.

"Coyotes," Mandenauer murmured. "Odd."

He was right. Why hadn't the wolves run the coyotes out of the area as wolves always did?

"Maybe foxes?" I proposed.

Wolves tolerated foxes. Lord knows why.

The old man shook his head. I had to agree. I knew the difference between a coyote and fox. Something strange was going on in these woods, but then, what else was new?

"What happened?" I indicated the pyre.

Mandenauer had been staring into the forest in the direction of the coyotes' calls. He blinked and forced his attention back to me. "You wish for a tall tale?"

"Just the truth, thanks."

"Truth. What is truth?"

My patience, nothing to brag about on a good day, snapped. "Spare me the existential bullshit and tell me what happened."

He smirked. The guy certainly was a jolly old elf tonight.

"I trailed the animal. It leaped at me from the night. I shot it."

"Yee-ha."

He shrugged. "You wanted the truth. The truth is not very 'yee-ha,' I have found."

Right again.

"How did you know the wolf was rabid?"

Mandenauer shoved a stone closer to the fire with the scuffed toe of his boot. "Does it matter?"

"Of course it matters! We can't just go around shooting every wolf in the forest."

"The DNR has given me leave to handle this situation as I see fit."

That didn't sound like the DNR. Control freaks thrived in government positions, and they rarely gave carte blanche to anyone. Certainly not trigger-happy old farts like Mandenauer.

"If we eliminate them all, your wolf problem will be resolved much more quickly. And who is to say that the uninfected wolf today will not be an infected wolf tomorrow?"

"Then we'll have to shoot the coyotes, the raccoons, the opossums. This could get messy."

"Yes, it could."

He reached out his bony hands and warmed them on the flames. We stood shoulder to shoulder as the fire died to embers. Then we stood until a cool breeze picked up the ashes and flung them into the forest.

As we returned to the car I had to squelch the nagging thought that Mandenauer had not just been talking about animals.

Chapter 20

The Gerard house was dark and silent, as was the rest of the neighborhood. Considering it was about four in the morning, this wasn't a big shock.

I wasn't sure if Cherry was sleeping or if she'd gone to the hospital with Mel and not yet returned. Either way, I wasn't going to interview her until a more humane part of the morning.

By then I'd be able to read over Brad's notes. I patted my pocket, relieved to discover the notebook was still there. I'd forgotten about it in all the excitement. If I was lucky, Brad had done a bang-up job and my interview with Cherry would be blessedly short. But I wasn't counting on it.

I checked in with Zee. I should have known better.

"Christ on a crutch, Jessie. Where have you been?"

"With Mandenauer. In the woods. Where else?"

"You were gone half the night. Isn't he some hot-shit hunter? Like you."

"*He's* right here."

I slid a glance at Mandenauer, but he'd leaned his head back on the seat and closed his eyes. At his age it was definitely past his bedtime.

"I didn't think you'd left him in the woods," Zee snarled.

She obviously couldn't care less if she insulted our guest. Why should he be any different from the rest of the planet?

"Did you get anything?" she asked.

"One."

"What did it look like?"

I frowned at the radio. What an odd question. Besides, I had no idea. I'd only seen the wolf through the flames.

"Cinnamon-shaded female," Mandenauer said, his eyes still closed. "About one year old."

I repeated the information to Zee. Silence came over the line. That was a first. I shook the mike. "Zee? Where'd you go?"

She coughed—long and hard—her lifelong smoker's hack. By all rights, she should be dead from the cigarettes, if not the mileage. In the end, the force of her cough would probably be the death of Zelda Hupmen.

"Sorry," she wheezed. "Got a call. Since it's been so damn boring for the last hour, I couldn't contain my excitement."

"You want me to take it?"

"Nope. Nothing but a dead deer on the road. Officer is already en route. Why don't you take creepy-crawly home and then go there yourself?"

"Now?"

"Now. You came on early today and stayed late yesterday. Clyde told me to even out the overtime. He can't afford it."

There was the Clyde I knew.

Ten minutes later I parked next to the car Mandenauer indicated was his. Long and black, all it needed was curtains on the windows to be mistaken for a hearse.

"Any dead bodies in the back?" I asked.

Mandenauer sniffed. "This is a Cadillac. A classic. Worth three times what I have paid for it."

"You must have paid a penny."

Mandenauer ignored my jibe, climbed in his car, and rumbled into the fading night. I climbed the steps to my apartment, the bandolier still strung across my chest, my rifle unfired. At least I wouldn't have to clean the thing tonight. I planned to dive right into bed as soon as I put all my weapons away.

I was tired—an unusual occurrence for me. Even when I had a night off I stayed up until breakfast and slept through the day. I know I'm backward—just ask my mother.

But I'd found that keeping to a schedule made my schedule easier to keep. Most people who worked third shift attempted to live like real folks when they weren't working. This, in my opinion, was what led to them being too tired to function for most of their life.

At any rate, I was exhausted at 4:00 A.M. and that just wasn't like me. Which was my only excuse for not noticing right away that I wasn't alone when I stepped into my apartment.

I unloaded the rifle as I walked down the hall and into my bedroom. Call me paranoid, but a loaded gun in the house is a very bad idea.

Replacing the weapon in the safe, I hung the bandolier alongside it and locked the door. I drew the totem over my head and laid it on the dresser. I'd learned my lesson about wearing the thing to bed. It had taken all day for the red marks to fade.

The overhead light hit the wolf's face and reminded me of something I'd been meaning to do. Quickly I rooted around in my nightstand until I found a magnifying glass attached to an old key chain. I checked the markings on the totem. Like Cadotte had promised, they were there. But did they mean what he said? I still couldn't buy it.

As I unbuttoned my uniform blouse, I realized I hadn't removed my gun belt and pistol. Leaving my shirt hanging open, I retraced my steps and performed my usual ritual with the Magnum. I wasn't going to lock all my guns in the safe. When I turned away from the refrigerator, I saw him.

The sliding glass doors were open and a pre-dawn breeze fluttered the drapes. Had they been like that when I'd come in? Surely I would have noticed.

A man stood in the opening. With no light from outside, no light from within, I could barely discern his outline from the ebony sky. But I could hear him breathing. I reached for my gun and he rushed me.

I'd learned to fight as a kid, which meant I'd learned to fight dirty. While rolling around in the dirt with little boys, a little girl quickly learns she'd better get mean or she'd get hurt.

I'd refined my street skills at the academy, where we'd learned hand-to-hand combat—the kind of fighting that usually went down in bars.

Except when I had to fight drunks, they were slower and stupider than me. My intruder was none of the above.

On my initial strike to the face, he grabbed my wrist, twisted me around. I kicked backward, going for his knee. He did a fancy sidestep, twirled me like a dancer, and kissed me on the mouth.

The first taste and I knew. Cadotte. Who else?

My racing pulse slowed as he deepened the kiss. Had he been here all along, waiting for me to return? Or had he climbed up the building again and slid inside?

I yanked my lips away. "What in hell are you doing here?"

He didn't answer. I couldn't see his face. Unnerved, I struggled to get free. He only pulled me tighter against him, where I discovered he was very glad I was home.

Though my body shouted for me to take him to the ground and climb on top, my heart still pounded with an excess of adrenaline, and my emotions were too tangled for me to be anything but angry.

"Let me go."

"No." He nuzzled my neck, scraped his teeth along a throbbing vein, licked my collarbone—

I stiffened, remembering the dream. "Right now, Cadotte!"

His laugh rubbed his chest against mine. My shirt was still open, my bra a mere wisp of lace. I bit my lip to keep from moaning out loud at the friction. How could I be angry, aroused, and frightened all at the same time?

"Don't make me hurt you."

"Why don't you go ahead and try?" he whispered.

Now how could I resist an offer like that?

Before he could think, I brought my knee up hard and fast. He twisted quicker than a cat, and all I hit was his thigh.

"Ah, ah, ah. If you did that, there'd be no fun later."

I shoved him away and he let me. For a tall, lanky geek with glasses, he had more muscle mass than I would have figured. But since I'd seen him naked, I should have known better.

I tried a flat-handed shot to his chest. He blocked that and did some fancy Oriental jump-kick that I was barely able to deflect.

"What the hell was that? Kung fu?"

"Tai chi. It's very good for you."

"I bet."

He became less and less the geeky egghead with every passing moment. So the professor knew martial arts? Time to get serious.

I couldn't see much beyond a shadow in the starless

darkness that filled my apartment. But I caught no glint of glass on his face, so punched him in the nose.

Or at least I tried to. He grabbed my fist inches from his nostrils. How in hell did he *do* that?

"Say uncle," he murmured.

"Bite me."

I'd never been very good at giving in.

"Jessie, Jessie. You aren't going to win."

Why it annoyed me so much that he was besting me in a physical fight, I have no idea. He was a guy. They were stronger. It was a medical fact, which had always pissed me off.

Maybe part of the reason I didn't want to give up and say uncle was because his macho-man muscling me around was the most arousing foreplay I'd ever experienced. So I hooked my ankle around his and took him down to the floor.

Chapter 21

I was supposed to land on top, where I could then crow victory and give in to my urges as a reward. Instead I ended up on my back, Cadotte settled firmly between my thighs. I was winded; he wasn't even sweating.

"Tell me that you love me." I heard the laughter in his voice and I smiled, too.

"Kiss my—"

His mouth covered mine. My brain melted as my body ignited.

It had been so long since I'd had sex, and I had never had sex that began like this. I was so excited I could barely keep myself from arching and coming right now. But I was tired of getting off with my clothes on. I wanted him, all the way, so I gave up fighting.

He kissed me forever. In my experience, limited as it was, guys don't waste much time on kissing, especially when they know they're on the fast track to something more.

But Cadotte seemed to like kissing. Hell, if I was that good at something, I guess I would have liked to do it all the time, too.

He nibbled at my lips, tasted me with his tongue, framed my face with his long, sexy fingers, stroking my chin with his thumbs, caressing my cheeks with his palms.

And he didn't stop with my mouth, giving equal and arousing attention to my neck, my eyelids, my ears. I never realized that the insertion of a clever tongue into the bend of my ear could make me damp a whole lot farther south.

I explored the solid muscles of his back with my fingertips, then ran my nails over the quivering flesh at his side, before palming his extremely nice ass. It wasn't enough. I needed to feel naked skin against skin more than I needed to breathe.

"Can we take this to my room?"

He lifted his head from a teasing lick across the lace-covered peak of my breast. Dawn threatened; just enough light filled the room so I could finally see his face.

No more laughter, the need was as stark in his eyes as it was in my gut. Without a word, he got to his feet in a fluid, graceful motion and held out a hand for me.

I could have made a smart comment. I could have ignored his hand. I wasn't so far gone that I couldn't stand up by myself. But the loss of his warmth, even in the heat of a summer night, made me shiver.

I put my palm against his, let him bring me to my feet. Then hand in hand we entered my bedroom.

It wasn't much. A bed, a gun safe, a dresser. I slept there—nothing more. Until now.

I had never brought a man into this room. The question of why not flitted through my head. I didn't answer. I had better questions to occupy my mind right now.

How quickly could I get him naked? How many times could he make me scream? Would he think I was weird if I asked him to tie me up and lick me all over?

My first question was answered without my saying a

word. He pulled his T-shirt over his head and shucked his jeans one second later. He didn't wear underwear. Another mystery solved.

I was tempted to turn on the light so I could see him, but then he could see me, and that didn't tempt me at all. I was a big girl—everywhere. I swear that naked, I looked even bigger.

I hovered just inside the doorway, suddenly unsure. He crossed the carpet in a sinuous movement that made me remember the loose-hipped gait of the big black wolf.

The image disappeared when he reached out and unhooked the front clasp of my bra with a flick of his fingers. My breasts, suddenly free, popped loose with a near audible *thunk*. I had no time to be embarrassed. He lowered his head and rubbed his cheek against the fullness, breathed in as if he could catch my scent, then shoved my shirt and bra off my arms and latched onto a nipple with a scrape of his teeth and a push of his tongue.

I'd read in some woman's magazine that the larger the breasts, the less the arousal a woman gains from them. Considering how guys worshipped women's chests and wanted to touch them in an ascending chart based on their size, I'd figured this was nature's idea of a hysterical joke.

But after reading said article, I'd been relieved. I'd always thought something was wrong with me. I could care less if a guy touched my breasts. Such pawing and panting below my neck had usually made me lose whatever interest I might have had.

Now I understood I'd been with the wrong guys. Cadotte knew what to do. Gentle and sure, he aroused me with tiny suckles, openmouthed kisses, and murmured

words of praise. By the time he bent and lifted me into
his arms, my knees had begun to sag.

"Hey!" The room spun as he strode to the bed. "I do
not want to play kidnapped settler and Indian brave."

How rude, Jessie!

My mother's voice. Hell. I had to get rid of her.

Cadotte's laughter did it for me. "Maybe later."

He dropped me onto the mattress without warning and
I bounced. At least that shut me up.

My arms reached for him. He stepped back. Worried
I had insulted him, I lifted myself onto my elbows. His
gaze went from my face back to my breasts.

"You know, they're amazing." He brought his eyes
back to mine. "And so are you."

My chest had been my curse since the age of twelve.
Once I had breasts, my friends who were boys could no
longer seem to forget I wasn't one, too.

Since then guys had been trying to get their hands on
my breasts. I had been trying to keep them off. No one
had called my breasts amazing. The nicest thing a man
had said about them was that they were "fucking big."

But in Cadotte's dark, serene eyes I saw the truth. I
was beautiful. At least until the sun came up.

He flicked a finger at my pants. "Take 'em off."

Happy to.

I kicked my boots across the room, lifted my hips,
and slid the ugly tan trousers down my legs. My white
cotton granny undies joined them. I might wear hooker
bras, but I did not appreciate underwear that rode my
crack like dental floss.

I lay on the bed and he towered over me. "Such soft
skin." He trailed a finger up my knee. "Strong legs.
Everything about you is beautiful."

"I-I like to swim." Why I felt the need to talk, I have
no idea.

"I like it that you swim, too."

"I have a pond. On my land. The old Macray place."

"Shh." He leaned over and kissed my belly. The urge to talk left completely.

The bed dipped, but instead of covering me with his body and plunging away—which would have worked for me—he stretched his length next to mine, held his head with one hand, and trailed the other from my hip, across my belly, and back again.

"Let me touch you, Jessie. I've been waiting forever."

I nearly pointed out that I'd only known him a few days, but I hesitated at branding myself a slut. Besides, I felt like I'd known him a long time. I seemed to have wanted him for a lifetime.

Dangerous thoughts those, so I closed my mind against them and closed my eyes against all the things I saw flicker across his face as he touched me.

How long we lay there, kissing, discovering, trailing fingertips across chests, hips, thighs, I'm not sure. When I opened my eyes, the dawn had spun gray shadows through my bedroom. I'd neglected to draw the shades again. I didn't care.

His body was even more spectacular in the daylight than it had been by the light of the moon. Just seeing him made me want him.

He kissed me and got off the bed. The rustle of clothes, the crackle of paper, the snap of rubber—he'd come prepared. I was glad, since until this moment I hadn't even thought of protection. Would I have let him do me on the floor without it? I guess I'd never know.

When he rose over me and at last came inside, I kept my eyes open. I wanted to see his face; I wanted to watch my hands stroke his chest, my thumb tease a nipple. I wanted to know how he looked as I tightened and pulsed around him.

His eyes didn't cross, though mine did. He made no sound; I had to. He held me and stroked me both inside and out, until I was gasping, breathless, limp.

I came back to myself and realized he was still big and hard inside me. Heat flooded my face. "What—?"

He swallowed my question with a kiss, didn't stop tonguing me until I stopped trying to talk. Only then did he begin to move again.

I'd always considered reports of multiple orgasms an urban legend. Guess I was wrong.

He reached between us, stroked me where I was already sensitive until I was writhing and gasping, on the edge all over again. Then he lifted my hips and filled me with a firm, sure thrust. I felt him where I'd never felt anyone before.

His hands taught me the rhythm. First fast, then slow, then something in between. Seeming to grow, to swell, he throbbed to the beat of my pulse. I gasped, tightened, came again as his teeth scraped the curve of my neck.

He collapsed, his weight pressing me into the mattress. Trapped for a moment, I suddenly realized how big he was, how strong. Panic fluttered for an instant, until his palm cupped my hip and he rolled to the side. Our noses nearly brushed. In his eyes I saw uncertainty. Something I understood very well.

My chest tightened. My belly fluttered. My unease was pushed aside by the urge to make that expression go away.

So I touched his face and murmured, "Uncle."

Chapter 22

I fell asleep with my hand still on his face. I'd been exhausted when I got home. Incredible sex had given me a second wind, but there was only so much a girl could take.

When I awoke we were both under the sheets. Someone, not me, had drawn the heavy curtains. I glanced at Cadotte. God, he was beautiful.

His skin was smooth and dark, darker still against my plain white sheets. I wondered what he'd look like with long hair. The shorn ends curled just a little, making my fingers itch to twine between them. His earring twinkled against the warm flesh of his neck.

I remembered kissing that neck a few hours ago, being startled by the cool metal brushing my lips. When he'd trailed his mouth all over my body, the earring had tickled me here and there, adding a new dimension to every embrace.

His hand covered my hip. My eyes jumped from his earring to his face. He smiled. "Morning."

I waited for the usual morning-after embarrassment to descend. Before it could, he shifted closer and kissed me. Just a gentle brush of his lips against mine and then he pulled back. Something between my belly and my heart stuttered.

"I'll make coffee," he said, and then he was gone.

I took advantage of the solitude to head for the shower. The totem caught my eye from the dresser. I glanced at the bedroom door through which Cadotte had disappeared. I could hear him banging around in the kitchen, see his shadow flitting against the wall in the hall.

I opened a drawer and dumped the wolf on top of my underwear, then scooted into the bathroom and locked the door. I had nothing against sex in the shower—with Cadotte I would probably be agreeable to sex just about anywhere—but right now I wanted to think.

What had I done?

Had sex. Big deal.

Actually it had been. And maybe that was the problem.

I knew better than to fall for a guy like Cadotte. He was gorgeous, brilliant, a little bit strange. We had nothing in common. We probably never would.

Why on earth he'd wanted me I had yet to figure out. But I couldn't believe he'd want me much longer. The best way to get out of this without getting hurt was to dump him before he dumped me.

This resolved, I returned to my room. The slant of the sun through the windows told me the time was long past noon. I threw on shorts and a shirt, tucked the totem underneath a pile of socks in a drawer, and walked barefoot into the kitchen.

Cadotte leaned against the counter, drinking coffee completely naked. He smiled as if he weren't and poured another cup. My gaze lowered. I could get used to this.

He turned and I yanked my gaze upward. Raising a brow, he handed me my coffee. "Would you like to go out for breakfast?"

The thought of walking into The Coffee Pot with him

and ordering breakfast at . . . 2:00 P.M. was just too much for me. Besides, wasn't I showing him the door?

I took a sip, swallowed, nearly choked with shock. Cadotte made the best coffee I had ever tasted.

"What did you do to this?" I stared into the cup as if I could find all the answers to life's mysteries in the swirling black depths.

"A sprinkle of cinnamon mixed with the grounds makes all the difference."

"I have cinnamon?"

"In the back of the cabinet. Yes."

"Hmm. Wonder where that came from." I took another sip.

"Breakfast?" he reminded me.

"I . . . can't."

The same emotion that had flickered in his eyes when I'd refused to meet him for dinner returned.

"Why not?"

More coffee. That's what I needed. I gulped half the cup, let the heat bubble in my empty stomach. "Because."

Same lame excuse I'd used the last time. Unfortunately, it didn't work this time.

"Because I'm good enough to fuck but not to eat breakfast with?"

I spilled coffee on my shirt. "What?"

Having a serious conversation with a naked man was a new experience—and downright difficult. I kept getting distracted by the way his skin shone in the sunlight.

"I may not be from here, but I know how small towns work. If it got out you were screwing an Indian, there'd be trouble."

I was silent. There would be, but not the way he thought. I sighed.

"Will, I—"

He set his empty cup on the counter with a *click* and crossed the floor so fast he was crowding into my space before I knew he was coming. He captured my cup, set it aside, and took my hands.

"Don't," he whispered. "Why can't we just enjoy each other like we did last night?"

I frowned. "You want to do it again?"

He slid his fingers into my hair. "And again and again and again."

I hadn't expected that. Still, why risk my career on something that would never last?

He kissed me, his tongue teasing mine, his lips soft and warm. He tasted of coffee and cinnamon. I wanted to drink him in and keep him with me forever.

Lifting his head, he remained close enough that his breath mingled with mine. "Does this have to be complicated? I want you, Jessie. You want me. Let's just keep doing what we're doing. Okay?"

When a gorgeous naked man asks you something like that, what else are you supposed to say but—

"Hell, yes."

We ended up back in bed, but before things could get good, the phone shrilled. Why had I ever plugged it back in?

"Don't answer," Cadotte whispered against my belly. The warmth of his breath trailed along the moistness left by his tongue. I shivered and forgot all about the phone.

Until my machine clicked in and Clyde's voice came out. "Jessie, you'd better get over to the hospital. We got trouble."

I sat up, nearly knocking Cadotte off the bed in the process.

"Your victim from last night died."

I dived for the phone. "Clyde?"

"Sorry. I didn't mean to wake you."

"You didn't. I was just—" I glanced at Will. "Never mind. What's going on?"

"Mel. He died. Cherry is screaming blue murder. Said you told them to give him the vaccine and now he's dead. She's threatening lawsuit. It's a total goat fuck."

I blinked. *Goat fuck* was Zee's favorite term. Things must be very bad.

"I'll be right there."

I hung up. Cadotte kissed my hip. "Problem?"

"Oh, yeah."

"Can you tell me about it?"

I considered and decided that I could. The incident last night, and whatever had happened at the hospital since, would be public record soon enough. I filled him in.

He lay on the bed with his arm beneath his head and stared at the ceiling with a frown. I got up and pulled my uniform out of the closet.

"I don't like the sound of this," he murmured.

"You, me, and the rest of the Miniwa Police Department."

My gaze on the floor—my bra and underwear must be around here somewhere—I didn't see him get off the bed. I didn't hear him, either. The guy moved more quietly than a wolf.

"Here." I glanced up. He held what I was looking for in one hand.

I slipped into my panties. Why I didn't feel embarrassed I wasn't sure. Maybe Cadotte's ease with his own nakedness was starting to wear off on me. Although I doubted I'd be walking bare-assed in the woods anytime soon.

I was struggling with the hook on my bra when his hands covered mine. "Let me."

As I stood in front of the mirror, my eyes met his. He hooked the clasp, lowered his head, and kissed my shoulder; his earring brushed my skin. His hand slid across my belly—dark against light, slim against round. We were so different—and maybe that wasn't so bad.

My mind skittered away from the thought. "I've got to go."

He stepped back. "I know. Is it okay if I shower?"

"Sure. Just don't scare the hell out of me when I come home. Next time I might kill you."

"You and what army?" he threw over his shoulder.

I laughed. Not only did I want his body, but I liked his mouth—and not just on me.

Opening my sock drawer, I slammed it shut when Cadotte stuck his head out the bathroom door. "We should meet when you get done. I've got some ideas I'm going to check out today."

"Don't you have a little thing called class to go to?"

"It's Saturday."

Huh. Where had the week gone?

"You don't have to help me."

"I want to." He tilted his head. "Maybe we should work together on this, Jessie. It couldn't hurt."

Clyde would hurt me if he found out about it. But right now, Clyde was the least of my worries.

"I don't know how much you can help, since you think I'm chasing werewolves."

"You are."

I made an aggravated sound and threw up my hands. "Cadotte, you are certifiable."

"Maybe." He didn't appear concerned. "What time will you be home?"

"Morning most likely. Seven-thirty?"

"I'll be here."

He shut the door and the sound of the shower came shortly after. I waited another minute, opened the drawer, felt for the totem, then slipped it over my head and beneath my shirt.

What could it hurt for Cadotte to research his delusion? Who knows, he might even turn up something useful.

Chapter 23

"About time," Clyde muttered when I entered the morgue.

Since the drive from Miniwa to the hospital in Clearwater was forty minutes, I'd done the best I could, so I ignored him.

I'd flipped through Brad's notes as I'd walked in from the car. He'd done a decent job, though it wouldn't do Mel much good now. As I'd suspected, a reddish-brown wolf had bitten Mel. Since Mandenauer had already killed and burned the thing, the case would be closed—if Mel hadn't gone and died on us.

The morgue was bright with electric lights and shiny chrome. All the players were in place.

Clyde leaned against a counter, jaw ratcheting his chew like a mortar with a pestle. Bozeman was playing with his instruments—lining and realigning them on the pristine table. Anal, much?

As I wandered into the room, the door behind me opened and what must be a doctor, since he wore a white coat, walked in.

"You wanted to see me?"

Clyde pushed away from the counter. "What happened to Mel Gerard?"

"Got me. I followed the prescribed practice for rabies inoculation."

The doctor shook his head. His next words were low, near a mumble, almost as if he were going over it again in his head. And maybe he was. "But he started convulsing. Blood pressure skyrocketed. Cardiac arrest. Flat line. All in about five minutes."

"Allergic to the vaccine?"

"I don't think so."

"What, then?"

He shrugged and jerked a thumb at Bozeman. "Isn't that what he's supposed to find out?"

Clyde chewed faster, thinking long and hard before he nodded. "Thanks for your time, Doctor."

When the door closed again, Clyde turned to Bozeman, who was still playing with his toys. "Let's get on with this, Prescott. I've got things to do."

Bozeman sighed and yanked the sheet from the body. We all stared. The ME went pale. Clyde made a gagging sound and hacked his chew onto the floor. I took one step toward the door before I stopped myself.

I'd been at autopsies before. Seen a lot of dead bodies. But I'd never seen anything like this.

Mel's face was hideous. His nose was twisted, as if broken ten too many times. His lips were drawn back in a grimace; his teeth appeared to protrude. His eyes, open and staring, had bled nearly to black, with only a small rim of yellow around the edge.

Had Mel had yellow eyes? I think I would have remembered that.

"What the—?"

I crept closer. Clyde stopped gagging and joined me.

The oddities didn't stop at Mel's face. His fingernails and toenails were unnaturally long. Fu Manchu had nothing on him. And his beard was longer and coarser than it should have been if he'd only shaved yesterday.

"A reaction to the rabies?" I asked.

"Or the vaccine," Clyde murmured. "But why didn't the doctor mention this?"

"He wasn't like this when he came in." Bozeman was still staring. He lifted his gaze from Mel to us. "I saw him. He was dead. But not like this."

"Rigor mortis?" I suggested.

"I've never seen rigor set in this fast or . . . or . . ." He waved a hand at the table. "This bad."

"That doesn't mean it couldn't."

"I suppose not." The ME went back to staring.

Clyde made an impatient sound. "Prescott, I need to know what happened before I talk to Cherry again. That woman is sue-happy."

"Her and the rest of the known world," I muttered.

"Um, yes. I . . . uh— Yes," Bozeman managed. He went to work while Clyde and I watched. Not the most appealing pastime for a Saturday afternoon, but I'd done worse.

Bozeman muttered and mumbled, cut, measured, recorded. When he was done, his hands hung at his sides as he shook his head.

"I've never seen anything like this," he said. "Come here."

I didn't want to and I could tell Clyde was thinking of about a thousand other things he'd rather do, but we went. We looked and we listened. We learned.

"The spinal column is altered. Twisted as if it were . . ." Bozeman's voice trailed off. He appeared to be searching for a word but unable to find one.

"What?" Clyde snapped.

"Changing."

Oh, boy, I thought. *That doesn't sound good.*

"Changing how?" Clyde asked.

"I don't know. He's also got hair growing out of his back."

"Some guys do," I murmured.

"Not like Mel's." Bozeman manipulated the body. He was right.

The hair, long and blond, resembled fur, but how could that be?

"What's going on?" I asked.

"I have to do more tests." Bozeman continued to stare at the body as he talked to me. "Maybe send out some samples. I wouldn't be surprised to discover bizarre changes in his DNA."

"From a wolf bite?"

He started, blinked, glanced at me. "Hell if I know."

Clyde had been amazingly quiet all along. He, too, was staring at the table. His expression was one of horror. I'd never known him to have such a weak stomach before. Clyde must have seen things in his years on the force that I'd only imagined. So what was the matter with him now?

"Clyde?"

I touched his arm and he jumped, yanked free, and spun away from the body. Any expression that had been on his face before was gone. Clyde was a good cop, a good guy. It probably just bothered him to see Mel this way.

"Do whatever you need to do, Prescott, and get back to me. Jessie, I want you to go to the Clip and Curl."

My hand went to my hair. The feminine nature of the gesture made Clyde scowl. "Yours is fine. And since when do you care?"

I blushed. If I didn't watch it, I'd be painting my nails and buying a dress.

I lowered my hand and curled my treacherous fingers into a fist. "What for?"

"Tina didn't come home last night. I got the call just before you came in. You gonna check that out?"

"I thought you didn't want any overtime."

"Looks like that idea is shot to hell." He sighed. "I gotta talk to Cherry. I don't know what I'm going to tell her."

Since I didn't want that job, I took the one that had been given to me.

However, on the way out of the hospital I ran into the ER doctor. He recognized me and paused. "The ME discover what was up with that guy?"

I shook my head. Even if he had, I wasn't sure if I was supposed to tell. But I *could* ask . . .

"Do you think that maybe this new strain of rabies needs a new strain of vaccine?"

His forehead furrowed. "What new strain of rabies?"

"The one that's creating supersmart wolves very fast."

He stared at me for a moment, then burst into laughter. "Right. You've been watching *Tales from the Crypt* reruns, haven't you?"

"I'm serious."

"So am I. There's no such thing as a new strain of rabies."

"But—"

"If there was, an ER doctor in the north woods would be the first to hear about it."

The speaker right above our head blared, "Dr. Benson to the ER stat."

"That's me."

I stood in the hallway and watched him go, but I didn't really see him. I needed to talk to Mandenauer. But first . . .

I pulled out my notebook and my cell phone, but I had no service. Sometimes being in buildings was worse than being in the forest. I found a pay phone, dialed the CDC, and asked for Dr. Hanover.

"Who?" the receptionist asked.

"Hanover. Dr. Elise Hanover."

"Hold on." She clicked off, returning a few moments later. "There's no Dr. Hanover here. Never has been."

That should have surprised me. But it didn't.

I was also not surprised to discover that Mandenauer was unavailable. The man I talked to at the Eagle's Nest said he'd been gone all day. Since Herr Spooky didn't have a cell phone, I'd have to hold my questions until I could get my hands on him. I had no choice but to head for the Clip and Curl.

By the time I returned to Miniwa it was nearing the supper hour—usually the least busy time of the day. Even tourists had to eat. Today the tourists appeared to be fleeing.

I rolled my patrol car in the opposite direction of all the other cars. Their backseats full of children and their roofs full of crap, everyone was leaving. Since most rentals were from Sunday to Sunday and no one would give up a day if they'd already paid for it, I couldn't figure out what was up.

I had no problem parking right in front of the Clip and Curl. I'd have no problem parking anywhere on Center Street right now.

Tina's partner, Lucy Kelso, stared out the window at the departing exodus. When she saw me, her relief was evident and she waved me inside.

"Have you found her?" she asked before I even shut the door.

"No." Her shoulders slumped. "Do you know what's up with the tourists?"

"They're all scared of the mad wolf pack. There was a story on the news at noon."

I cursed. It had been pure luck that we'd been able to keep things quiet as long as we had. Our luck appeared to have ended.

Lucy sighed and glanced out of the window at the parking lot that was Center Street. "There goes the summer crowd."

She was probably right, and as much as I loathed the tourist season, I would loathe being out of a job even more. So I'd better do my job while I still had one.

"When was the last time you saw Tina?" I asked.

"Yesterday. We both had late appointments. Perm for me, a color for her."

"You left together?"

"No. Tina had to do one of the Chicago ladies." Lucy lowered her voice as if imparting a state secret. "Black roots. Platinum hair with highlights."

She shook her head, sympathy all over her face. I had no idea if she was sorry for the Chicago lady or Tina.

"I left around six. Tina said she'd lock up. This morning she had a nine A.M. cut. I ended up doing it. I ended up doing all her people today." Lucy's lip trembled. "This isn't like her. She knows if you miss an appointment, customers don't come back. There are too many other salons. People don't have much loyalty these days."

That I could agree with. "You called her house?"

"Yep. And went up there, too." She pointed at the ceiling, which I took to mean Tina lived in the apartment over the Clip and Curl. "She wasn't there."

"No note? No message?"

"Nothing."

"Family? Boyfriend?"

She gave me a strange look. "You know she lived with her gramma, who died last year."

I nearly said, "How would I know that?" before I

remembered. Popular high school prima donnas believed everyone knew everything about them and cared.

I nodded sagely and scribbled "Blah, blah, blah" in my notebook.

"Her boyfriend is on the road," Lucy continued. "He's a trucker. Karl Baldwin, remember him? He was the quarterback."

"Uh-huh." I didn't know Karl Baldwin from Karl Marx. I hadn't had much occasion to attend football games in high school.

"Could Tina have gone with him or met him somewhere? Little vacation?" I winked.

Lucy was already shaking her head. "I called Karl on his cell. He hasn't heard from her, either."

I frowned. This was not going as well as I'd hoped.

"All right. I'll check into it. Let me know if you hear from her." I handed Lucy my card. "Do you have the key to her place?"

She nodded. "And I found hers when I was in the apartment."

"Her keys were there, but she wasn't?" Lucy nodded. "What about her car?"

"Still in the lot."

"Her purse?"

"On the kitchen table."

That wasn't good. In my experience, you have to pry a woman's purse out of her cold, dead fingers. Women never left home without them.

I could tell from Lucy's expression she was having the same thought. She put the ring of keys into my hand and turned away blinking back tears.

I stepped outside, planning to go directly to Tina's and see what was up. But someone bumped into me, and when I turned around, all I saw was the gun.

Chapter 24

I grabbed the rifle right out of the guy's hands.

"Hey!"

He tried to get it back, but I shoved him with one firm hand on his chest. I nearly passed out from the beer fumes, but I managed to stay upright and keep him from snatching the gun.

Jerry Uber wasn't the brightest star in the sky. His shaved head only proved my point. Jerry didn't have the smoothest noggin or the best skin. Right now he looked like a lumpy egg with diaper rash.

"You can't carry a rifle without a case in the middle of town, Jerry. You know that."

"How am I gonna shoot rabid wolves if my gun's in the case?"

"Shoot?" I put my finger in my ear and jiggled it. "What?"

"Me and the other *men*." He puffed out his chest. His beer belly went with it. "We're gonna do what you cops haven't."

I glanced up and down the street. The tourists were gone. Only the gun-toting citizens remained.

Vigilantes. I hated these guys.

"Yeah, well you're gonna have a tough time without your gun." I headed for my car.

"Huh?"

Jerry danced around behind me as if the beer he'd already drunk today needed to be released right now. Maybe I'd get lucky and he'd relieve himself on the street. Then I could arrest him and there'd be one less drunken idiot in the woods.

"Thass my gun. You can't do that."

"Actually, I can." I unloaded the thing and pocketed the bullets, then laid it on the passenger seat of my car. "You can pick it up from Zee when you're sober. Bring along your case."

"Zelda?" He shook his head and put up his hands. "Aw, Jessie. You know she scares the crap out of me."

"You, me, and everyone else in town. That's why she's in charge of the guns."

Since Jerry and I had had dealings before, he didn't argue. He went home. No doubt to get another gun. I picked up my radio, not bothering to give my call sign, since I wasn't technically working. "I need to talk to Clyde right now."

"He isn't here. Can I help you?"

The voice was new—young, hopeful. She wouldn't last.

"Yeah, find him. Tell him we've got armed citizens all over town and the tourists are leaving."

I spent the next hour confiscating weapons. When my car was full and my pockets weighted with bullets, I drove to the station.

I knew I was fighting a losing battle. These guys all had more guns. They'd be out in the woods come night-fall. Someone was going to get shot. I could only hope that that someone wasn't me.

Clyde had never materialized, which was strange. For all his minor annoyances, he had always been on top of things.

No Mandenauer, either. Not so strange—considering the source.

After I'd tagged, recorded, then locked up all the guns, I did manage to find Zee. In the break room with a cup of coffee on her left, a lit cigarette on her right, and a roast beef sandwich the size of a small dog in the center.

I swear she ate red meat at every meal. Zee's longevity was a never-ending mystery, like so many others. I'd heard stories of Great-aunt Helga who smoked all her life and lived to be a hundred and four, contrasted with stories of jogging health-food fanatics who keeled over at forty-two. Go figure.

Since Zee was enjoying herself, I backed out of the break room so she could continue.

"Where you goin'?"

She didn't even turn my way. The woman had ears like a bat. And she looked like one, too.

"I need to find Clyde."

"Sit."

Zee indicated the chair to her right. With a glance at the smoldering cigarette, I took the one to her left.

"Want half?" She pointed at the sandwich.

The beef hung out of the bread—thick, red, and juicy. The scent, combined with that of horseradish, reminded me of the wolf pyre in the woods. I shook my head and swallowed hard.

Zee shrugged. "More for me."

She made short work of the sandwich. The woman could certainly eat. How she could be stick-thin was another of life's little mysteries. Although now that I thought about it, Zee had a habit of gorging a day here, a day there, then existing on cigarettes and coffee in between.

With a sigh and a pat for her distended belly, she sat

back and lifted her cigarette. I made a face. She blew smoke rings at me.

I waved them away. "You know I hate that."

"Which is why I do it." She winked. "I hear some evidence has turned up missing."

"Yeah."

"Since I'm in charge of the evidence room, that upsets me."

The sharp tap of her fingernail against the table punctuated Zee's irritation. I braced myself for the explosion. Instead, she took another drag and blew it out slower than slow.

"I didn't exactly want to dance a jig when I heard."

"Any clue where the stuff is?"

"If I knew, then it wouldn't be missing."

She lifted one eyebrow. "Are you getting smart with me?"

"No, ma'am. I need to find Clyde."

"Good luck. He went ten-seven after he left the hospital."

"Then I'll call him at home." I shoved back my chair.

Zee grabbed my arm. "Leave him be."

Something in Zee's voice made me stay where I was. "Why?"

She took another drag on her cigarette, blew the smoke out the corner of her mouth in a stream that shot away from me for a change. "He's taking it hard."

"What?"

"Clyde went to school with Mel's dad. He had to tell Tony what happened. Cherry's a mess."

"Oh." I didn't know what else to say.

"I told Clyde about the tourists and the gun freaks. He called in some extra help from Clearwater."

I thought of the amount of citizenry with guns, the depth, darkness, and expanse of the woods.

"That'll work."

My sarcasm must have been showing, because Zee snorted. "Who knows, maybe the idiots will thin out the wolf population."

"Or the other way around."

"Either way, we win."

I wasn't sure whether to laugh or cry.

"Heard from your mom lately?" Zee asked.

"Who?"

Zee lit another cigarette from the embers of the first. "Guess not."

She took a deep drag and let the smoke drift out on a contented sigh. She and I hadn't had a good talk in a long time. Considering our age difference, you wouldn't think we could. But Zee was young at heart, despite the probable black tar therein. She was the best friend I'd ever had, and I loved her.

"You gonna tell Mom about the guy?"

"What guy?"

"Don't screw with me, girl. Cadotte. Is he as good as he looks?"

"When did you see him? And how do you know . . ." I fumbled for a word. "Anything?"

"I have my sources."

She no doubt did. Sources she'd never reveal to me. The woman knew everything that went on in Miniwa. It was downright terrifying. And often quite handy. Unless it was me she knew everything about.

I narrowed my eyes. "You didn't tell Clyde, did you?"

Zee shook her head. "Clyde's got enough problems right now. He thinks of you as his daughter—or near enough. He'd kill Cadotte if he found out you were banging him."

"Nice," I murmured. Though *banging* was probably

a pretty good word, considering what we'd been doing.

But I was more interested in Zee's observation of Clyde's feelings for me. "Clyde thinks of me like a daughter?"

I heard the hope in my voice and cursed myself. I'd never had a father. I didn't need one now.

Zee contemplated me a moment. "Sure. Just like I think of you as the granddaughter I'll never have."

"No gramma worth her salt would ever use the word *banging*."

Zee cackled. "Aren't you glad?"

"Damn straight."

Zee and I had talked about many things over the years, but mostly present tense. What we'd done today, what we'd like to do tomorrow, whose butt was better than Jimmy Smits's.

She'd told me once that her family was dead. She'd come to Miniwa because she had nowhere else to go and stayed because she liked the trees. Her expression had been so sad at the time, I never had the heart to ask her anything about her past again.

"So what are you gonna tell Mummy Dearest about the guy?"

"Uh, nothing?"

"That would be my advice. She'd have a conniption."

"You got that right."

Zee had met my mother once. It had been hate at first sight—on both their parts. My mother said I clung to Zee like moss to a tree just to annoy her, and maybe she was right. But Zee had given me more affection and support in the years I had worked with her than my mother had given me all of my life. Pathetic but true.

"Although I might have to agree with Mummy on this one."

I gaped. "What?"

Zee shrugged. "Unless you're just doing him."

He'd actually been doing me—quite often—but that was my business.

"There's nothing serious starting up with you and him, is there?" Zee was staring at me too closely. I began to sweat. "You haven't mistaken sex for love or anything, have you?"

"Of course not. Do I look stupid?"

"Never said that you did. I just don't want you to get hurt."

"And that would happen because . . . ?"

"Mixed relationships never work out."

I knew Zee didn't much care for the Indians, but I'd never expected her to be so blatant in her prejudice.

"What are you trying to say, Zee?"

"I went out with a beautiful man once." Her eyes went dreamy. "It was nice at first. But not for long. He actually thought I should be grateful." She snorted. "Women propositioned him right in front of me like I wasn't even there."

I blinked. "By mixed, you mean—"

"Cadotte's hot, Jessie. You're . . ." She lifted one shoulder, then lowered it.

"Not. I know. Big deal."

"Now, now. No need to get testy. Face the facts. You aren't Marilyn Monroe. A guy like him, pretty soon he'll start listening to all those people who are asking him what he sees in you."

I'd thought the same thing. But the more I got to know Cadotte, the less I could see him caring what people thought.

Second Shift appeared in the doorway. She glanced at Zee, flinched, then focused on me. "Jessie, we got trouble in the woods."

"No shit," Zee muttered.

"If you can't be constructive . . ." I began.

"Shut the fuck up," Zee finished.

It was, after all, her favorite saying.

"What's the matter?" I asked the youngster, who appeared to have swallowed a frog.

"The um . . . uh . . ." She waved her hand back toward the command center.

"Two words?" I held up two fingers, then tugged on my ear. "Sounds like?"

She tilted her head and stared.

"Don't confuse her, Jessie." Zee slurped what must be, by now, ice-cold coffee.

"You never let me have any fun." I sighed. "The um . . . uh . . . what?" I asked.

"The other patrol. Two Adam Four."

Henry. "What about him?"

"Shots fired in the forest. Screaming. Something about an ambulance. Backup. Help."

My gaze met Zee's.

"Let the games begin," she muttered.

Chapter 25

By the time my shift was over and the sun had risen on another day, I'd decided to name the game "pandemonium."

We'd had four arrests, three accidental shootings, two dead dogs—

"And a partridge in a pear tree," I muttered as I filled out my reports.

I'd never had a chance to meet with Mandenauer. Hunting would have been pointless anyway, since the woods were overrun with morons.

Amazingly, not a wolf had been shot. I had to wonder if they'd all turned tail and run to the next county. It wouldn't break my heart any.

I was also unable to meet Cadotte. I'd called his house, but he wasn't there, so I left a short, apologetic message. I suspected he was at my place, and I felt kind of bad that I'd left him sitting on my doorstep. But I couldn't leave just yet. He knew where to find me.

As I was looking through my notes, I discovered that while I might thrive on third shift, my memory did not. I'd forgotten about Tina Wilson.

I decided to stop by her apartment later today, if not tonight. My days of working in the dark and sleeping in the light appeared to be over—for the duration of our wolf problem.

"Ha!"

The door slammed. Everyone in the room—me, First Shift, Brad, several of the Clearwater cops—jumped. Clyde held a legal-sized sheet of paper in his fist.

"Got it," he told the room at large.

We glanced at one another, then back at him.

"Got what?" I asked.

"A proclamation from the DNR."

"What's it say?"

"Any private citizen caught in the woods with a gun will lose their license for a year."

"Ouch," I murmured. Clyde just smiled.

While folks in and around Miniwa wouldn't blink at a few days in jail for illegal firearms transportation, threatening to take away their hunting and fishing privileges—which was the DNR's specialty—would make people sit up and take notice.

"Post this at the Coffee Pot." He handed the paper to Brad. "Then put out the word."

Which meant get some coffee, gas up your squad car, have a doughnut, and while you were at it, let everyone know that the DNR was behind us. The woods were going to be more deserted than a ski hill on the Fourth of July.

"This time tomorrow everything should be back to normal." Clyde went into his office and shut the door.

Great. Now he was delusional, too. Had he forgotten the *wolf* problem?

As everyone dispersed to spread the news, I knocked on Clyde's door.

"Come!"

I went in.

"What's up, Jessie?" Clyde's grin didn't mask the circles under his eyes, the pallor beneath his tan, the sag of his shoulders. He hadn't forgotten the wolf problem. In fact, he probably remembered it better than I did. Especially when I was in Cadotte's arms, where I forgot everything.

I straightened and got down to business. "I wasn't able to go out with Mandenauer last night."

"Of course not. That would have been suicide. Edward and I had dinner."

"Edward?"

He ignored me. "We also had quite a conversation." From the narrowing of Clyde's eyes, I knew what was coming. "Didn't I tell you Cadotte was trouble?"

"Yes, sir."

"Yet you're sleeping with him?"

"How the hell did you know that?"

He raised one dark eyebrow. "I didn't."

Damn Clyde. He was the best interrogator on the force—and he'd just played me like a green kid with her first felony.

"Jessie." He shook his head and sat on the edge of his desk. "I thought better of you."

I lifted my chin. "I haven't done anything wrong. I'm an adult. So is he."

"You find that totem yet?"

I blinked at the sudden change of subject. As if the stone had heard us, it swayed between my breasts. I jumped, then had to clench my fingers into fists to keep from reaching for the thing and rousing Clyde's suspicions.

"No. Why?"

"Ever ask Cadotte about it?"

"Why should I?"

"I don't know, Jessie; maybe because he's an expert

on totems. You find one, show it to him, then *poof,* the next thing we know, the stone is gone."

"You think he took the totem?"

Since I knew he hadn't, Clyde's attempt to make me suspicious of Will only convinced me to keep the thing under my shirt—so to speak.

"I'm not sure what to think."

Which only made two of us. Everyone was acting weird lately. Except Cadotte. But he'd been strange to begin with.

My cell phone rang. I glanced at the caller ID. Speak of the Devil. I hooked the thing back onto my belt. Raising my eyes, I met Clyde's. From the expression in his, he knew who'd been on the phone.

He heaved a sigh. "Be careful. I don't want you to get hurt."

Zee had said the same thing. Was I such a social reject that everyone took one look at Cadotte and labeled *me* "soon to be hurt"?

That was a rhetorical question.

A knock on Clyde's door had us both lifting our heads. Mandenauer walked in.

"Just the guy I wanted to see," I began.

He raised a slightly yellowed brow and shut the door behind him. "I am at your service."

He bowed, just his head and shoulders in what I was beginning to think of as the German fashion. I half-expected him to click his heels, but he didn't.

"The doctor at the hospital didn't know anything about the super-rabies."

"Of course not."

"*Why* not? Don't you think that's something the doctors ought to know?"

Mandenauer shrugged. "Rabies is rabies to them. The vaccine works on both."

"Not so much. Didn't you hear that Mel died? Have you seen the body?"

"Yes to both questions. Sometimes that happens."

"Well, don't get too broken up about it," I mumbled.

"Jessie," Clyde warned.

"Yeah, yeah."

I rubbed my forehead. I was getting tired, dopey, crankier than usual. I had another question for Mandenauer—it was on the tip of my brain.

"Oh!" I smacked my forehead. "Ouch." I forced myself to lower my hand so I could see Mandenauer. "I called the CDC."

He didn't react.

"The Centers for Disease Control?"

He spread his bony hands wide.

"Something is funny there."

"I have never known the CDC to be very funny."

"Exactly. The first time I called, they had heard about the virus. When I called back and asked to talk to the doctor, they'd never heard of her."

Mandenauer and Clyde exchanged glances.

"Sounds like someone was yanking your chain, Jessie."

"At the CDC?"

"How long since you slept?"

"I forget."

"Sleep." Mandenauer turned me toward the door. "Forget about anything but ridding your forest of the wolves. Tonight we hunt at dusk."

"Dusk?"

"When the sun just sets."

"I know when the hell dusk is. But why then?"

"It is the time when the wolves come to life. I will be at your house an hour before that."

"Fine. Whatever."

I was starting to wonder about that first phone call to the CDC. *Had* someone been screwing with me? How could that be?

A tap on the phone? Interception of my calls?

Put me and Oliver Stone in the same padded room, thank you.

Chapter 26

There was no sign of Cadotte when I let myself into my apartment. I checked my messages. None—on my home phone or my cell. Strange.

But he should get the message I'd left him. I was so tired, I unplugged all my bells and whistles, then fell into bed. I had another doozy of a dream.

I was at Mel's funeral. Closed casket for obvious reasons.

Cadotte was with me. He cleaned up nice. The dark suit made his hair appear darker, and his eyes seemed endless.

I was in uniform, which wasn't strange. But Cadotte holding my hand was. Even stranger . . . I liked it.

We sat at the back of the church. I could tell by the stained glass it was St. Dominic's right at the edge of town. The place was full. A sea of humanity rippled all the way from our pew to the front, where Cherry sat dolled up in killer black heels, a silky dress, and a hat with a veil.

The priest went into his endgame. I tried to pay attention. Really. But out of the corner of my eye I saw the casket move. Before I could shift my gaze, the top slammed open and Mel popped out.

At least I think it was Mel. He was a wolf now. Huge, muscular, sleek, and blond.

People started screaming, running, but he paid them no mind. He set to devouring everyone in the front pew.

"Does that seem like rabies to you?" Cadotte asked.

I hated being wrong. Hated it even more when my being wrong cost lives. I headed for the front of the church unimpeded since, in the way of dreams, everyone else had disappeared.

"Mel!" I shouted as he began to eat a mourner's face.

He looked up. The wolf's eyes were Mel's. The blood dripping from his muzzle ended any hesitation I might have felt.

I emptied my gun into him. He didn't flinch. He didn't die.

Instead, he gave up on the appetizer and came for me.

I awoke to a pounding on my front door that echoed the one in my chest and my head. One glance at the clock revealed I'd slept the day away. The slant of the light told me who was at the door. Mandenauer was nothing if not prompt.

Since I'd fallen asleep in my uniform, all I had to do to get ready for work was fill my rifle and my pistol with silver instead of lead. Mandenauer's bandolier was a regular buffet line for ammunition.

I didn't believe in prophetic dreams. I didn't believe in werewolves. However, I did believe in being prepared, and what could silver hurt? Hopefully nothing but the wolves.

I opened my door and joined Mandenauer in the hall. He took one glance at my face and kept quiet. Smart man.

The streets were deserted. Without the tourists, who would wander the shops at this time of day? I only hoped that the threat of the DNR had cleared the forest. I certainly didn't want to spend my tomorrow filling out more accidental shooting reports.

Mandenauer drove his hearse . . . I mean Cadillac. After my dream the thought of riding in it nearly caused me to insist on the Crown Victoria. But since I hated being scared even more than I hated being wrong, I forced myself into the passenger seat. Not that I didn't check the back for stray corpses. There weren't any.

He drove away from town, in a different direction from Highway 199 and the place where we'd first seen the black wolf, in the opposite direction of the Gerards' place and the wolf pyre of the night before.

"Where we going?"

"North."

My teeth ground together, but I managed not to snarl my next question. "Any reason why?"

"Because we have not gone there yet."

I guess that was as good a reason as any other.

He turned off the main road and onto a dirt track. The Cadillac fishtailed. Luckily we hadn't had much rain or we'd have needed an ATV to get wherever it was we were going.

The road was surrounded on all sides by towering pines. I wondered how Mandenauer had found it or if he'd just picked a road, any road, and turned. I considered asking, but really, what did it matter?

The track stopped abruptly and so did the car. We were surrounded on three sides by thickly set trees. There was barely enough room for a raccoon to squeeze between them. How we were going to, I had no idea.

Nevertheless, I followed Mandenauer deeper into the woods. He had a sixth sense for finding the way. There wasn't exactly a path, but we made progress. We seemed to walk for hours, but when he stopped at last, darkness still hadn't fallen.

We stood on the south side of a fern-covered hill. Mandenauer shimmied to the top on his belly. He beckoned me and I followed his lead.

The ferns whispered as I slithered through them. Soft, spidery leaves brushed my cheek, tickled my neck. The scent of fresh greenery and damp earth pressed against me like a fog.

Peeking over the hill, I frowned. About one hundred yards distant stood the opening of a cave.

Caves were not all that common around here. Farther west, toward La Crosse maybe. But in the deep woods? I'd never seen one—until today.

"What is this?" I whispered.

"I found it while the others were running mad through the woods last evening. You wonder why no wolves were shot?"

"The question did cross my mind."

He smiled. "Your answer is here."

Night came on long thin fingers of darkness that spread through the trees, walked over the ground, and smothered the mouth of the cave. The moon and stars sparkled in the sky as wolf-shaped shadows slunk out.

One, two . . . Five, six. . . . Eleven, twelve.

I cursed beneath my breath and my hand crept toward my gun.

Mandenauer stopped me. "Let them go," he breathed. "For now."

He ignored my incredulous gape. Seemed to me we could pick off quite a few before they knew what hit them. But since there were more wolves here than I'd ever seen before, and he was the expert, I let my hand fall back to my side.

The animals slunk into the forest. Silence descended, broken only by the breeze through the branches, and then—

A chorus of howls shattered the night. I started, gasped. They sounded as if they were right behind us. But when I turned, nothing was there.

The rustle of leaves beneath boots yanked my attention back to my companion. He was headed for the cave.

I scrambled to keep up, reaching his side in time for us to enter shoulder to shoulder. He produced my city-issue flashlight—guess I'd forgotten to get it back, so bill me—and shone the artificial light inside.

The night was hot against my cold, cold skin. "What is this place?" I murmured.

"They always have a lair. Always."

The cave was damp, as caves were. But that wasn't what made me go all clammy.

The piles of bones in every corner didn't even bother me. We were, after all, in the lair of the wolf. No, what made me squirrelly were the scraps of cloth, the unmatched shoe, the glint of an earring beneath the startling white of a rib bone.

Nausea rolled in my belly and I turned away. "Wolves don't do this," I said.

"These wolves do."

An unnatural clatter made me spin around. He was poking through the pile of bones. His boots scuffled in the dirt as he continued around the room.

"What are you looking for?"

"A clue."

"What kind of clue? They're animals."

"You'd be surprised what animals like these will leave behind."

"After this, not much will surprise me."

Once again I couldn't have been more wrong.

The howl of a wolf reverberated around the stone enclosure, so loud Mandenauer and I both flinched and spun toward the entrance. He shut off the flashlight, but it was too late. We were trapped.

I lifted my rifle. This time Mandenauer didn't stop me. The shadows on the rock's surface did.

The moon hit the mouth of the cave and sent silver light cascading across the opening. The silhouette of a man appeared.

I lowered my gun, opened my mouth to call out, and Mandenauer's hand slapped over my face. He shook his head, and his expression was so odd—equal parts of fury, disgust, and fascination—I didn't struggle. Soon all I could do was watch.

At first I thought the man was bending to touch his toes. Calisthenics in the forest. Sounded like something Cadotte would do.

But he didn't return to a standing position. Instead, the shadow remained folded over as it changed.

One moment there was a silhouette of a man touching his toes. The next he was on all fours, his head hung down so low I couldn't see it.

The shadow rippled. The sound of bones popping, nails scratching, filled the cave, punctuated by a series of grunts and moans I would have associated with really great sex if I hadn't seen what was happening instead.

Between one blink and the next the man became a wolf, threw back his head, and howled. Others answered and he was gone.

Sometime during the show Mandenauer had dropped his hand from my mouth. I couldn't have spoken if he'd poked me with a stick. I couldn't stand, either, so I sat in the dirt and put my head between my knees. Mandenauer left me there as he continued his hunt for clues.

I'm not sure how long my mind spun and my voice refused to work. I jumped a foot and yelped when Mandenauer patted me on the back.

"We must go, Jessie."

I lifted my head. "W-W-What was that?"

His rheumy blue eyes met mine. "You know what it was."

I shook my head. "How would I know?"

He pulled me to my feet—I would never have been able to get there under my own power—then tapped his forehead. "Ignore what you know." His finger moved to his chest and tapped there, too. "Believe what you feel."

"You sound like Cadotte."

"The boyfriend?"

"He's not my boyfriend."

"Lover then."

I made a face. That sounded so . . . girlie. "Leave him out of this."

"I did not bring him up."

Right again. I needed to get back to the matter at hand. Whatever it was.

"Did you find anything?" I made a vague gesture to indicate the cave at large.

"Nothing I did not expect."

"What did you expect?"

He stared at me for a long moment as if gauging my sanity. Since I was wondering about it myself, I let him. Then, as if he'd made a monumental decision, he lowered his head in that bowing thing he did and sighed. "We need to talk."

"I'll say."

"Let's go back to your apartment."

"My apartment?"

"What I have to tell you is for no one's ears but your own."

"Sounds serious."

"More serious than anything you could ever imagine."

Well, hell, I didn't like the sound of that. He'd told

me to trust what I felt. What I felt was scared and angry and confused. Three emotions that brought out the worst in me.

"Shouldn't we do a little hunting before we call it a night?"

"Not tonight. Tonight we talk. Perhaps once you know the truth you will be of more use to me." He picked up his rifle and headed for the mouth of the cave.

"Hey." I scrambled to catch up. "What's that supposed to mean?"

He paused at the entrance, looked both ways as if crossing the street, before he leaped out, spun around, and pointed his gun at the roof of the cave. I flinched and ducked. But he lowered the weapon, straightened, and beckoned for me to join him.

"You will be more motivated when I have told you the truth."

"All right. Tell me."

"Ever hear of Josef Mengele?"

A chill of dread rolled from my neck to the small of my back. "The Nazi?"

"That would be him."

"Isn't he the wacko who did all those experiments on the Jews?"

"Yes."

"He's dead."

"But some of his experiments live on."

Chapter 27

No matter what I said, Mandenauer refused to tell me any more until we reached my apartment. Which left me plenty of time for thought.

But thinking only got me more confused. Theories ranged from rabid wolves to werewolves, from an Ojibwe legend to a Nazi nightmare. None of them made any sense.

We reached my place at midnight. At least no one was out and about. Zee believed we were still in the forest. I should have told her otherwise and planned to as soon as we reached my apartment. I'd shut off my radio in the woods and as of yet, I hadn't turned it back on.

However, as soon as we entered my place, the dam broke on Mandenauer's silence. I didn't think about anything but his words for a long time.

"I am not who you think I am."

He strode through my apartment and yanked the drapes shut before he turned on a light. Then he sat with his back to the wall, where he could see both the window and the door.

I didn't like to sit near windows, either, but now that I thought about it, I'd never seen Mandenauer without a

gun, never known him to relax to a level lower than red
alert or put his back to any entrance. It was the behavior
of a man with enemies, a man who was as much the
hunted as he was the hunter.

"Who are you then?"

"I am a *Jäger-Sucher*."

"Hunter-searcher. I know. So does everyone else
around here."

"No, they think they know what a *Jäger-Sucher* is,
but they do not, because what it is, is secret and special."

A puzzle piece snapped into place in my head with a
near audible click. "As in Special Forces?"

His lips twitched. "Yes."

"Who do you work for?"

"Not the DNR, to be sure. Though they think so."

"Does Clyde know?"

"No one knows but those of us who belong."

"Then why are you telling me?"

"Because I may need you as more than a hired gun.
I believed I could handle this case myself, but it is far
more complicated than I at first understood. And my
compatriots are all occupied elsewhere."

"Compatriots? How many *Jäger-Suchers* are there?"

"Enough."

"Obviously not, if you need me."

"Touché." He flipped his forefinger toward his temple, then away, in a jaunty salute. "Will you help me?"

"Aren't I already?"

"Yes. But it is not fair or safe for you to continue
without knowing the truth."

"Then let's hear it."

"I will start at the beginning."

"An excellent choice."

His eyebrows lifted. I shut up.

"You've heard of Mengele and his horrible experiments at Auschwitz?"

"Who hasn't?"

"You'd be surprised how many people know nothing of it. Or if they have heard, they have pushed it out of their minds, even refused to believe in the truth of such inhumanity to man."

"Are these people familiar with the term *Nazis*? Which I believe is the German word for inhumanity to man?"

Mandenauer's lips twitched. I'd nearly gotten him that time.

"There was more going on with Mengele than the documented terrors he performed at Auschwitz."

"Why am I not surprised?"

"He had a secret laboratory off-site where he worked on his pet project." Mandenauer choked, a sound that resembled a laugh. "Pet. That should be funny under the circumstances. But it isn't."

"What are you trying to tell me?"

He cleared his throat and took a deep breath. "Monsters, Jessie. They not only wore the uniform of the Reich; they were made by them."

"I don't understand."

"Mengele made monsters."

"What kind of monsters?"

"The ones we have here."

"Which would be?"

He tapped his head, then his chest, as he'd done in the cave. "You know."

I did. "Werewolves."

"Yes."

I might have begun to wonder about shared delusions, psychotic paranoia, something in the water. Except I'd been there a few hours ago when that shadow of a man had become something else. I wasn't saying I believed in werewolves. But I wasn't such a skeptic anymore.

"How?" I asked.

"One of Mengele's famous experiments was the effect of contagious diseases on different races. He used Jews of course, as well as Gypsies. Hitler didn't like them, either."

"Who did he like?"

"Blue-eyed, blond-haired white men."

"Like you?"

"Exactly."

"You knew Hitler?"

"Only in passing."

I blinked. "How old are you?"

"Old enough."

"Wait just one damned minute." Without my even thinking about it, my hand had crept to my rifle, which lay near enough to touch. "Whose side were you on then? What side are you on now?"

"The side of right."

"Haven't you ever heard that a villain is the hero of his own story?"

"I do not understand."

"Hitler thought he was right, too."

"But there's one difference between him and me."

"What's that?"

"He was wrong."

I didn't know if I was supposed to laugh at his skewed logic or not.

"Relax, Jessie. Take your hand off the gun. I am not a Nazi or a werewolf."

"Well, that sets my mind at ease. Like you'd tell me if you were. Bad guys don't usually have a swastika tattooed on their foreheads." I frowned. "Except for Manson."

I was starting to confuse myself. Thankfully Mandenauer knew when to ignore me.

"I was a spy then. A very good one. I spoke the language and looked the part. I was born in Germany and lived there until I was ten years old. Some would say I was a traitor."

"Some wouldn't."

He smiled. "Thank you. I was given a mission and to accomplish it I did many things of which I am not proud."

His eyes went distant; sadness haunted his face. I remembered him saying he'd lost his soul long ago. I wondered what else he had lost while trying to save the world.

"What was your mission?" I asked.

"To discover what Mengele was up to in his secret laboratory and destroy both it and him."

"I take it that went well."

"*Nein.*"

"What happened?"

"By the time I located the laboratory . . ." He glanced at me. "Have you ever been to Germany?"

"No."

"There are beautiful cities, acres of rolling countryside. There is also what is known as the Black Forest. In the old days wolves by the thousands roamed. Mengele kept his secret lab in the depths of that forest."

I nodded. I had a feeling I knew where this was going.

"I saw hundreds of wolves as I crept toward the secret place. I thought nothing of them. I saw shadows of other things, too. But I ignored them, since what I saw with my eyes would not agree with what I knew as the truth in my brain."

"I hear you," I muttered.

"However, when I reached the laboratory it was

empty. Everything Mengele had made was gone."

"Where?"

He made a fluttering motion with his fingers. "Released."

"Why?"

"Hitler wanted a werewolf army."

"Uh-oh," I muttered as another puzzle piece went *click*.

I had heard that term before. I opened my mouth to mention it, but Mandenauer cut me off.

"When the Allies hit the beaches at Normandy and the Russians started marching in from their side, Mengele panicked. He released the monsters and hustled back to Auschwitz, leaving the lab abandoned."

"You're saying we've got Mengele's wolves running around loose in Miniwa sixty years after the war? Sorry, Ed, I find that hard to swallow. I find all of this hard to swallow. I've done some reading on Mengele."

Nazi information was like a train wreck. No matter how awful it was, you just couldn't keep yourself from looking, then looking some more.

"I've never heard a whisper of Mengele's secret monster-making lab."

"You think because you haven't read about it, this makes it untrue?"

"Something this large-scale and horrific would have been documented."

Mandenauer laughed. "The amount of things undocumented would amaze you, Jessie McQuade."

"Does the federal government know about this?"

"My dear, the federal government knows about everything."

I snorted my opinion of that. Mandenauer and Cadotte each had their own conspiracy theory, and I, who had never believed in conspiracies, was now beginning to believe both of them.

"How long do these things live?" I demanded.

"They are quite hard to kill, as you may have noticed. I have devoted my life to this endeavor."

"You've been hunting werewolves since World War Two?"

"Among other things."

I frowned. "What things?"

He shook his head. "One monster at a time."

Part of me wanted to argue; part of me agreed. If I had to worry about other monsters, I just might need that padded room today.

"How many werewolves were released?"

"We have no way of knowing. Mengele destroyed all his records from the secret lab."

"Then how do you know—"

I broke off. I could be buying into one huge delusion, except . . .

"I saw them, Jessie. So did you."

Except for that.

"It does not matter how many there were."

"No? I would think that would matter quite a bit."

"What matters is how many there *are*. How many there will be if they continue to be made at the rate they seem to be being made here in Miniwa."

Made. I'd heard that before. From Cadotte. Though I wasn't going to say I was buying this, there were a few too many coincidences for my liking.

I sighed. "There isn't any super-rabies, is there?"

"No. Although the werewolfism," he shrugged, "or perhaps I should say lycanthropy for want of a better term, is a virus of sorts. Remember Mengele's tests on contagious diseases?"

"How could I forget?"

"He blended viruses. Mutated them. This one passes through the saliva."

"But if the rabies vaccine works, why don't you just use it?"

He shook his head. "You saw how well the rabies vaccine worked on one who was bitten."

My eyes felt like they'd bugged out. "You mean that was *supposed* to happen?"

"Werewolves can't shift until dusk. Except the first time. Once bitten they change within a few hours—day, night, rain, shine, it does not matter. The only way to delay the change is an immediate and thorough cleansing of the wound. Delay, but never stop."

I recalled the ER doctor's praise of Brad's first-aid skills. It had taken Karen Larson several hours to lose her mind, and she hadn't changed—at least not while I was watching.

"I could not let Mel become a wolf. Would you rather I put a silver bullet through his brain in front of half the town and a television camera?"

"You recommend the rabies vaccine knowing it will kill the victims?"

His pointed stare was answer enough.

"Why not just inject all the monsters?"

"The rabies vaccine only kills the bitten before they have shifted for the first time. After that, only silver will do. The more they change, the stronger they become. The older ones are able to control the change, move around as human under the moon. But even they must shift at some point when the moon is full."

So much information, so little time.

"How do you know all this if Mengele's records were lost? Did he tell you?"

"No. But others were persuaded to do so."

From the chill in his eyes, I could imagine how the

others had been *persuaded* to tell him. I gave a mental shrug—all's fair in love and war. And it had been war. Looked like it might be war again, since there seemed to be a werewolf army on the move.

I shook my head. I still couldn't quite buy all this. Seeing might be believing, but to truly believe, I was going to have to see a whole lot more than a shadow on the wall.

Chapter 28

My cell phone shrilled into the silence that had fallen between us. I glanced at the caller ID.

The station. *Oops.*

"Hello?"

"Why is it that I'm constantly asking, Where the *hell* are you, girl?"

I winced. "Sorry. Is there a problem?"

"Yeah. That Lucy Kelso chick has been calling every hour on the hour."

Hell. Tina. I'd forgotten her again. Obviously she hadn't shown up yet.

"I'll get back to her."

"Where are you?" Zee repeated.

"With Mandenauer. We had business to discuss."

"Kill yourselves anything tonight?"

"Not tonight."

Zee's exhale was so heavy, I nearly saw the smoke curl out of my phone. "You comin' in soon?"

"I need to do one more thing."

"Fine. But do me a favor?"

"Anything."

"Turn on your fucking radio. You think it's for decoration?"

Zee slammed the receiver down hard enough to make my ear ring. I flicked on my radio, then caught Mandenauer's eye. "I need to get back to work."

He stood. "Me, too."

"Where do you think you're going?"

All this talk of monsters and Nazis had me worried. I'd seen enough in my life to know that evil was damn near impossible to kill, and suddenly I didn't want to let Mandenauer out of my sight.

"I must return to my cabin and check in with my people."

"Your people?"

"The other *Jäger-Suchers*. They are scattered from west to east and north to south all over this world. I am their leader since I began the journey. We keep in contact now on the lovely Internet." He shook his head. "What an invention."

"Who do you work for?" I asked again.

"That federal government you are so fond of."

"Of the United States?" My voice squeaked.

He smiled. "What other one is there?"

I shook my head. "I have never heard of a unit like yours associated with the U.S. government."

Mandenauer just raised a brow and didn't comment.

Well, duh. *Secret* Special Forces. But a monster-hunting society and a Nazi werewolf army division? Please.

"You said Clyde doesn't know who you really are."

"The DNR sent a hunter, which is what I am. We have contacts with resource departments everywhere. In this way we are kept informed of any odd situations and we can investigate, then deal with whatever we find."

"But—"

Mandenauer held up a hand. "Enough for one day, Jessie. You know what is important. You must be careful. We will talk again tomorrow." He started for the door.

"Wait."

He had told me what I needed to know to be safe. The least I could do was return the favor. Though Cadotte had asked me to keep what he'd discovered between us, after what I'd seen and heard tonight, the time for that was gone.

I quickly filled Mandenauer in on Cadotte's theory of the Matchi-auwishuk.

"The Evil Ones," he murmured. "And a wolf god. He may be right."

"But how do an ancient Ojibwe legend and a Nazi experiment fit together?"

"I am not sure. I will have some of my people investigate. In the meantime, you keep an eye on the professor."

I didn't think I'd have any problem with that.

Mandenauer opened the door, then paused. "But be careful," he murmured. "Do not trust him too much."

"Why?"

"I have discovered over the years that the one who knows the most about a secret is often the one behind the secret."

"You think Cadotte is a werewolf?"

"He could be."

"Why would he tell me about them if he's one of them?"

"To gain your trust. And you must trust no one, Jessie. It is the only way to stay alive."

"Why do you trust me?"

He shifted his rifle in my direction. "I could always shoot you with silver and see if you die."

"I'll pass, thanks."

He smiled and left. I wasn't all that sure he'd been kidding.

I patted my pocket where the weight of Tina's keys still rested. I was going to her house and dealing with this case before it slipped my mind again. I was starting to have a very bad feeling about Tina. Instead of returning my rifle to the safe, I took it with me to the car.

Even though it was past midnight, I knocked on Tina's door. I hoped she'd open it, pissed off that I'd woken her. No such luck.

Maybe she was a heavy sleeper and I'd walk in on her. Or maybe she was a thorough lover and I'd walk in on *them*. I didn't care. At least she'd be alive and off my to-find list.

I pulled her keys out of my pocket. Something fell to the floor with a clatter. I bent and picked up the key I'd found next to Mandenauer's wolf pile. Holding that one in my left hand, I used my right to try all the keys on Tina's key ring.

None of them fit.

I tried again, tilting them every which way, jiggling them in the lock, trying to entice one to open the door. Maybe these were a friend's keys. The car keys. The keys to the Clip and Curl. Hell. I was going to have to wait until tomorrow and get Lucy's copy.

I shoved the key ring into my pocket, switched the single key I'd found in the forest from left hand to right, then—I have no idea why—tried the mystery key in Tina's door.

It slipped right in.

My breath caught; I turned my hand. The lock clicked. One tiny push and the door swung open.

A cold wave of dread washed over me, but I stepped over the threshold anyway. "Tina?"

Come on; come on. Be here. Be mad. Be very, very mad.

My plea did no good. As I walked from room to silent room, I heard nothing, saw no one.

I checked her messages and heard only frantic pleas from her boyfriend and Lucy to call them.

I went through the mail. Nothing but bills and junk.

I didn't see a computer. She probably kept that downstairs in the shop. I was sure Lucy had already checked Tina's e-mail if possible.

Tina Wilson appeared to have vanished.

I opened my hand and stared at the key. What did it mean? I had a niggling, nasty suspicion.

Mandenauer had killed a cinnamon-shaded female, then burned the body. I'd found Tina's key next to the fire.

I reached out and picked up a photo of Tina and Lucy outside the Clip and Curl. The blonde and the redhead. although Tina's hair had been more reddish brown. Auburn, some called it—perhaps cinnamon.

I set the photo down with a *click,* then collapsed onto the sofa.

What I was thinking was crazy. Tina had run off with some guy. It happened all the time.

Of course, how did I explain that her purse, her car, her keys, her clothes were still here?

She'd run off with a rich guy who'd promised to buy her the world?

Maybe.

I remembered the last time I'd seen her, when she'd questioned me on the street. Had she truly been concerned about mad wolves or more interested in discovering what we were doing about them? Hard to know when she wasn't here to ask.

Well, I'd follow procedure. Report her missing and

send out the appropriate information to the media and other police stations. But I didn't think Tina was going to turn up.

My gut feeling was that the local hairdresser was one dead werewolf.

How was that going to look on a report?

Chapter 29

As I was leaving, a pile of books on the counter caught my eye. Since they were the shape and size of textbooks and Tina did not strike me as the textbook type, I was curious.

College algebra, biology, and intro to Indian studies. Before I even opened her notebook and peeked at the course list, I knew.

Tina had been in Cadotte's class. How was that for a coincidence?

I spent the rest of my shift driving around, handling the usual. Speeding, reckless driving, bloody bar fight—all in a night's work. I could deal with them in my sleep, which was lucky, since I was pretty damn distracted.

Memories swirled though my mind, little things and big, followed by questions. By the time I got off and went home, I was a mess. Had I been screwing a were-wolf? Thank goodness we'd used protection. I certainly didn't want any puppies—or would that be cubs?

On my way up the stairs to my apartment I started to giggle; then I couldn't stop. I passed my landlord, Mr. Murphy. Still snickering, I nodded in lieu of hello.

"What's so funny?" He smiled along with me.

"Puppies," I managed between desperate attempts to catch my breath.

His smile disappeared immediately. "You know there are no dogs allowed in this building."

I couldn't help it; I erupted with laughter. Waving good-bye, I escaped into my apartment. This was all just too ridiculous.

Once inside, however, I sobered. As much as I hated the concept of woo-woo, I couldn't deny that something weird was going on in Miniwa.

Only fools ignored the evidence, and I liked to think of myself as one step above a fool, at the very least. I sat down and listed all that I knew to be true.

Karen Larson bitten by a wolf. Loses her mind and rips out the throat of her principal. Despite her having her brains blown out, both she and the principal disappear.

The evidence gathered from the scene of the Larson accident vanishes from the evidence room of the Miniwa police station.

Someone breaks into Cadotte's office and ransacks the place, taking nothing.

Mel Gerard bitten. Rabies vaccine administered. Dies of as yet undetermined causes, with strange changes in the body.

Tina Wilson turns up missing. But the key to her apartment is found next to a wolf bonfire in the woods.

I watch the shadow of a man become the shadow of a wolf on the wall of a cave.

Sitting back, I chewed my lip and examined the evidence, none of which made much sense. However, when I combined facts and fantasy a clearer picture emerged.

Obviously Clyde had not used silver on Karen Larson. Hence her ability and that of her principal to get up and walk out of the morgue. Or perhaps her change had merely been delayed as Mandenauer had predicted and she'd run out of the place on all fours.

The disappearance of the evidence from the police station indicated the involvement of the department. But who?

The ransacking of Cadotte's office led me to believe someone had been searching for the totem. But why had they been searching there? Again, police involvement was indicated—unless someone was following me. Also a possibility.

If I believed Mandenauer's claim that the rabies vaccine had killed Mel, then there could be something to his theory of lycanthropy. If Mel had had rabies, he should have been cured, not killed.

If I believed Mandenauer that far, why not go the entire way and buy into a Nazi werewolf army? I wouldn't put it past them.

So who was a werewolf and who wasn't? It was impossible to tell, unless I shot everyone with silver. I wasn't willing to do that. Yet.

Sunlight filled the room. I should be in bed, but I wasn't the least bit tired. I got out of my uniform and into my swimming suit. Then I tossed what passed as a purse for me—a small plastic makeup case sans makeup, with just enough room for a few personal necessities, my keys and my ID—into a gym bag along with a towel, some water, my gun of course, the totem—I wasn't letting the thing out of my sight—and headed for my pond.

I needed the exercise. I needed the release. I needed the peace of my own special place just to think. Theoretically I should be safe—it was broad daylight.

Half an hour later as I swam back and forth, back and forth, across the pond I pondered some more.

Who could I trust? Mandenauer said no one, but he

could be nuts for all I knew. I certainly didn't trust him. No more than I trusted Cadotte.

Closing my eyes, I remembered the big, sleek black wolf I'd encountered the first night I'd hunted with Mandenauer. The way the animal had moved reminded me of Cadotte. Or maybe it was the other way around.

I swam until my head stopped spinning, pushing myself until all I could think about was the next stroke, the next kick. The sun was warm first on my back, then on my face. Peace settled into my soul. This was what I had come here for.

When I couldn't drag myself any farther, I crawled out of the water and sat on the bank, trailing my toes along the surface.

The sounds of nature surrounded me—bees buzzing, birds twittering. A frog splashed into the pond on the far side. A fish flipped its tail in the center. I rooted around in my bag for my water, tilted my head, drank.

And the forest went silent.

I swallowed what was left in my mouth, but my tongue was still dry. I lowered my head, and my eyes scanned the tree line just as he stepped out of the woods.

He was as naked as he'd been the first time I'd seen him. As he walked across the meadow separating us, the birds started to sing again. A crow swooped nearly down to his head, then up to the treetops. He didn't notice. His gaze was focused on me.

I watched him walk and was reminded again of the wolf. Loose hips, long strides.

I frowned with a sudden memory. His hip. The night I'd met him he'd had a nasty bruise there.

Again I experienced the mythical *click* in my head of a puzzle piece. I'd forgotten about the bruise, since it bore no relationship to anything. Unless you considered a wolf could become a man. And what if that wolf had just been tapped by the bumper of a great big SUV? Would the man then bear the bruise?

Keeping my eyes on Cadotte, I let my hand slide over to my gun. He stopped several feet away.

"What are you doing here?" I asked.

"Don't you want to see me?"

"I'm seeing quite a bit of you. Where're your clothes?"

He glanced down, blinked as if he was as surprised to see all of him as I was. "I was working out."

"You work out in the buff?"

"Don't you?"

I swept my free hand down my body to indicate my perfectly modest one-piece swimming suit. "Obviously not."

He shrugged. "I was practicing my tai chi."

The ripple of lean muscle beneath his skin, the shine of the sun across his belly, his shoulders, his hair, was making me forget I should probably shoot him.

"Was that what you were doing the night we met?"

"Of course."

How convenient. Too bad I wasn't buying it.

"You were practicing at four in the morning?"

"I couldn't sleep."

Because he'd been chasing—something—through the woods and been hit by a car.

"How did you know where I was?"

"I didn't. I called." He looked away as if embarrassed. "All your numbers. When you didn't answer I thought you might be here. So I walked over."

I glanced at the trees, gauged the direction and distance.

"You walked five miles naked?"

"For you I'd walk a hundred."

I snorted.

He was acting strange—too nervous and shy for Cadotte. What was the matter with him? Was I right in my assumption? And if so, what was I going to do about it?

He didn't give me a chance to think. Suddenly he was moving toward me and my gun was pointed at his chest. He froze, lifted his eyes from the barrel to my face.

"Jessie?"

"Are you a werewolf, Cadotte?"

His eyes widened. He was either very good at feigning surprise or truly surprised. "Yesterday you called me insane for suggesting there were such things in the world. Today you accuse me of being one. Tough day at the office, dear?"

Now that was more like him. I smiled. "You have no idea."

"Want to tell me about it?"

"Want to answer my question?"

"Why in hell would I tell you about them if I were one of them?"

"That's not an answer. That's another question."

Cadotte and Mandenauer had more in common than I would have thought.

He sighed. "I am not a werewolf."

"Like you'd tell me if you were."

"Good point." He flicked a finger at the gun. "Now what?"

"I could shoot you and see if you die."

"I'll take Door Number Two."

I wanted to laugh. I wanted to put down the gun and make love in the sun. I wanted to believe that the only man who'd ever made me scream and writhe and want him over and over and over again wasn't a werewolf— so I did.

He must have seen surrender in my face, because he began to walk toward me again. I lowered the gun. He threw back his head, howled like a wolf, and charged.

I was so shocked I just sat there, expecting to die. He did a cannonball into the pond and drenched me.

I waited for his head to surface. Instead, something wound around my ankle and yanked. My shriek became a gurgle as I sucked pond water.

He could have drowned me. He could have done anything and I couldn't have stopped him. My gun was on the bank. I was at his mercy. I didn't mind.

Before we even surfaced his mouth was on mine, the heat a contrast to the coolness of the water. His tongue tickled my lips.

We broke past the surface and into the sun. I tore my mouth free and breathed deeply. He took the opportunity to run his lips down my neck and lick the water from the tops of my breasts.

Near the middle he could stand; I could not. But he held my head above water with his hands at my waist.

"What's with the howl?" I demanded.

"Wolf clan." He shrugged. "I do it sometimes for fun."

"Fun. Right."

His idea of fun and mine were worlds apart.

"Do you ever swim in the nude?" he asked.

"Never."

"Wanna try?"

He didn't give me a chance to answer, just slipped the straps off my shoulders and yanked. The suit stuck at my hips.

"Not as easy as it looks, huh?"

He shrugged and gave another mighty tug. Suddenly my swimming suit was gone. Really gone.

"Hey! Give that back!"

"Sorry, lost it."

I blinked. "You mean—"

"Yep. Bottom of the pond. Good riddance."

"That's my favorite suit."

"No offense, but it's butt ugly."

"That's because my butt's ugly. The suit covered it nicely."

His hands slid from my hips to my ass. "Your butt isn't ugly. There isn't anything ugly about you. I'm going to buy you a new suit. One that suits you." He smiled.

"I'm glad you amuse yourself."

"Me, too."

He lifted, then plunged into me in one smooth thrust. I squeaked in surprise and clutched his shoulders.

"Wait, wait." But he was rocking against me, not pulling out, just rocking. Slow, deep, pushing against a part of me so rarely touched before. There was something I had to do, but I couldn't think.

"That's it," he murmured against my breasts. Soft kisses, gentle licks, and a tiny, soft nibble on the nipple. "That's it."

"Puppies," I muttered, and shoved him away with all my strength.

I had no delusions that he couldn't keep me right where he wanted me. He was stronger than I was. But he let me go.

"Puppies? Is that some new form of curse word?"

"Uh. Yeah. I'm trying to cut down."

He reached for me again and I slid out of his reach. "What's the matter, Jessie? You can't actually think I'm a werewolf. You don't believe in them, remember?"

He was right. I didn't believe in woo-woo. There was another explanation for all that had happened, everything I'd seen. If I kept on searching, I'd find it. The world was black-and-white. Had to be. I didn't know how to deal with it any other way.

While I'd been thinking, he'd gotten close again. Damn, he was fast—by land and by sea. His hand slid around my waist and he pulled me to him. "Talk to me." He nuzzled my neck, took a bit of my skin into his mouth, and sucked.

His erection pressed against me. My legs widened, wrapped around his hips. Damn, I was doing it again.

"Protection," I managed. "I don't have anything with me and I can bet you don't, either."

He cursed and the word wasn't *puppies*. Our foreheads touched as he sighed.

"Sorry. I've never been irresponsible. Not once. But you make me crazy, Jessie. I see you and all I can think about is being inside of you."

As if to prove the point, his penis shifted and pulsed against me. I groaned. His hands clenched at my hips, and I tensed, prepared to get physical if he tried anything again without a condom. He'd never had sex without one, and neither had I, which took care of one worry. Puppies aside. Luckily all he did was lift me out of the water and onto the bank.

The slight breeze played along my wet, naked skin and I shivered. I groped for my towel, but his hand wrapped around my wrist.

"Not yet." His fingers tightened. He wasn't hurting me, but I let the towel go.

I sat on the bank. He stood in the water. His mouth was level with my hips, which gave me an interesting idea.

"Lie back," he murmured.

Huh, great minds do think alike.

Chapter 30

His mouth hot against my chilled skin, my legs hung into the water. My back was cushioned by mossy green grass. His shoulders parted my thighs as the sun sparked diamonds against my closed eyelids.

For an instant, reason shouted that we were outside, naked, anyone could see. I tensed and he kissed me, but not on my mouth.

"Trust me," he whispered, and his breath brushed the damp curls between my legs.

Trust him? Was he nuts? His tongue flicked over me. *Okay, what the hell?*

My fingers clenched, pulling out handfuls of grass as my head thrashed in the moss. How did he make his tongue so stiff, so acrobatic, so clever?

From his earlier kisses, touches, the few seconds of intercourse, I was swollen and needy. He tormented me with his mouth, then soothed me with his hand. I heard myself breathing and begging. At the same time full and empty, I was on the verge and yet so far away.

"Hush," he whispered. "I'll make everything all right."

His fingers filled me; his mouth locked onto me and with his tongue he gave me what I needed.

A splash woke me from a doze. A shadow blotted out the sun. I opened my eyes; his face hovered inches from mine. The uncertainty I saw there made my heart flutter, so I lifted a hand and touched his cheek.

He was still hard against my hip so I turned, rubbing along the smooth length of him. I shifted my hand from his cheek a few feet lower. "Let me make everything all right for you, too."

He was on the edge, just as I had been. A few sharp pumps, a flick of my tongue over the tip, one deep draw into my mouth, and he shoved me away. I admit I fought him. For the first time in my life, I wanted to go down on a guy and stay there. But it was pretty erotic to watch as he took himself in his own hand and finished what I'd started.

When he opened his eyes, our gazes met. "Wow," I said.

He smiled. "Yeah. Wow."

Getting to his feet in a lithe, supple movement, he jumped into the pond, ducked under the surface, then came up and shook his head, spraying me with water like a dog. I laughed and he swam over to the edge. We couldn't seem to stop staring at each other.

"What?" he asked.

I shrugged and dropped my eyes. I didn't want to say what I was thinking.

"Hey, I thought you trusted me."

Did I? I wasn't sure. I wanted him. Badly. But trust? That was so much harder to give than my body.

He touched my ankle. "Jessie?"

I met his gaze. "I was just thinking that I wished we had a condom."

His fingers tightened on my ankle, like a hug almost. He lifted himself out of the pond. I got distracted by the bulging muscles in his arms and the way the water streamed down the length of his body. He sat next to me on the bank and kissed me—soft, slow, and sweet.

"Me, too," he whispered.

Our mouths met, hard this time, a deep, searching, sexy kiss that sent my body spiraling into arousal once more. Whenever I was around him I had absolutely no control.

He broke away, breathing heavily, then tugged my hair. "We could always take a little chance."

"Or not."

He laughed. "That's what I love about you, Jessie. You keep me in line."

Love? That had to be a figure of speech. Had to be. So I let it pass.

"I've got to get back," I said.

"You could come to my place." The uncertainty returned—to his face, his voice.

"I need to sleep."

"So sleep. In my bed. With me."

God, it was tempting. But I was afraid if I went to Cadotte's bed, I'd do everything *but* sleep. And as appealing as that was, I had to work tonight. The nonstop cop schedule was starting to wear on me.

"I can't."

His eyes shifted away as he sighed.

"What's the matter?" I asked.

"Is it all about sex between us?"

I wasn't sure what to say. I'd thought we were fucking each other because we couldn't seem to stop. In fact, I distinctly recalled him agreeing to just that. When had things changed?

I probably should have set him straight. Less hassle later that way. But the dejected set of his shoulders touched me. Though I should have stayed where I was, I couldn't keep myself from going to him.

The muscles in his back bunched and rippled beneath my hands. I smoothed my fingers over his skin in a gesture I hoped would soothe. I was no good at soothing. But I'd give it a shot.

"I'm not sure what this is," I admitted. "Do we have to decide right now?"

"I wish you would."

I didn't like being pushed. But Cadotte had issues. Didn't we all? However, since I'd never been an Ojibwe man in a white, white world, I decided to cut him some slack.

"You're smart," I said as he turned to face me. My hands fell away from his shoulders to hang loose and empty at my sides. "Funny, too, when you aren't being a pain in the ass. You aren't half-bad in bed. Even better without the bed."

"Well, gee, Jessie, I'm all warm and fuzzy."

I tilted my head. He was angry, but I couldn't figure out why. What guy didn't like being called good in bed?

"Why are you mad at me? I think you're okay. For a glasses-wearing geek."

He didn't even smile. "Are you embarrassed to be seen with me?"

I sighed. He wasn't going to let me tease my way out of this. "You want the truth?"

"Dazzle me."

I couldn't believe we were having an argument sitting naked under a noonday sky. But there were a lot of things I'd done with Cadotte that I couldn't quite believe.

"Yes, I'm embarrassed to be seen with you."

He blinked and his face paled against the inky darkness of his hair. He looked like I'd slapped him. Hell, I felt like I had.

I grabbed his hand. He tried to pull away, but I

wouldn't let him go. "I'm embarrassed, Will, because I know what people will think."

He sighed. "Here we go."

"Where?"

"People will think less of you because you're with me. It doesn't matter what I've done. Who I am. What we have together. All that matters is who my parents are."

"Huh?"

"Jessie, I've been dumped a hundred times and it isn't because I can't dance. It's because I'm Indian."

Now I was mad.

"Women can't see that the first time they see you? Your heritage comes as a surprise to them later? You date a lot of morons, do you?"

"Maybe they just can't take the stares, the whispers, the pressure."

"Do I seem like I can't take the pressure?"

His lips twitched. "No."

"Thank you."

His amusement died as quickly as it had sprung to life. "Then why are you embarrassed to be seen with me?"

I didn't want to tell him, but I had promised the truth. Still I hesitated long enough for him to squeeze my hand. "Jessie?"

"Because everyone will wonder what you're doing with me," I blurted. "You're hot, Cadotte. I'm not. For a guy like you to be with a woman like me . . ." I shrugged. "I must give great head. I must fuck like a rabbit. I must—"

He put his hand over my mouth. "Shh," he whispered. "You do. So what?"

Silence fell over us both. We stared at each other as

what we'd said hung between us. Then I laughed, and he laughed with me. It felt good.

I went into his arms and just held him while he held me. I couldn't remember the last time I'd hugged a guy for more than a minute. I'd never missed it, either. But I would now. Cadotte gave very good hug.

"Come back to my place," he murmured. "Sleep with me. Stay with me."

He kissed my brow and I snuggled closer, held on tighter.

I'd never felt like this. Too bad I wasn't sure what *this* was. I liked him a lot. I wanted to be with him too much. I wanted to say yes, to anything, everything. Where William Cadotte was concerned I had no control. And it scared me.

Nevertheless, I went home with him. It was the best damn day I ever had. Which worked out well, since everything went to hell soon after.

Chapter 31

Cadotte drove my car. I kept having visions of being stopped by one of my co-workers and trying to explain why the driver was naked and I was near enough. I wore a long T-shirt that just covered my cheeks, but no underwear. If someone saw me like this I'd never live it down.

But he was a careful driver, and we reached the end of the dirt trail that led to his cabin without incident. He parked my car next to his, a Jeep, and we set off toward the house.

I'd never been inside his place, only looked in the front window like a voyeur. I'd forgotten that occasion until I followed him inside and got another scare from the wolf hanging in the hall.

"What's with that?" I asked.

He didn't seem like the kind of guy who'd display dead things on the wall.

"Gift from a friend."

Now that I could see more closely, the wolf's head was a hat and the skin a cape. I'd seen pictures of men wearing them at powwows and such. People wore all sorts of interesting things when they danced in ceremonies.

"Do you use this?" I asked, thinking it must have something to do with the wolf clan.

"No. That's a Plains tribe affectation. The Navajo believe a witch becomes a werewolf by donning a wolf skin." Cadotte nodded toward the one on his wall. "Like this."

"Believe? As in present tense?"

"Yes. Or at least some of them do."

"Like your friend?"

"Maybe."

"What about you?"

"I believe in werewolves. But I've tried on that skin and I was still me—wearing the head of a wolf."

He continued into the main part of the house, leaving me to stand alone in the hall or join him. Since the wolf skin creeped me out more than it should, I hurried after.

Cadotte wasn't in the living room. Or the kitchen, which I could see from where I stood. The place was cleaner than I'd expect for a guy who lived alone, but not neat by any means. Papers and books were strewn over every flat surface, and the paraphernalia of life was stacked in the corners and behind the furniture.

I let my gaze wander over his stuff, then around the room. Wood shutters graced every window. Huh. I'd seen storm shutters attached to the outside of a cabin. I wondered why he had them on the inside, too. Must be better insulation.

A door to the left stood open, so I went in. He was already in bed.

I raised a brow. "In a hurry?"

"I thought you were tired."

Seeing him there with the sheet pooled at his hips, chest all bare and beautiful, I wasn't so tired anymore. I dropped my bag, lost the shirt, and crawled in beside him. But when I ran my hand up his thigh, he put his over mine.

"I promised we'd sleep."

"I didn't."

He tugged my head onto his shoulder. "Rest, honey. Let me hold you awhile."

I jolted at the endearment. "You know, if any other guy called me 'honey,' he'd be having his teeth for lunch."

"I guess I'm not just any guy."

"I guess you're not."

His lips brushed my hair. "That might be the nicest thing you've ever said to me."

"Don't let it go to your head."

"I won't."

Fingertips trailed along my spine, gentle, light, a relaxing touch that made my eyes drift closed. But I didn't fall asleep. There was something I had to ask.

"The night we met, you had a bruise on your hip."

"I get a lot of bruises."

"You do? Why?"

"I'm kind of a klutz, or I used to be. Which is why I started practicing martial arts. It helped my balance. I don't stumble over my own feet nearly as much as I used to."

A good excuse, but he still hadn't answered my question. I asked him again.

"Why don't you tell me where *you* think the bruise came from?"

When I tried to articulate my doubts, I found I couldn't put anything so silly into words. So I didn't. However, Cadotte had no such compunctions.

"You think I got hit by a car while in wolf form, and by the time you saw me I had a bruise."

I started, colored, shrugged. "Well, the bruise *was* gone by the first time we . . . you know."

"Made love?"

I winced. I hated that term. Love was a foreign emotion to me. I wasn't exactly sure what it meant. My father hadn't loved me, obviously. My mother had an odd way of showing it. I'd never loved a man and a man had never loved me. Maybe what I felt for Zee was love—maybe.

"Whatever," I muttered.

"I heal quickly. Always have. Healthy lifestyle. And some Ojibwe medicine."

"What kind of medicine?"

"My grandmother was a member of the Midewiwin."

I frowned and he quickly clarified. "The Grand Medicine Society. She was what people refer to as a medicine woman. She used natural remedies—herbs, bark, eye of newt." He winked. "She knew the old ways, and she taught them to me."

"Knew?"

"She died of pneumonia when I was ten. Some things can't be cured."

"I'm sorry."

"So was I."

My hand rested on his chest. His heart beat steadily beneath my palm. The room was quiet and I drifted toward sleep.

"Why do you think so little of yourself?" he asked.

"What?" I struggled to follow the sudden change in subject. "I don't."

"Right. That's why you're so worried about what people will say. Beauty and the Beast, but I get to be the beauty. There's a switch."

"I know who I am. I have my strengths. Being a girl isn't one of them."

His free hand slid over my hip, cupped my butt. "I think you're wrong. You make a very nice girl."

"You would say that."

"Yes, I would, because I think you're beautiful."

"You're slow *and* blind."

"Don't be sarcastic."

"But I'm so good at it."

"You are. That's true." He kissed me on the head again. "Don't tell me you aren't beautiful. I know that you are."

I shifted, squirmed. Talk like this made me more uncomfortable than facing a drunk with a broken bottle. I knew what to do about that. But compliments? I wanted to run, hide, never come back.

Because if I believed them, I'd only be hurt more when I discovered he'd lied. But why would he lie? I couldn't quite figure that out. Yet.

As if he knew what I was thinking, Cadotte tugged me closer. "You're special to me, Jessie. Don't run away before we figure out what that means, okay?"

"Okay," I said, before I could stop myself.

"So when did my werewolf delusion become yours, too?"

I hesitated. Should I tell him, or shouldn't I? I wanted to tell someone and why not Cadotte? I knew he wouldn't laugh at me. Much.

I told him everything. I couldn't shut up. About Mandenauer and his secret society. About the wolves I'd seen. Tina. The cave. The man-wolf shape on the wall.

He listened. Not once did he interrupt. At certain points in the story, I'd hear his heart speed up—but then so did mine. Other times he'd tense, then relax. When I was done, silence fell over the room.

It went on too long and I lifted my head, turned to look into his face. I stiffened, half-expecting him, despite his belief in all things woo-woo, to be staring at me as if I'd lost my mind. Hearing the story out loud had made me wonder again myself. But his expression was thoughtful, considering. He peered across the room.

"What?" I asked.

He jumped, glanced down at me, smiled, but the smile was distracted—not the smile I was beginning to adore.

"Quite a story," he murmured.

"What do you think?"

"I think the government always knows a helluva lot more than they're letting on."

"Gee, what a surprise."

He laughed. "That's my girl. I'll have you seeing conspiracies around every corner soon enough."

"I already do," I muttered.

"Mmm."

He'd gone off again, thinking. I'd never dated a brainiac professor before. I suspected he went off like that a lot.

"Do you know Tina?" I asked.

"Tina?"

"The missing girl?"

"I'm sure I do. But I can't place her right now."

"Neither can anyone else."

"I thought she was ashes to ashes."

"Maybe. Don't you think it's weird that she was in your class?"

"Not really. We've established that someone is trying to raise a wolf god. That's an Ojibwe ceremony. If this Tina was one of them, it made sense for her to be in my class."

"Why?"

"Maybe she was trying to discover something obscure that would help her leader."

I frowned. "Did you ever get that book you ordered?"

"Huh? Ah, no. Not yet." He went back to staring.

I cuddled closer and the beat of his heart beneath my cheek, along with the sure, steady stir of his breath against my hair, relaxed me. Combined with very little sleep and a whole lot of stress, I was out in thirty seconds.

I awoke to the sun slanting through the windows at an angle that signified early evening. Cadotte was still asleep beside me. I had to go to work, but I needed my clothes.

Slipping out of bed, I watched his face. He really was too pretty for me. Strangely, I was starting to like it.

He never moved, even when I kissed him on the brow. I tiptoed into the living room, stopped to get a drink of water in the kitchen—and found it.

At first I thought he'd left notes scattered across the counter. I was even smiling at his absentmindedness as I drank from a Flintstone jelly glass.

Then my own handwriting caught my eye. The words registered in my brain a second later. I nearly dropped the glass, which would have been a shame—the thing was damn near an antique.

I snatched the papers. One was the receipt I'd had Cadotte sign for the totem; the other was the crumpled, torn page of the evidence log. And beneath them both was the bag of fiberglass and plastic that I'd swept off the pavement after Karen Larson's accident.

What was the missing evidence doing in Cadotte's kitchen?

I had no idea. But before I beat it out of him, I was going to find out what else he was hiding around here that I wanted to know about.

I didn't have far to go. Spread across his coffee table were books and notes. All of them related to Miniwa's little problem.

He'd been very helpful, highlighting the pertinent passages. One book in particular—*Legends of the Ojibwe*—was fascinating. Was this the book he'd been waiting for? The one he'd told me hadn't arrived? From the amount and nature of information highlighted I suspected this was the case.

I swallowed the thickness at the back of my throat that tasted too much like tears. I did not cry over men. Hell, I didn't cry over anything.

I glanced at the bright and shiny yellow highlighting, which swam before my eyes. I closed them tight, gritted my teeth, and when I looked again the words were all too clear.

The ceremony must take place beneath a blue moon. Which, by my calculations, was tomorrow night.

I felt as if time were rushing past, pulling all of us inexorably toward that second full moon.

I forced my attention back to the book.

The way must be paved by a werewolf army.

"Yada, yada, yada," I murmured. "Been there, know that."

I turned the page. A jagged edge was all that was left. Will, or someone else, had torn out the rest of the information. That couldn't be good.

I found nothing more of interest in the book, so I went through Cadotte's papers again. I didn't find the missing page, but I did discover one tidbit.

A wolf totem with the markings of the Matchi-auwishuk was needed to complete the ceremony. Sadly, his notes didn't say how.

I put everything back where I'd found it; then I snuck out of Cadotte's house and went searching for Mandenauer.

Chapter 32

I hurried home to get dressed, where I found a message on my machine from just the man I wanted to see.

"Jessie, I went back to the cave last night. Now I must do some burning. I will meet you at the station for your shift."

"Can't leave him alone for a minute," I muttered as I put on my uniform. After checking my weapons, I grabbed more ammo and slipped the totem over my head. "Don't leave home without it."

It wasn't hard to find my man. I only had to drive to the place we'd been the night before, then follow my nose.

Mandenauer stood watch over a much larger bonfire than he'd made the last time. Thankfully, when I arrived what he was burning was no longer discernible— although I knew very well what it was. I'd never had a weak stomach, but those days appeared to be gone.

"You said no hunting last night."

He glanced my way. "No hunting for you. You'd had a shock."

"I have shocks every day. I can still do my job."

He shrugged. "I did not need any help. When they returned to the cave it was like . . . how do you say . . . ? Shooting ducks in a pond?"

"That's what we say."

Lord knows why. The image was not very appealing.

"Why did they come back?"

He stared at me as if I'd just announced, "I was screwing a werewolf all afternoon."

I gave a mental wince. Better to not go there right now. That was one shock I wasn't quite up to handling, despite my brave words to the contrary.

"This is their hidey-hole. Where they go to change."

I frowned. "Why not just change . . . wherever?"

"They come in human form. They need a place to leave their clothes."

Such mundane problems had not occurred to me.

"There were clothes in the cave?"

"Of course."

"Any ID?"

"They are werewolves, not idiots."

I moved closer to the bonfire. "They don't change back when they die?"

He shook his head. "A myth. If they die as a wolf, they remain a wolf."

I sighed. Having the wolves return to human form would have been too easy. But couldn't something be easy just once?

"I was thinking . . ." Mandenauer made a noncommittal murmur. "Karen Larson hit a werewolf. Maybe we should be asking around about broken legs, hips, severe bruising."

He was shaking his head before I finished.

"Another myth?"

"Unless she hit the wolf with a silver car, any injury would have healed almost immediately."

Well, that let Will off the hook—for the bruise at least.

My radio crackled. "Jessie?"

I frowned. Zee was at work early again. "Yeah?"

"We got a call from Clearwater. About twelve campers have gone missing. They'd like us to keep an eye out."

"Ten-four." I turned my gaze on the flames. "I think I know where they are."

Mandenauer didn't answer. When the silence became too loud, I asked, "Now what?"

"We keep hunting."

"Here?"

"No. The others will not come back to this place now."

"Where, then?"

"I am not sure. Have you discovered anything new since I saw you last?"

I didn't want to tell him, but I had to. This entire situation was getting out of hand, and Mandenauer was the only one doing anything to stop the madness.

So for the second time in twenty-four hours I spilled my guts. I told him everything and then some. When I was done, he stared into the dying fire for a long time.

"We should shoot your lover." I opened my mouth to protest, but he kept talking. "But shooting people always gets me into trouble. Better to wait until they are wolves."

Hard to argue with that.

"I've been thinking," I said. "Why would Cadotte need to research the ceremony? Why would he want to help me discover the truth?"

"Perhaps he was making sure you didn't discover it?"

"How?"

"By telling you enough to make you trust him, but not enough so you could stop it. He has also had his foot firmly in the enemy camp. Have you told him what you know?"

My face heated. He glanced at me sharply and sighed. "Jessie. He could have killed you while you slept."

"But he didn't. Another thing bugs me. Why would he give back the totem if it's so important to the ceremony?"

"You have the totem?"

Me and my big mouth. "Uh, yeah."

Guess I hadn't told him everything.

"You've had it all along?"

I nodded.

For once his expression reflected respect instead of annoyance. "Good. From what you read, they can do nothing without it."

"They can't make another one?"

"If it was that simple they wouldn't be searching for it so hard."

"Are they?"

"Someone stole the evidence from the police station."

"Cadotte."

"Perhaps."

I frowned. "But someone tossed his office, so it couldn't be him."

"Perhaps." I gave him a dirty look and his lips twitched. "He could have ransacked the place himself."

"Maybe. But it still makes no sense for him to hand the totem back to me. He could have said he lost it. Or it was stolen. I would have been in trouble."

"True."

"Do you really think he's one of them?"

"In my mind everyone is one of them, until I know differently. Thinking in that manner has kept me alive for a long, long time."

I found a stick and bent over the fire, spreading the embers apart, trying to kick dirt over what was left. My boot caught on a rock and I stumbled. Mandenauer grabbed my arm to keep me from eating ashes. His body was between me and the forest.

As if from a long way off I heard an odd *thunk*. It wasn't until something whistled through the air that I realized what I'd heard.

If I hadn't known the sound from memory, the arrow sticking out of Mandenauer's shoulder would have clued me in. He fell to his knees, narrowly missing the remains of the fire.

I pulled my weapon, crouched in front of him, and searched the tree line. Nothing was there.

Mandenauer shoved me with his foot. "Go. I'll be fine."

He'd hauled his rifle into his lap, but with the arrow sticking out of his shoulder, he wouldn't be able to shoot very well.

I sighed. "I'm not going to leave you."

"He's getting away."

"He's gone and you know it."

I peered at the arrow more closely. A chill went over me. "This is from a crossbow."

"So?"

Pictures flashed in front of my eyes. Cadotte's semi-messy house. Papers. Books. Wolf head on the wall. Crossbow in the corner. Hell.

I glanced at Mandenauer and decided not to share. "Never mind."

He tried to see the arrow, twisting this way and that. Blood stained his shirt in an alarming flood.

"Hey. Quit moving around!"

"How can you tell what kind of bow it came from?"

"Shorter."

"It feels long enough to me." Sweat had broken out on his brow. His pale skin had gone a whole lot paler.

"Come on." I helped him to his feet with his good arm. "Let's get you to a doctor."

"Just pull it out. I'll be fine."

"You want a bullet to chomp on, big boy?"

"What?"

"Never mind. I'm not pulling that out."

"This is what they want. For us to be taken away from the hunt. If we do not destroy the werewolf army before the blue moon, evil will walk the earth."

"Evil always walks the earth, in one form or another."

He stumbled and I held on tighter. "You are right. Even if we succeed here, there is always another monster somewhere else. It never ends."

"Thanks, pal. Just what I needed to hear."

Along with the knowledge that Cadotte had tried to kill me, the idea that monsters were everywhere, for always, made my day complete. For a woman who had scorned all things woo-woo, I'd become awfully accepting of monsters. I suppose that was bound to happen.

I loaded Mandenauer into my car and headed for the emergency clinic, calling my whereabouts and the situation in to Zee on the way. She said she'd inform Clyde, if she could find him. He had a habit of disappearing when he wasn't on duty. I couldn't blame him. A man needed some time away from the chaos.

Mandenauer closed his eyes. I thought about crossbows. They weren't common—it was illegal in this state to hunt with one unless you were over sixty-five or physically incapacitated.

However, *owning* one wasn't illegal, so its presence in Cadotte's house hadn't bothered me—until five minutes ago. He had a right to buy one and use it for target practice. I winced at the memory of who had been the target.

I had kissed Cadotte, touched him, let him touch me

in ways I'd never let anyone else. Half an hour out of his bed, and he'd tried to kill me. He could have told me he wanted to be just friends.

"Does anyone else know you have that totem, Jessie?"

Mandenauer's eyes were still closed. He faced me, his uninjured shoulder against the seat, the arrow sticking out of the other and pointing at the passenger window. Looking at it made me slightly nauseous, so I concentrated on the road.

"Just you and me."

"Best to keep it that way, hmm?"

"Sure."

"Better safe than dead," he murmured.

"Which brings me to the question: If they wanted us dead, why not use a bullet?"

"Why not indeed?"

"This answering with a question stuff isn't answering at all, you know?"

"No?"

My back teeth ground together so hard they hurt. "Maybe I *should* pull that arrow out."

"Be my guest," he said, but his voice was fading and there was blood on the seat.

I drove faster. By the time I reached the clinic, Mandenauer had passed out. I drove right up to the door and shouted for help.

The same doctor was working. He glanced at me and frowned. "I'm starting to think you're bad luck."

"Me, too."

They whisked Mandenauer away. An hour later I got to see him. He was fine but dopey. I figured now was as good a time as any to get a clear answer to any question I might ask. And I had quite a few.

Why did we have to shoot all the wolves? Wasn't

there an easier way to get rid of them? Why couldn't we put them back the way they'd been before all this started? If anyone would know how to cure a werewolf, wouldn't it be the man who'd been hunting them for most of his life?

I sat in a chair next to his temporary bed. The small emergency section of the clinic didn't have rooms, only curtained partitions. If someone needed to stay longer than a night, they were sent to the hospital in Clearwater.

Thankfully Mandenauer wasn't that bad off, although he didn't look good. He'd lost a lot of blood, which was being reintroduced via an IV. I hated those things. They felt like someone had stuck a knitting needle into a vein.

"The doctor says you can leave in the morning."

He opened one eye, then closed it again. "Yee-ha."

I snorted. "You've been hanging out with me too long."

"Or perhaps not long enough." He opened both eyes. "You saved my life. Thank you."

"I think you saved mine. But you're welcome."

"You will not hunt tonight."

The words were not a question, but I answered anyway—in a manner he could understand. "No?"

"No. You are not trained to do so alone."

"We don't have much time."

"True."

"Is there anything else I can do?"

"Bring me some vodka."

"I doubt that will mix well with the drugs. Anyway, I meant is there anything else I can do to the werewolves? Isn't there a cure?"

"None that I know of."

My heart flipped and settled like a stone in my belly. "None?"

He sighed. "That I know of that work. There are innumerable theories, myths, legends. I prefer to be sure and use the silver. But I have an associate who has researched the cures. As of yet she's found nothing."

It was bad enough that Cadotte might be a werewolf, but I couldn't accept that there was no way to fix him. I wouldn't.

"Can I talk to her?"

Mandenauer's eyes popped open. He'd nearly been asleep. He waved a hand at his trousers, which were slung over a chair. "Her number is in my wallet. Elise Hanover."

I already had the pants in my hand. "Dr. Hanover?"

"You know her?"

"She works at the CDC. Or maybe not." Confused, I stared at Mandenauer. "She's one of yours?"

He nodded.

"You had my calls rerouted, didn't you?"

"Do not be angry. I had all the calls out of Miniwa sent through my people. Do you think we want the entire world descending on this town before we get it cleaned up?"

I thought we'd been lucky to avoid media mania. Instead we'd been manipulated.

I stood there with Mandenauer's trousers hanging from my hand and watched him drift off to sleep. Every time I turned around there was a new secret, another conspiracy, someone who wasn't who I thought they were. It was getting old.

Chapter 33

"What happened?" Elise cried. "Has he been killed?"

"Of course not. Why would you think that?"

"This is my private line. Only *Jäger-Suchers* have this number."

"Mandenauer gave it to me. I need information."

"I need to talk to him."

"He's sleeping."

The line went dead. I cursed and hit redial. When she didn't answer, I hit redial over and over again until Dr. Hanover picked up. "What?"

"I need information," I repeated.

"Without Edward's okay, you get nothing."

"Listen." Quickly I told her what had happened that day and what I wanted. "I'm not waking him. You can forget about it."

Silence met my declaration. For an instant, I thought she'd hung up while I ranted. I waited for a dial tone. Instead I heard a soft sigh.

"Fine. But I want to talk to him as soon as he's able."

"And my information?"

"You'll have it. What harm can it do?" she mumbled. "Fax number?"

"Hold on." I got the number from the nurses' station and gave it to her.

"You'll stay with him?" she asked. "He shouldn't be alone when he can't protect himself."

"You think the wolves will come after him here?"

"With Edward, there are more than wolves to worry about."

"Peachy."

Moments later a nurse brought me the faxed information from Dr. Hanover.

"Interesting reading, Jessie," she said.

I glanced at the top sheet. "Ways to Cure a Werewolf." Well that was succinct and to the point. Not very secretive, either. But then again, who'd believe this shit was real—unless they'd seen what I had?

I gave the nurse a sheepish smile and pointed to Mandenauer. "It's for him."

"Uh-huh," she said, and left.

I spent the next hour reading Elise's fascinating material. Not only were there several methods for curing a werewolf; there was a lot of historical information included.

From the Romans through the Greeks, to the Middle Ages, then on to the present time, there were tales of strange goings-on, explicable and inexplicable behavior. Funny, but most of the documented cases of lycanthropy in the twentieth and twenty-first centuries had never come to light in the newspapers or on television. Imagine that?

Up until a few weeks ago I'd have said this made them untrue. Now I knew better. There were ways to make the truth disappear along with the evidence. Obviously *Jäger-Suchers* were involved with more than just the elimination of the monsters themselves; they also had a hand in the elimination of any evidence of the werewolves' existence.

"Pentagram," I read. "Protection against a werewolf."

I could imagine wearing a symbol of witchcraft in this neck of the woods. I might find myself the victim of a little Jessie bonfire. Twenty-first century or not, folks in the north woods didn't take kindly to pentagram-wearing women.

"Skip that," I murmured, even before I saw Elise's notation in the margin.

"No good."

I kept reading. Next to many of the cures Elise had written the results. Most of them didn't work, as Mandenauer had said. But there were several next to which she'd jotted encouraging words like: "Sometimes," "maybe" and "what the hell?"

I was beginning to like Elise.

" 'Call the animal by its human name while in wolf form.' Well, that works if we know who in hell it is in the first place."

That *could* work with Cadotte. Wouldn't hurt to try.

" 'Remove ten drops of blood from the beast. Hold a piece of steel over its head.' " I scowled at the paper. "Those could hurt. Me. I'll pass."

" 'Cut off a limb. The werewolf will change back, sans limb.' "

"I don't think so."

There were quite a few ideas that hadn't been tried. Most of them were violent and involved hacking the beast in some way. Not only was I not willing to get that close to a werewolf, but I didn't want to injure Cadotte in the process.

If I had to kill him, so be it. But I wasn't going to torture him on the off chance he might be cured. That smacked a little too close to the Nazi way of doing things, which was what had gotten us into this mess in the first place.

In the end I had two methods I could try. The name

game and one other. "Profess your love to the man within the beast. If your love is true, he will become human again and stay that way forever."

I didn't know if I loved Cadotte, but I'd give it a shot. I'd be a lot less embarrassed to profess true love to a wolf than a human anyway. If my love was true, I guess we'd both win.

I used my cell phone to contact Brad. He was an idiot, but he was my idiot. Brad was as loyal as a Labrador retriever and only half as stupid. If I told him to watch Mandenauer like a hawk, he would. If I told him to protect the old man with his life, he'd do that, too.

Ten minutes later, Brad arrived. I explained the basics: Mandenauer had been shot; I wasn't sure by who, so I wanted him protected.

"I'm going to check out a few leads," I said, and left the two of them together.

I headed for the emergency room exit at the back of the clinic. I planned to find Will and test Dr. Hanover's theories.

Since it was after midnight in a small northern town, the parking lot was deserted. A few cars, most likely belonging to employees, butted up against the bank of trees that made a half-circle at the back of the clinic.

Beneath the bright and shiny moon, the hood of my car sparked silver shreds of light into my eyes. Which was my only excuse for not seeing the huge black wolf until he growled at me.

My hand went to my gun. The wolf was between me and my car, where I'd left my rifle. And I'd called Brad stupid. Although at this range I shouldn't need anything stronger than my pistol.

I stared at the wolf. God, he was huge. I'd never seen one bigger. I recalled reading somewhere that black wolves were the largest. The zoologists couldn't figure out why.

I tightened my fingers around my gun. The wolf snarled.

"Smarter than you look, aren't you?" I murmured.

The wolf cocked his head like a dog. The eyes nearly blended into the fur—black pupils, dark brown irises, a little bit of white at the edges. This was the same wolf I'd seen that first night with Mandenauer.

"William Cadotte," I said.

The animal's lip curled and a low, vicious rumble came from his chest. The hair on the back of my neck tingled.

"That went well."

Either the wolf wasn't Cadotte or the name thing didn't work. I'd have to tell Elise. If I lived.

I'd gone this far. I took a deep breath. "I love you, Will."

The wolf stopped snarling and tilted his head in the other direction. Sadly, he remained a wolf.

Either the animal wasn't Cadotte or my love wasn't true. I was back to square one.

Now what?

We could stand here staring at each other all night. I could shoot him, just for fun. I could let him bite or kill me. None of those options was very appealing.

My radio crackled and the wolf jumped straight up in the air. "Nervous?" I asked.

He lifted his lip in a silent snarl, or maybe a sneer, then sat down again.

"Three Adam One, where the hell are you?"

The way Zee was behaving lately, you'd think I was MIA every minute of my shift.

I reached for my radio with my left hand. It was times

like these when I wished Miniwa had the tax base to afford shoulder mikes.

"I'm outside the clinic. I've got a little situation here."

"What kind of situation?"

"Big black nasty wolf doesn't want to let me leave."

Silence met my declaration. The doors swished open behind me and voices swept out ahead of the young couple.

"Stay back!" I shouted.

They did, and so did the wolf. But the woman shrieked—an ear-piercing sound that made me blink on a wince. In that split second, the wolf disappeared. I was left standing in the parking lot, gun drawn and trained on thin air.

I turned to the couple but kept my eyes peeled and my gun ready. "He's gone. You can stop screaming now."

As if I'd pressed a button, she shut off.

"Who's gone?" the man asked.

"The wolf."

"What wolf?"

"You didn't see him?" I glanced at the trees, saw nothing, and reluctantly holstered my weapon. "Then what was she yammering about?"

The woman's bottom lip puffed out. She sniffed and turned away.

"I think the gun might have upset her, ma'am."

"Oh. Uh, well, carry on."

They hadn't seen the wolf. How could they have missed him? I *knew* he had been there. I wasn't delusional. I watched them get in their car and drive away.

Crackle. Pop. Zee was back.

"I'm here."

"Did you get rid of the wolf?"

"He ran off."

"Good. Clyde wants to know if you ever found that missing evidence."

I crossed the parking lot, watching every corner, twitching at every shadow. After climbing into my car, I locked all the doors. The wolf might lack the opposable thumbs necessary to open the doors, and then again he might not.

"Let me talk to him."

"Have you looked at your watch? Right now he's probably glued to TBS. It's all Clint, all night."

"Must have missed that."

I sat in my car and thought awhile before I answered Zee's question in regard to the evidence. "Trust no one," Mandenauer had said. And though I hated to continue lying to my best friend and my colleagues, in this instance I'd just have to do it anyway.

"Jessie?" Zee prompted.

"No," I said as I rolled the totem between my fingers. "I never found anything."

She cursed, low and quite viciously, even for her.

"Sheesh, lighten up. It's not your ass."

"I know. I'm just sick of hearing him bitch. Get over it already."

I had to agree. I spent the rest of the night trolling the town, the highway, the woods. I even went back to Cadotte's, but he wasn't there. That made me more nervous than anything. Where in hell had he gone in the middle of the night?

When morning came, I returned to the clinic and drove Mandenauer home. He was still tired, but he'd be all right.

"Get some rest, Jessie." He collapsed onto the ancient stained couch in the cottage. "We win or we lose tonight."

"But how can they perform the ceremony without the totem? Haven't we already won?"

"I do not know. Perhaps they will find another totem."

"How?"

"If I knew, then I could prevent them from doing so. But how they got the first one is a mystery."

"Swell," I muttered.

"Since blue moons are few and far between, for the most part, I doubt whoever is behind this will let something so small as a missing item keep them from becoming."

I pulled the totem from beneath my shirt. "Maybe we should destroy this?"

He lifted a brow. "Maybe we should."

"Got a hammer?"

"In the kitchen."

I found the tool and came back. After placing the icon on the floor, I lifted the hammer and hit the thing as hard as I could. The blow reverberated up my arms. I peered at the stone.

There wasn't a mark on it.

"That's impossible," I muttered.

Mandenauer sighed. "More impossible than humans becoming wolves?"

He had me there. "What next?"

"Fire won't melt rocks—or at least any fire we can produce."

"I could throw it into the lake."

"You could. But I've seen mystical items float right back to the surface. What if the one who wants the totem the most finds it?"

"I could bury the thing."

"It could pop out of the ground like a zombie."

"Zombie? Are you serious?"

"You'd be amazed at the things I have seen." He

shook his head. "Perhaps Elise will discover some way to use the icon against them. Then we will need it, yes?"

I shrugged and dropped the stone back down the front of my shirt. Being unable to destroy the thing had creeped me out more than I wanted to admit.

What was the totem made of? Moon rock? Had it been forged in hellfire? I didn't want to know.

The icon shifted between my breasts and I shuddered, then slapped my hand over it. "Stop that," I muttered.

Mandenauer coughed. I blushed. I'd come a long way from believing in nothing I couldn't see, hear, or touch to talking to stones and telling wolves that I loved them.

"Do you need help getting into bed?" I asked.

"Not since I was two." He rose, swayed, then glared when I would have grabbed his elbow.

I lifted my hands in a gesture of surrender. "Fall on your face. See if I care."

"Ah, Jessie, you are so good to me."

I left him in bed with a high-powered rifle and a laser scope, which was the most action he got at his age.

Chapter 34

I slept with a pistol and a rifle. Probably the most action I'd be seeing for years at the rate I was going. This time tomorrow night, I could be minus one . . . what?

Boyfriend? Lover? Really cute guy who made me scream? Hell, I could be minus a limb, my sanity, or my life. Better get my priorities in order.

As soon as I walked into the apartment, I glanced at my machine. The message light was blinking.

"Dammit, Jessie. Where are you?"

Cadotte sounded seriously pissed. Had he realized I'd read his notes, seen his book, knew he'd lied? Or was he just mad he hadn't gotten a little early-evening delight?

I set traps in front of the picture window, the door, hell, every window. I didn't plan on being surprised by any furry friends, or enemies. I had to sleep today, or I'd be no good at all tonight. Nevertheless, I awoke in the heat of midday and knew I wasn't alone.

I'm not sure what woke me. The mousetraps by the windows? The bells on the front door? The marbles in front of the balcony entrance?

None of the above or all three? I heard nothing now. But I felt someone. I crept out of bed, taking along both guns for company.

Barefoot and in my underwear, I checked every room, every closet. Not a single trap, bell, or marble was out of place. I was losing my mind.

When I glanced out the picture window, the bright light of midday hit my eyes and made my head ache. When I turned around, I saw stars. When the stars went away, I saw him.

I cocked my pistol. He crossed his arms over his chest and leaned against the wall in the hall. His earring swung merrily as he tilted his head. "Are we back to this again?"

"How did you get in here?"

"It wasn't easy."

"Get out."

He started to walk toward me. My heart sped up.

"I mean it, Cadotte!"

The gun shook. I lost the rifle so I could steady the pistol with both hands. He laughed. "Got silver bullets in there?"

"I've been packing silver since I met you, Slick."

He stopped a foot away, blinked, snorted. "Good girl. You may need it."

"Have you come to finish the job?"

"I thought I finished pretty well." He wiggled his brows.

Cadotte was behaving oddly for a man who'd tried to murder me a few hours back. He didn't have any weapons that I could see. Of course he could strangle me with his bare hands, if I let him get close enough.

"You know damn well I meant finish me off. Kill me. Murder me. Dump my body somewhere it'll never be found."

His mouth fell open. "What?"

"Someone shot a crossbow at me."

His gaze drifted over my body. "You seem all right."

"I'm fine. Mandenauer isn't."

His eyes snapped back to my face. "Dead?"

"Is that what you'd like?"

"I don't even know the man. Why would you think I'd try to kill you with a crossbow? I could have done pretty much anything I wanted to you at my place."

And had. My cheeks warmed.

"You've got a crossbow."

"Me and about a hundred other guys."

"What's it for?"

"My grandfather. It's a gift." He threw up his hands. "If I'm a werewolf, I don't need a damn crossbow to kill you. Why would I be that stupid?"

He had a point.

Cadotte took one huge step and grabbed the barrel of the gun. God, he was fast. I held on tight, figuring he'd wrench the thing out of my grip. Instead, he put the business end to his chest.

"Shoot me. See what happens."

"Have you lost your mind?"

"Yes. I love you, Jessie. I'd rather die than have you look at me as if you think I'm going to hurt you."

As declarations go, it was pretty impressive. I never thought a man would tell me he loved me. Especially one like this.

Of course my skeptical mind whispered: *Is he telling you he loves you because you told him? When he was a big black hairy wolf?*

Did it matter? My chest ached. My eyes burned. No one had ever said they loved me before, not even my mother. Suddenly I understood why people did anything for love.

I eased my finger from the trigger. I'd rather die than be the one to kill him. Even if he was a werewolf . . . I couldn't do it.

The pistol was too heavy to hold any longer. I let it fall back to my side, then placed the weapon on the couch. Cadotte pulled me into his arms, buried his face in my hair. "I missed you."

He smelled like the wind and the night, the forest. When I was in his arms, everything I believed became jumbled and confused. I could only think of touching him skin to skin, of feeling him move inside me, of letting him make me forget who he was or what he might be.

I pulled his T-shirt from his jeans, slipped my fingers beneath, spread my palms across his back, his shoulders. He had the most beautiful skin, smooth planes, hard muscles. I could touch him forever and never grow tired of the game.

He stepped back and drew the shirt over his head. I became fascinated with the ripples across his stomach and chest. I wanted to taste his skin while his muscles danced against my lips.

I dropped to my knees and did what I'd only dreamed of, placing openmouthed kisses across his hard, supple belly, sucking his flesh between my teeth, laving my tongue over the curve of his navel. He groaned and forked his fingers into my hair, pulling me closer, showing me he liked my fantasy as much as I did.

His erection pressed against my chest. The rasp of his jeans across my nipples, covered only by an old, thin T-shirt, was as arousing as his hands or his mouth.

Suddenly he slid to the floor and crushed his face to my breasts, filling his hands with me. It was my turn to thread my fingers through his hair and press him ever closer.

His earring dragged across one tight nipple as his mouth closed on the other. For a minute I wished he had long hair and that he would swish the tresses all over my body.

The thought was soon gone when he ripped my T-shirt down the center. My breasts spilled free, and he moaned as if he'd been given a gift.

"Hey!" I protested.

"I'll buy you another. I'll buy you a hundred. With lace. Red, blue, purple."

The words were muffled against my skin. The puff of his breath against me made my hands clench on his shoulders. I wanted to say something sarcastic about me in purple lace, but I couldn't quite manage it.

"That shirt was old anyway."

"And ugly. You should wear silk, Jessie. As soft as your skin right here." He placed a gentle, sweet kiss at the curve of my hip and I shivered, then smoothed my palms over his biceps.

No man had ever spoken this way to me. Hell, in my experience men didn't do much chatting during sex. Mostly, "oh, yeah," or, "right there." Cadotte seemed to like to talk nearly as much as he liked—

His hand slipped into my panties and stroked me. "Oh, yeah," I muttered. "Right there."

"How about right here, right now?"

My answer was to slip the button from his jeans and slide the zipper down. My hand followed. Heated, hard skin met my palm.

"Do you even own underwear?"

"What for?"

He lost his shoes and his jeans, fumbling a bit in the pocket for a condom. I thanked my lucky stars he'd remembered, because I continued to forget a lot of things. And the whole puppy issue just wasn't funny anymore.

He covered himself and tossed the empty package to the floor. My underwear soon followed. He thrust into me just as he had in the pond; one smooth stroke and he was all the way home.

I expected him to be wild, rough, fast. I wouldn't have minded. I wanted to forget that this could be the last time we were together. I imagined the blue moon hovering just below the horizon, waiting to pounce. Neither one of us knew what would happen tomorrow—if there'd even be a tomorrow.

I'd never done it on the floor. The men I'd known hadn't ever been so anxious to have me they couldn't wait awhile. I discovered the idea that he needed me, now, was as arousing as his mouth at my breast and his body within mine.

Instead of desperation and frantic need, a pounding, pulsing coupling, he gave me love. His kiss was sweet and gentle as he traced his lips across my cheekbone to the corner of my eye. His breath a breeze that ruffled my hair, I sighed and he drank me in.

The pace slowed. His hands almost reverent as they soothed and aroused, I wanted to crawl inside of him and stay there forever.

"You feel so good," he murmured against my neck.

I ran my hands down his back, rocked my hips, and took him as deep as I dared. He quivered, then stilled.

"Look at me, Jessie."

I couldn't focus on what he wanted until he kissed me, then took my lower lip between his teeth and tugged.

My eyes popped open. He was so close I could see where the black of his pupil and the dark brown of his iris met. For an instant I was staring into the eyes of the black wolf, and I stiffened.

"Hush." He kissed the corner of my mouth. "I love you, Jessie. I'd never hurt you."

He punctuated every other word with a slow slide and

firm thrust of his body into mine. All I could do was nod and clutch him tighter.

Taking my hands, he placed palm against palm, clenching our fingers together. I felt him growing inside of me, pulsing, coming.

"Come for me," he whispered. "I want to go there together."

My attention drifted lower, to where our bodies joined. My eyes fluttered closed. He stopped moving.

"Look at me," he demanded. "See *me*. Please."

I frowned and opened my eyes. His expression was so sad, I wanted to touch his face, but he wouldn't free my hands. I lifted my mouth inviting his, and he kissed me, long, deep, wet, while he remained buried inside.

"I see you, Will," I whispered against his mouth. "I've always seen you."

He lifted his head and together we reached what we'd been searching for. At the moment of climax his eyes went intense, fierce. He thrust into me faster, harder, and I clenched around him, the waves of pleasure so intense I could do nothing but ride them and call his name.

He didn't collapse on top of me in a heap of satisfied male flesh. Instead he rolled to the side, taking me with him, keeping us joined through some acrobatic maneuver that would have been even more impressive if I could think.

My hands free at last, I touched his cheek, his hair, and he nuzzled my palm. My heart did that nauseatingly slow flop toward my belly. Oh, boy, I had it bad.

"I love you," he repeated and before I could force the words back where they belonged—a secret in my heart until it was safe to set them free—they popped out of my foolish mouth.

"I love you, too."

Chapter 35

Will disentangled himself from me and jumped to his feet. Startled, I just lay on the floor, naked and alone. This wasn't going at all as I'd imagined it might once I loved a man and he loved me back.

Leaning down, Will scooped me into his arms and lifted. Then he strode toward the bedroom.

"Hey! What the hell?"

"I'm taking you to bed, Jessie. I want you again."

That was mighty obvious from the steady poke I was getting in my backside.

"What, are you a machine?" I asked.

He laughed. "I just want to enthrall you sexually while I have the chance."

"I think you have."

He carried me as if I weighed no more than a child, and I knew that wasn't true. I was not now nor have I ever been a small girl. I probably weighed as much as he did, or near enough.

That he could sling me around like a sack of potatoes should have annoyed me. Instead, I found myself enchanted by his great big muscles and aroused by his Neanderthal tactics. Yep, I definitely had it bad.

For a man who could be a werewolf.

I figured the sex would be better in the bed, but it wasn't. The sex was spectacular wherever we had it—in a bed, at the pond, on the floor.

His fingers lazily played with my hair, then drifted across my spine. I lay facedown, arm hanging limply off the bed, legs all tangled with his. When I turned my head, he was so close his nose brushed mine.

"Jessie?"

We were still nose to nose, breath mingling, hips touching.

"Will?"

He smiled. "You hardly ever call me that."

"Really?"

"I think you called me Cadotte until about an hour ago."

"It seems bad form to call a guy who's making you scream by his last name."

His smile faded; uncertainty flickered in his eyes.

"Hey, what's the matter?" I reached for him, but he was already moving away.

"You aren't with me for the sex, are you?"

I sat up. "Are you that insecure?"

"Yes."

My eyebrows shot up. He'd never seemed insecure to me. He was beautiful, built, brilliant. What did he have to be insecure about? I asked him.

"Do you know how many women have slept with me because of my face? Because I'm good in bed?"

"Do I want to know?"

His lips twitched, relieving some of the tension. "Probably not."

"Then let's leave them in the past where they belong. Don't we have enough to worry about right now?"

His gaze met mine. The uncertainty was gone, replaced by a wariness that made the hair on my forearms

prickle. We had a helluva lot more to worry about tonight than old lovers.

He nodded and opened his arms. "Come here."

"Again?"

"Got a problem with that?"

I pretended to think. "Not really."

I slid across the bed and kissed him. I didn't want to
stop; I didn't want to think. There'd be time enough for
that later. Maybe. Right now I only wanted to be with
him, to feel the things only Will could make me feel.

But as he moved inside of me, my treacherous mind
went *clickety-clack*. The blue moon threatened. Tonight
was the night when everything changed—or maybe
everyone.

What if Will was not only the love of my life but the
monster I'd been searching for? What if he'd killed people? What if he'd eaten them? What if he was a power-
hungry nutcase bent on ruling the world? What if . . . ?

My body betrayed me, shutting down my mind, making me come apart in his arms. Love was wearing me
out—and the sex wasn't bad, either. I could no longer
keep my eyes open.

As I fell asleep with his cheek nuzzling my hair, the
answer to my questions came to me with brilliant clarity.
Whatever he was, I loved him. If he was cursed, I'd try
to cure him. There must be a way. I only had to find it.

I awoke to the twilight and an empty bed. I wasn't
worried; not at first. I actually believed he loved me.

But as I wandered through my empty apartment and
realized Will was gone and the moon was rising, uncertainty set in. I reached for the totem I'd been wearing
around my neck for weeks, but it wasn't there.

My heart gave one painful, panicked thud before I
remembered I'd taken it off as I always did when I went
to bed. If I'd actually been wearing the thing, it would

have strangled me during our energetic bedroom activities. Not to mention I'd have had to explain to Will that I'd had the thing all along.

I went back into my room, crossed to the dresser, reached for the totem. My fingers came up empty.

I dropped to my knees, crawled around the floor patting the carpet. Tore the room apart in a frenzy. But nothing changed what I knew in my gut.

Will was gone, and so was the stone.

Chapter 36

I would have liked a shower, but I didn't have the luxury. Instead, I threw on my uniform, retrieved my weapons, and was on my way out the door when the doorbell rang. Expecting Mandenauer, I could only stare stupidly at Clyde.

"Where you goin' in such a hurry?"

"Um. Uh."

I should tell Clyde everything, but I was in a bit of a rush. Besides, he hated Will already. He'd be thrilled to shoot him with silver and say "whoops" later.

"Mandenauer," I blurted. "I said I'd come over early."

"I was just there, and I woke him up. Definitely a 'don't go away mad; just go away' moment. *Heartbreak Ridge* was on last night. Not exactly Clint's words, but near 'nough. Mandenauer was going back to sleep. Since you've got hours yet before your shift, why don't we have a little chat?"

I glanced through my living room toward the window. I might have hours before my shift, but sundown was soon.

It was then I saw my panties lying on the carpet in the middle of the room.

Clyde sniffed, once, twice, and I turned to find him so close I leaped back.

"What the hell?" I demanded, embarrassed, nervous, betrayed, and cranky.

"I can smell him on you."

I didn't know what to say to that. Luckily I didn't have to say anything, since Clyde kept talking.

"Jesus, Jessie, I'd have thought you of all people would be able to resist a pretty face. Have you no pride?"

Apparently not.

"Clyde, I've got to go."

"Where?"

"None of your business."

"When you're wearing that uniform, everything you do is my business."

I had a flash of what I'd been doing a few times in this uniform. Definitely *not* Clyde's business. But I wasn't going to tell him that. My cheeks heated in spite of myself.

"I need to see Mandenauer," I repeated. "I'll just have to wake him up."

"Where's Cadotte?"

"Not here."

I stepped into the hallway and Clyde had no choice but to move back; then I closed the door firmly behind me.

"I want to talk to him."

"Join the club." I started down the hall.

"He sneak out on you?"

I turned. "Why are you so damned interested in Cadotte all of a sudden?"

"I want to talk to him about the attempted murder of Edward Mandenauer."

"Have you lost your mind?"

"Have you?"

"What possible reason could Will have to shoot Mandenauer? He barely knows the man."

"Mandenauer and I had quite a chat when I stopped into the clinic earlier. I hear he was shot with a crossbow."

"And?"

"Cadotte has a crossbow."

"So does every old man between here and Minoqua. That doesn't make him guilty." I turned and headed down the hall. "He's got no motive."

Trust Clyde to fuck that up.

"Wouldn't a werewolf want to kill the wolf hunter?"

I froze. "A what?"

"Come off it, Jessie. Mandenauer told me everything."

Slowly I faced him. "And you believed him?"

He shrugged. "I was raised Ojibwe. Just because I've had to play that down to get where I am doesn't mean I don't believe in the legends. I've seen things . . ." He shook his head. "Let's just say werewolves are the least of them."

I couldn't quite get my mind around the fact that my boss believed in the unbelievable. Had everyone gone over to the dark side?

I set my rifle against the wall. The weapon was getting too heavy to cart up and down the hallway. "So you know about the blue moon? The werewolf army? The wolf god?"

"Everything." He held out his hand. "Why don't you give me that totem for safekeeping?"

I stared at his palm, then lifted my gaze to his face. "I don't have it."

Anger flickered in his eyes. "Jessie, you're playing with something you don't understand."

It was on the tip of my tongue to tell him that Will

had taken the stone, but he grabbed me by the upper arms and shook me. My teeth rattled, and I decided to keep the information to myself. I didn't care for the way he was acting.

"I don't have the totem, Clyde. I swear."

"Only one way to find out."

He spun me around and patted me down. I was tempted to fight back, but Clyde was a lot bigger than I was. Besides, he wasn't going to find anything, thanks to Cadotte.

My boss released me with a little shove and a mutter of annoyance. I stepped out of his reach and nearer to my rifle. My fingers rested on the butt of my pistol.

Clyde ran a hand over his face and sighed. "He's been keeping an eye on you. Discovering what you know. Putting you off balance. If he's got you in his bed, then you aren't out doing your job, are you?"

"I've been doing my job," I snapped.

"You've been doing him." Clyde bit off a stub of chew and chomped ferociously for a few seconds. "I like you, Jessie, and I don't want to hurt your feelings."

"Why stop now?" I muttered.

Clyde ignored me. "I've seen the women Cadotte fucks. You don't fit in."

What else was new? I never had. But I'd started to think that I might, with him.

"Cadotte's up to something," Clyde continued. "I just can't figure out what."

I wanted to say Cadotte loved me. He thought I was beautiful. Funny, sexy, special. Everything I'd ever wanted to be, I was to him. But I wasn't so sure anymore.

He *had* taken the totem. To protect me? Or to ruin me? Until I knew, I was keeping my mouth shut.

"Did he tell you anything about the ceremony?"

"No."

He hadn't *told* me. I'd read it in a book.

I frowned. But not all of the ceremony. There'd been a page missing. Which was more troublesome now than ever before.

"What do you know?" I asked.

"Blue moon. Werewolf army. Matchi-auwishuk totem."

Clyde knew about as much as I did.

"Blood of the one who loves you."

I blinked. "The what of the who?"

"Blood of the one who loves you," he repeated slowly. "It's needed for the ceremony."

I turned and headed for the door.

"Jessie? Where you going?"

I didn't answer. I couldn't very well tell the sheriff that I was going to kill someone.

Chapter 37

I tossed my rifle into the Crown Victoria and climbed in after. Clyde raced out of my apartment building just as I left the parking lot. He tried to flag me down, shouted something, but I was on a mission. I didn't need any company while I kicked Cadotte's ass.

Could I kill him? I wasn't sure. But I could beat him bloody. He'd made me believe in love right along with the werewolves.

I'd wondered why love had come along so soon. I'd wondered why me? The answer was crystal clear. He'd needed someone to love him fast, and what better patsy than a woman who'd never been loved before? I must have been so easy.

My hands ached from clenching them on the steering wheel. I welcomed the pain. It made me forget the one in my chest, the bubbling agony in my belly, the burn of tears in my eyes and my throat.

I'd been such an idiot.

I reached the turnoff to his place and left my car next to his. The sun was almost down; the moon was not yet up. Usually all this woo-woo shit took place at midnight anyway. If so, I had plenty of time.

I paused at the edge of the clearing. Lights yellowed

the windowpanes of his cabin. Either he was home or he liked to waste electricity.

I braced myself to cross the yard and walk inside. I didn't plan on knocking. I wasn't a complete moron. Or maybe I was. I took one step and someone grabbed me from behind.

My rifle flew into the underbrush. Strong arms pinned mine to my side. I struggled, kicked backward, tried to flip my assailant over my shoulder. Nothing worked.

I took a deep breath, and I smelled him. "Will?"

He nuzzled my shoulder; then his mouth latched on to my neck and his teeth grazed my skin. I shuddered. "Let me go."

He lifted his head; his breath brushed my hair. My body went limp with wanting him. I was pathetic.

And suddenly I was free. My hand went to my gun, but it was gone.

I spun around. Cadotte had my pistol. He'd also managed to retrieve my rifle. He looked a little silly holding two guns while stark naked.

Well, he wasn't completely naked. He wore the totem around his neck. I guess he wasn't going to deny stealing it.

"You need to go home, Jessie."

"Ha. I don't think so."

"Please. I don't want you hurt."

"Too late."

He frowned. "What are you talking about?"

"I know about the ceremony. I know what you need to become the wolf god."

"Me? I'm not going to become the wolf god."

"Then what's that for?" I pointed to the totem.

"I'm trying to stop it."

"How?"

"I discovered a ritual." His hands clenched on the

weapons. His gaze shifted behind me. His agitation was evident. "It's too complicated to explain right now. I need to finish before the blue moon rises."

"How do I know you aren't raising the wolf god?"

He sighed. "You don't. You're going to have to trust me."

"I don't think that I can."

Hurt flickered over his face and for a minute I felt bad. Then my gaze lowered to the totem, and I remembered one of Zee's favorite sayings that didn't involve a curse word.

Fool me once, shame on you. Fool me twice, shame on me.

"Shame on me," I muttered.

He shook his head. "Sarcastic to the end. That's my girl."

"I am *not* your girl."

His lips tightened; his eyes narrowed. I'd managed to annoy him, and that wasn't easy.

"I don't have time to argue. Are you going to behave, or do I have to tie and gag you?"

There was no way I was going to let him tie and gag me, not even for fun. "I'll behave."

He grunted and took a wide berth around me, then headed for a cairn of rocks at the far side of the clearing. Since he had my guns, there wasn't a whole helluva lot I could do about it—yet.

Besides, according to Clyde he needed my blood to do the deed. When he came to get it, I'd be ready.

I sat on the porch steps. Cadotte lit a fire in the center of the rocks. Sprinkled what appeared to be dirt on top, except the flame turned green, then purple, then blood-red. No dirt I'd ever seen could do that.

I couldn't take my eyes from the fire, from him. The colors of the flames played over his skin. His muscles flexed and released—across his stomach, down his thighs, up his arms. He was so beautiful he made me yearn.

He began to chant in Ojibwe. The words ebbed and flowed, a beautiful song in a language I could not understand. As the fire burned higher, hotter, he danced around the stone circle.

The oddity of a naked man dancing in the forest snapped me out of my trance. I began to get nervous. I glanced at the eastern horizon, but the sky was still pink. Not a sliver of silver to be found.

A sound in the brush to my right caught my attention. When I followed the rustle, I saw the wolf. "Will!"

He froze, followed my gaze, cursed. More wolves appeared, sliding from the underbrush all around us. At least fifty of them ringed the clearing.

Suddenly Will was at my side, shoving me toward the door. Good idea, since the wolves had begun to advance. Legs stiff, hackles raised, they snarled.

"What do they want?"

"What do you think?" He tapped the totem, which still hung around his neck.

We stumbled over each other and into the cabin. He slammed the door just as a heavy body thumped against it. My eyes went to the glass window just as Will slammed a wood shutter into place and flipped the lock.

"Help me!" he shouted, running from window to window.

He didn't have to tell me twice. What little light was left in the sky was blotted out as we boarded up all the glass.

I'd puzzled over the dual shutters. Now I thanked God for them. If Cadotte's cabin had only been equipped with outdoor storm protection we'd be dead or foaming at the mouth.

The windows shattered as the wolves tried to get in. The shutters shimmied, but they held.

"Hell," Cadotte muttered.

I glanced at him and found myself distracted again by all that smooth, perfect skin and those supple muscles. I turned my back. "Can you put on some clothes?"

"What? Oh, yeah."

He went into his room and returned, pulling a bright yellow T-shirt over his head. The top button of his jeans hung open, and I swallowed the urge to put my mouth against the strip of skin.

This wasn't the time. There might never be a time again. That upset me more than it should. Cadotte had used me, lied to me, and I wanted him still. I loved him.

The shutter behind my head rattled. I flinched. "Can I have my gun back?"

"Are you going to shoot me?"

"Are you going to bite me?"

He wiggled his brows. "Maybe later."

I made an impatient sound and he sighed. "I thought you loved me."

"That's what you wanted all along, wasn't it?"

He appeared confused. "Of course I want you to love me."

"Because you need the blood of the one who loves you to become the wolf god."

"I do?"

"Don't tell me you didn't know that!" I shouted. "Don't lie to me anymore, Will!"

"You think I've been lying to you? That I told you I loved you . . . why?"

"You *made* me love you."

His lips narrowed. "No one has that power. Either you love me or you don't. I can't make you feel anything. No matter how much I might want you to."

The eternal sadness that had drawn me to him so many times before was back, but I wasn't going to let him seduce me again.

I stalked into the kitchen, shuffled through the minutiae on the counter. Found the bag of plastic and held it up.

Confusion pushed away the sadness in his eyes. "Where did that come from?"

"Don't play stupid with me. You stole this from the evidence room."

"Me? If I went anywhere near the police station your boss would have a stroke. Someone planted that."

"Spare me the O.J. delusion." I moved into the living room and picked up the book on Ojibwe ceremonies. "What about this?"

"What about it? I've had that book for years. It's useless without the page that's missing, which is why I ordered another one." He frowned. "But it hasn't arrived. That's what I get for ordering a used copy off the Internet."

"Isn't it convenient that the one page we need is missing?"

"It's weird, that's for sure. I picked that book up in a secondhand store, never even looked through it until last week when I found a page missing." He shook his head. "You actually think I was trying to raise the wolf god?"

"I don't know what to think."

"Those wolves attacked us both. Why would they go after me if I made them? If I were a werewolf, wouldn't I have changed? Like them?"

I spread my hands and shook my head. I wasn't sure of anything anymore.

He crossed the room and I tensed. I didn't want him to touch me. I wasn't sure what I'd do. Slug him or hold him—neither one appealed at the moment.

Cadotte handed me my pistol, shrugged when I lifted my gaze to his. "If you want to shoot me, Jessie, go ahead. I'm tired of trying to make you believe that what we have is special."

I opened my mouth to say . . . I'm not sure what, and my cell phone rang. It was Mandenauer.

"I am waiting for you, Jessie."

"You'll be waiting quite a while. I'm a little . . . trapped."

"Where?"

"Cadotte's place."

"I will be right there."

"Bring a lot of ammo. There are at least fifty of them out there. And . . ."

"Yes?"

"Be careful."

"Fifty is nothing to me, *Liebchen.*"

Then he was gone.

Cadotte had moved to the other side of the room with my rifle. His back to me, the set of his shoulders was dejected. "I didn't finish the ritual," he said.

"I know."

"We can't let them get the totem."

"I know that, too."

Silence descended, broken only by the intermittent thud of wolf bodies against the door and the windows. I wanted to ask him so many things, but he was right. I didn't trust him.

Gunshots sounded outside. Our eyes met. "It's too soon to be Mandenauer," I said.

Cadotte flipped the lock on the window in front of him and peeked out. "It's the sheriff."

He must have followed me here. Damn.

I crossed the room and glanced outside. It was Clyde

all right. He shot a few wolves. They whimpered, but they didn't die.

"Lead bullets," I murmured. Clyde must not have had time to find any silver.

He shot his way through the circle, then backed toward the cabin. The wolves advanced again.

I locked the shutter and hurried to let him in, taking my pistol along. I remembered how Clyde had tried to convince me that Will was the werewolf leader—and I wasn't exactly unconvinced of that yet—but I wasn't going to let my boss kill him. I couldn't.

So as soon as I opened the door I asked for Clyde's gun. He froze, frowned, stared at the pistol trained on his chest. "You nuts?"

"Hand it over, Clyde, or stay outside with them."

"Fine." He slapped the weapon into my palm and stomped into the house.

"What are you doing here?" I demanded.

"What do you think?" His attention was captured by something behind me. "You've brainwashed her, you bastard."

Before I could stop him, Clyde charged Cadotte. They went down in a heap. Clyde was bigger, heavier, but Cadotte was younger and stronger. They rolled across the floor, banged into the furniture. Papers and books flew every which way.

Clyde yanked Cadotte's earring from his ear and tossed it across the room. The golden feather skittered into a heating vent. Damn, I'd really liked that earring.

Blood flowed down Cadotte's neck, a graphic illustration of the dangers of pierced ears—one reason I didn't have them.

I took a step forward just as Cadotte hooked his leg around Clyde's and flipped the larger man onto his back.

I blinked, and he had his knee on Clyde's chest, his forearm at his throat.

"*Aanizhiitam?*" he growled.

"Fuck you."

Cadotte pressed harder, and Clyde turned purple.

"*Aanizhiitam?*" Cadotte repeated.

Clyde gave a sharp nod and Cadotte jumped up. He held out a hand, but Clyde smacked it away and clambered to his feet on his own.

Blood spattered across Cadotte's shirt and Clyde's. There were drops all over the floor. I resisted the urge to get a towel. This wasn't my house.

"What is your problem?" Cadotte asked.

"This." Clyde reached out and yanked the totem from Will's neck.

Will grabbed him by the shirt with both hands and lifted him off his feet. "Give it back."

My mouth fell open. My boss had to weigh 300 pounds.

"Jessie!" Clyde called. "Don't you think I should hang on to the totem?"

I looked back and forth between the two of them. I honestly didn't know.

Another volley of shots sounded from outside. This time they were followed by surprised yips and agonized howls.

"Let him go, Will," I ordered.

"No."

Mandenauer pounded on the front door and shouted my name. I didn't have time for these games. I cocked the gun. Will's gaze flicked to mine. He shrugged and let Clyde go.

"Play nice," I admonished, and let the old man inside.

He was wearing his Rambo outfit again—commando chic, with a whole lot of bullets. I couldn't conjure up a snappy retort. I was too damn glad to see him—and his ammo, too.

Before I could grab a bandolier for myself, Mandenauer stalked past me and into the living room. The expression on his face made me hurry to keep up.

"Which one of you is wolf clan?" he demanded.

"Why?" I asked.

"A member of the wolf clan must take part in the ceremony."

I flicked a glance at Will. "Did you know this?"

"Sure."

I let my breath out on a long, slow sigh of disappointment.

"Before you get all bent out of shape, I'd like to point out something."

"What?"

"He's wolf clan, too."

My head jerked up. Will was pointing at Clyde.

"You are?"

"So what? Nobody holds with that stuff anymore. Except for him." He jerked his head at Will. "Most people don't even know what clan they are these days. Don't you find it interesting that he does?"

Mandenauer drew his revolver and pointed it at Will.

"Hey!" I grabbed his arm just as he fired.

Training took over and I cracked his wrist over my knee. The gun fell to the floor. I kicked the rifle out of his other hand, then pulled his arms behind his back. He didn't fight me. Instead he stared at Will.

Terrified, I followed the direction of his gaze. There was a neat hole in the fleshy part of Will's arm. He was a mess, but he was alive, which also made him human. I could breathe again.

I tightened my grip on Mandenauer. "What the hell are you doing?"

"Proving that he is not one of them. And quite nicely, don't you think?"

"No," Will snapped.

He pressed a hand to the hole, but blood seeped through his fingers. Black dots danced in front of my eyes. Since when had the sight of blood bothered me? Since it was his.

Mandenauer had just proved Will wasn't a werewolf. The knowledge wasn't as comforting as it should have been. We still didn't know who was.

Mandenauer tugged on his hands, which I still held behind his back. "Give me back my guns."

"I don't think so."

"Then shoot the other so we know."

I glanced at Clyde. He frowned and shook his head.

"Isn't there a less bloody way to go about this?"

"I have never found one."

I was at a loss. I wanted to bandage Will's arm, but I couldn't leave Mandenauer alone. I couldn't hold on to all the guns myself. I couldn't bring myself to shoot Clyde and be done with it.

A chorus of howls rose in the yard. Others joined in, louder and louder, until I wanted to put my hands over my ears to blot out the sound. But I couldn't do that, either.

At last the noise stopped. The resulting silence seemed to echo with their cries.

"How many are out there?" I whispered.

"There were more than seventy when I arrived," Mandenauer answered. "Probably well past a hundred by now."

"That can't be right."

"What part of 'werewolf *army*' did you not understand, Jessie?"

I dumped Mandenauer's guns on the couch, holstered

my pistol, and took him with me to the front window. I unlatched the shutter. We stared at what appeared to be a sea of wolves in the yard.

"What are they here for?"

"This."

The voice wasn't Mandenauer's; it was Clyde's. I glanced toward him just as he opened the front door.

"No!" I shouted, but the wolves didn't charge. Instead, they sat like dogs, tongues lolling.

I released Mandenauer and ran, but I was too late. Clyde tossed the wolf totem high above the crowd. All heads tilted up, then followed the stone back down.

Before it met the ground a small ash-blond wolf leaped into the air and caught the rawhide between her teeth. She hit the ground running. The others followed.

I could do nothing but stare at Clyde. His face bathed by the silver light of the rising moon, he began to sweat, to shake.

To change.

Chapter 38

I should have slammed the door, but I couldn't. I was rooted to the floor in the hallway, unable to drag my eyes from the sight in front of me.

Clyde's body contorted; his shoulders hunched; his legs bowed. He threw back his head and howled. The sound shot ice down my spine. The wolves in the forest paused in their flight and answered.

His clothes split open with a shriek of rending cloth and bursting seams. His shoes seemed to explode and paws popped out. He dropped to all fours and the hands that caught him had claws.

Black hair sprouted from every pore, thickening, lengthening, becoming fur. A tail erupted from his spine. The last thing to change was his head.

I sensed movement behind me, but I couldn't tear my gaze away. I braced myself, expecting Mandenauer to shoot. But he didn't. Odd, he'd never hesitated before.

The popping of bones, the stretching of skin, caused a horrible sound. I winced as Clyde finished the change.

His nose and his mouth stretched, melding into a snout. His teeth grew; his tongue must have, too, since it lolled out the side of his mouth. His brow bulged. When he swung his head in our direction his face was that of a skinned wolf with Clyde's eyes.

Nasty. I wished for the fur to arrive. My wish was soon granted.

Black hair flowed over his face, obscuring the bones that marred his cinnamon skin. He shook himself as if he'd just come out of the water, then turned toward me.

I gasped. Clyde was the black wolf that had dogged my steps and haunted my dreams. He was most likely the wolf that had bitten Karen Larson and countless others.

The gunshot made me scream and fall to the floor, throwing my hands up in front of my face. My ears rang, but I still heard Clyde shriek. I didn't want to look, but I had to.

Flames burst from a neat hole near his heart. The scent of scorched hair and cooking meat filled the air. The howl of a wolf, the cry of a man—he writhed in pain, twisting, turning, his claws scrabbling against the planks of the porch as he died.

I stayed on the ground. I couldn't gain my feet. Mandenauer stepped around me and shoved at Clyde with his boot. The wolf's head lolled sickeningly.

I leaned my back against the cabin wall. I was weak, limp. I couldn't stop staring at what had once been my boss. I'd liked Clyde, trusted him as much as I trusted anyone—except maybe Zee. I couldn't get my mind around the idea that he'd forever be a wolf. That Clyde would never again spit chew or quote Clint.

"Why did you let him finish the change before you shot him?"

"It is easier to explain a dead wolf than a dead sheriff." His gaze swept the forest. "We must go."

"Go? Where? We got him."

"The sheriff was nothing more than a minion of evil. The one who will become remains."

"How you figure?"

Mandenauer flicked me a contemptuous glance. "If he was the one, why did he give the totem to the others?"

I hadn't thought of that. Damn.

"Listen," Mandenauer whispered.

In the distance the wolves called to one another. There were more of them now. The ones who had been here had joined those who waited there. With their leader.

I glanced at the sky. The blue moon had not yet reached the apex. Our night had only begun.

I struggled to my knees, gained my feet without help. I looked for Will and didn't find him.

Had he passed out from blood loss? I took a step toward the door and Mandenauer stopped me. "Your lover is putting a bandage on his scratch. He does not need your aid."

"You call that a scratch?"

"You do not?"

"I say a hole through the arm is a wound and not a scratch."

"I say if you can walk, then walk."

I tore my gaze from the cabin. "You trying to tell me something?"

"Follow those wolves."

"I just knew you were gonna say that."

I stalked inside, retrieved my rifle, went searching for Will. To hell with Mandenauer; I wasn't going to leave until I saw with my own eyes that Will was all right.

I followed the blood trail to the bathroom. Will struggled to fasten gauze around his arm with one hand. He glanced up and his eyes met mine in the mirror. He didn't appear happy to see me.

"Let me." I stepped into the room, leaning my rifle against the wall.

"It's done." He grabbed one end of the gauze with

his teeth, the other with his free hand, and jerked. His breath hissed in sharply when the material tightened on the wound.

"Maybe you should go to the clinic and get stitches."

"I don't need stitches. It's just a scratch."

My lips twitched. "Scratch. Right. What about your ear?"

He shrugged one shoulder. The blood that had bathed his neck cracked, and rust-colored flecks rained down on his already ruined clothes. "I'll live."

"Jessie!" Mandenauer shouted. "Today if you please?"

I stepped closer and smoothed his hair away from his brow. "I have to go."

He shifted abruptly, his body bumping against mine in ways that would have been interesting if he weren't covered in blood and I didn't have places to be, werewolves to kill.

"Let me change my shirt."

"You aren't coming."

"Yes." His eyes met mine. "I am."

"Now that Clyde's dead they need a wolf clan member. Bringing you along would be downright stupid."

"I can take care of myself."

"So can I. Stay here. Clean up. Rest. I'll come back when it's over."

"You think I can just sit here while you face a werewolf army? Wait like a good little boy until you have time to come to me again? I love you, Jessie. If you die, so do I."

The thought of him dying made my palms clammy and my voice sharp. "I'm not going to die and neither are you. Just let me do my job, Will."

"Let me help."

"I don't need your help."

"Of course not. You don't need anyone." His voice rose and anger warred with the pain in his eyes. "You certainly don't need me. You never did."

"Jessie." Mandenauer stood in the hall. Urgency tightened his features.

I glanced at Will. I wanted to stay, but I had to go. I wanted to kiss him, but he turned away and started the shower.

"I'll be back," I promised.

He didn't answer, and that bothered me more than his anger and pain had. Torn between my job, my duty, and my love, I hesitated.

In the end, I had no choice. I followed Mandenauer and he followed the wolves.

Chapter 39

"What's the plan?" I asked.

The trail widened. I was able to quicken my pace and walk shoulder to shoulder with Mandenauer.

He gave me a quick glance and a rare smile. "You are not moping about leaving your lover behind?"

I frowned, confused. "Should I be?"

"Most women would. I like you, Jessie. You are an able officer."

"Gee, thanks. I'm so glad you approve."

I hadn't felt like an able officer lately. I'd broken a shitload of rules, withheld information, stolen evidence, and protected a suspect. I'd most likely be thrown off the force, if I didn't die first.

Mandenauer, who either didn't get my sarcasm or was learning to ignore it, continued. "The plan is to follow the wolves to the ceremony and put a bullet in every single one."

"I can do that."

"However, if the wolf god rises, we may have a problem."

I gave him a quick glance. "What kind of problem?"

"I do not think the wolf god can be killed with silver."

"Why the hell not?"

I must have sounded slightly hysterical, because he reached over and patted me on the shoulder with a heavy, awkward hand. "Otherwise it would be no more than a werewolf, yes?"

I saw his point. I didn't like it, but I saw it.

"Then how do we kill a wolf god?"

"I have no idea."

"Great. Swell. Wonderful."

"My sentiments exactly."

We had no trouble following the wolves. The trail was damp. It must have rained while I'd been sleeping— and doing other things. Unnaturally large paw prints padded to the west like a neon arrow.

"They aren't trying to hide where they're going," I said.

"No."

"That can't be good."

"I agree. But what choice do we have?"

None.

"I don't suppose you have any idea who's behind this?"

Mandenauer adjusted his bandolier, which kept slipping to the edge of his bony shoulder. "Do you?"

"Question with a question," I muttered.

Was he *trying* to annoy me?

"I thought I did."

"You believed your lover was the one."

I shrugged. Hard to admit you'd been sleeping with the enemy. Easier to just do it—or do him, as Clyde had so kindly pointed out—than talk about it.

My eyes burned at the thought of Clyde. I'd miss him. Werewolf or not, he'd been good to me. He'd been a decent boss, a likable guy. What had happened?

I thought back on all that had occurred in the last week. Clyde had made me suspicious of Will. He'd given me false information. He'd out-and-out lied.

That left a bad taste in my mouth. We were the good guys—or at least we were supposed to be. But who was I to throw stones after all I'd done?

"You are thinking about your friend the sheriff?"

I nodded.

"And how he could have done what he did?"

"Yeah."

"He had little choice in the matter. Once you are bitten, you do what you are told."

I didn't like the sound of that. I'd never been very good at doing what I was told.

I stopped and he glanced at me with a raised brow. "Problem?"

I'll say.

"If everything goes to hell . . . I mean if we—"

"Are unable to stop them and are bitten?"

I couldn't speak, so I nodded.

"We have a saying in the *Jäger-Sucher* society: Always save the last bullet for yourself."

The stark words made me wince, but I could see their practicality, and I'd always been a practical gal.

"Didn't I hear that in an old Western once?"

"I never said it was an original saying." Mandenauer winked and kept walking.

"There's one thing that bothers me."

"Only one?"

"Actually there are about a hundred, but for now—" He waved a thin, heavily veined hand. "Ask."

"Why did you tell Clyde who you were?"

"I didn't tell him anything."

I stopped again, but this time Mandenauer kept walking. I hurried to catch up. "He told me that he knew what you were. That you'd told him everything."

"He told you a lot of things, Jessie."

True. What was one more lie on top of all the others? I'd never been a trusting soul. I had a feeling I'd be even less so now.

Another thought occurred to me. "The crossbow."

"I'd rather not think about that any longer, thank you."

"Just a sec." My mind churned, trying to put all the pieces in place. It wasn't easy. "He told me that Will had one. But how would he have known that unless he was in Will's house?"

Mandenauer shrugged.

"Will said someone had planted the evidence." I rubbed my forehead. "I'm such an idiot."

"Clyde manipulated you. He had his reasons."

"Do you think he shot you?"

"Does it matter now?"

In the scheme of things . . . ? "I guess not."

We continued to walk, and then we walked some more. Where in hell were these wolves headed? Canada?

I was in good shape, but a timber wolf could run me into the ground any day. I wondered if that was what they were up to. They knew we were coming. We hadn't been quiet. What was the point when they could hear a pin drop one hundred yards away?

Mandenauer wasn't even breathing hard. I hoped I could walk a million miles at his age. I hoped I could walk at all in the morning.

He stopped, raised a hand, gestured for silence. The sound of chanting rose toward the blue moon.

I peered through the trees, which wasn't easy. The forest was thick, the trail we were on a deer trail and very narrow. But several hundred feet ahead I saw the flicker of a flame.

Mandenauer fixed me with a serious stare from his eerie blue eyes and patted his rifle, then he pointed toward the flames. With his finger and thumb he made a motion. I nodded.

Bang, bang, bang. They would all be dead.

His pace picked up. We were nearly there.

The trees rustled with a summer breeze, and I saw the clearing, recognized it instantly. They'd led us to their lair at the cave. I should have known.

Mandenauer didn't hesitate. He braced his back against a tree and started shooting.

I followed his lead, finding a nearby tree with a decent view. The view was what screwed me. I'd have been all right if there'd only been wolves. But there weren't.

The sight of several naked people—men, women, white and Indian—made me hesitate. The hesitation got me knocked over the head with something really hard.

I fell on my face. A gun was pressed to my head.

Man, I hated when that happened.

"We've been waiting for you."

The voice made me blink. I tried to turn so I could see with my own eyes what my brain refused to accept. But the poking of the gun barrel at the base of my neck stopped me.

A groan from Mandenauer's direction, and the cessation of the shots, told me he was in the same predicament. Too bad we hadn't climbed a tree this time. Of course there were no handy tree stands around—no doubt one of the reasons this place was theirs.

My weapons and ammo disappeared. The pressure of the gun lessened, and I raised myself to my knees. My head hurt like a son of a bitch. Thankfully I didn't have to lift it very far to have a confirmation on that voice.

Perfectly manicured toes peaked out of obscenely high-heeled sandals right beneath my nose.

High heels in the forest. What a moron. But then, look who I was dealing with.

"Get up," Cherry demanded, tapping me again with the barrel of the gun.

My breath hissed in as a shaft of pain went through my head. But I got up before she could smack me a third time. I glanced toward Mandenauer, but he was already gone. My eyes met Cherry's and she smirked. "Not so smart now, are you?"

"Guess not. I never would have believed you'd let yourself get furry. Doesn't that ruin your makeup?"

"You'd be surprised." She motioned toward the clearing with the gun.

Cherry was the culprit? I had a hard time with that. She didn't have the brains, and I couldn't imagine Clyde taking orders from her.

Mandenauer sat in the center of a snarling, snapping circle of wolves. The ones he'd shot smoldered, the scent of burning flesh reminding me of a tailgate party at Lambeau Field. BBQ was always on the menu.

The chanting had continued right through our altercation. I didn't recognize either of the men or the woman at the bonfire. I did, however, recognize the totem hanging over the flames.

The only word I understood was *Matchi-auwishuk*. I figured they were calling on the Evil Ones to raise the wolf god.

Cherry shoved me across the clearing with several nicely placed jabs to the small of my back with her pistol.

"Sit." She kicked the back of my knees and I hit the ground. She certainly was a nasty little thing, but I'd figured that out a long time ago.

"Now what?" I asked.

"Now we wait for—" One of the wolves snarled and she bit her lip. "You'll see."

I frowned. "You aren't going to become the wolf god?"

Her eyes widened. "Me? Hardly."

Sheesh, how many surprises did I have in store for me tonight? At least a few more.

"Why did you let Tina bite Mel?"

Surprise flickered in her eyes for a moment before they started to water. "I wanted him to be like me, but I couldn't do it. He would have been, too, but you killed him!"

The gun wobbled alarmingly. Why had I felt the need to chat?

"I thought I was helping."

"You thought!"

"Didn't you know better?"

"I thought once he was bitten it wouldn't matter. And everyone was so damn determined that he have the shot. I got confused." Her mouth trembled, but she tightened it and gave me a glare. "You'll get yours soon enough."

"I will?"

She smiled. The expression did not bode well for me. "You know how to make a wolf god, bitch?"

"Kind of."

"Blood. Yours. Soon." She licked her lips. My stomach rolled—from the headache or the discussion of my blood I wasn't sure, maybe both.

I took a few deep breaths, stared at the ground awhile and not the gun. I had just started to feel better when Cherry whispered, "They come."

I lifted my head too fast; the world spun. I had to swallow back bile. I heard footsteps, more than one person, perhaps two.

The brush parted and Will stumbled into the clearing. My heart gave a hard, painful thump. Confusion clouded my mind. He wasn't a werewolf, so . . . why me?

I saw the lump on his forehead, new blood on his clean shirt, the way his hands were bound.

He had not come willingly.

The brush rustled once more, and I turned my gaze toward the new arrival. The wind kicked up and seemed to whisper: *The blood of one who loves you.*

I'd wondered, *Why me?* Now I knew.

Zelda Hupmen stepped out of the forest.

Chapter 40

"Quit starin' at me like you're brain-dead, girl. Don't tell me you didn't imagine I was the one."

I hadn't. Not for a minute. Not once had I suspected my best and only friend of being a werewolf.

But now . . . so many things made sense.

She smoked like a chimney, drank like a fish, Lord knows how old she was—yet she had the nose and ears of a . . . wolf.

Most important, she ran this town—or near enough. She received all the information before anyone else. She could control what the police learned, where they went.

Having the sheriff as her compatriot was brilliant. Between the two of them it was little wonder they'd been able to get this far.

"I should have known," I muttered. "If Clyde wasn't the leader, it had to be you."

"How you figure?"

"Because no one told Clyde what to do."

"Except for me."

"Bingo."

The Indians continued to chant; they seemed to be in a trance. I glanced at Will and he took one step in my direction. A wolf lunged for his crotch. He jumped back and the animal's teeth snapped shut centimeters away from his jewels.

"Ah, ah, ah, Horace," Zee admonished. "I need him for a little while. You can eat him later."

The wolf sat in front of Will and stared at him as if he were a lamb chop.

"You know why you're here?" she asked him.

"I'm a bit fuzzy on the details since my book has a page missing."

She smiled. "Clever of me, hmm?"

"You took the page?" I blurted.

Zee nodded. "I broke into his office looking for the totem, but I found the book. I didn't want to steal it, too obvious, so I tore out the end of the ceremony."

"You didn't think he might order another one?" I asked.

"Of course. That's why I had Horace here keep an eye on pretty boy's mail. Any packages he was to bring to me, which he did."

I glanced at Horace and realized he was the mailman. He was a little hard to recognize all furry like that. Did Zee have a werewolf planted in every walk of our lives? It appeared so.

"What was on the page you tore out?" I asked.

"The part that matters the most. What happens tonight."

"Which is?"

"I become invincible."

Mandenauer, who'd been unnaturally silent until now, snorted. Zee turned in his direction. A snap of her fingers and the wolves parted. She crossed the distance between them. "You have something to say, Herr Mandenauer?"

"No one is invincible. I have learned that much in all my years on the hunt."

"You will learn something new tonight. The wolf god

cannot be destroyed. I will live forever and I will rule everyone."

"Why?" I asked.

I couldn't think of anything I'd less like to do than rule the world. What a shitty job.

Zee spun toward me, and the wolves encircled Mandenauer once more. Anger brightened her eyes. "Because once I was powerless and Mengele made me a monster."

"Mengele?" I remembered what Mandenauer had told me about the Nazi. "You were one of his experiments?"

"Yes."

"But you haven't got an accent," I blurted.

Zee's penciled-on eyebrows lifted. "That's all you can say?"

I was in shock. I knew that much. But I'd never met a native-born German who could lose the accent.

She waved her hand. "I had plenty of time to practice my English. That was the least of my worries."

I glanced at Will. He made a swirling motion with his finger. Horace followed the movement as if Will's hand were a prepackaged doggy treat.

I got the message. Keep her talking. Why not? I didn't want to get to the part where she needed my blood.

"What were your worries?"

She gave me an incredulous snort. "Look at me. Mengele couldn't have infected me with his crap when I was twenty and beautiful? No, he had to do it when I was eighty and ugly."

I blinked. "You were eighty in the nineteen-forties?"

"Werewolves don't die, Jessie. Unless you shoot them with silver."

"I can take care of that for you!" Mandenauer called. "If you just return my gun!"

"I could have killed myself if I wanted to die. If I do,

that pig wins. I wanted a cure. I spent decades searching for one. I traveled the globe, investigated every werewolf legend, tried lotions and potions and incantations until I was so damn tired."

"And then?"

"Then I came to Wisconsin, and I found something much better than a cure." She smiled. "Ever hear 'if you can't beat 'em, join 'em'? I much prefer 'if you can't be cured, then become.' "

"I'm a bit confused as to how you get to rule the world by becoming a wolf god."

"It's not all that hard. If my army spreads, bit by bit, country by country, soon everyone is a werewolf."

Aha!

"And you are their god."

"Works out quite nicely, doesn't it?"

Abruptly Zee crossed to the fire, grabbed a machete that had been heating at the edge of the flames. She beckoned to Will and to me.

"Nuh-uh," I said at the same time Will muttered, "No, thanks."

Zee gave an impatient sigh. "Jessie, I need your blood, but it really doesn't matter to me if I get it after you're dead."

"I thought you were my friend."

"I was. I am. I will be again if you help me. In fact . . ." Her once dear face took on a feral yet speculative gleam. "You could join me. The world isn't going to be fit for just plain folks. Let me give you a little nip—after, of course." She wiggled the huge knife. "Then we can be together forever."

"As appealing as that sounds, I'll have to pass."

"Sorry, you don't get to decide. Now get over here, and your little friend, too."

"What do you need Will for? If I come, you can let him go."

"Jessie." Will sounded exasperated.

Zee ignored him. "You haven't been listening, girl, and that's not like you. I need wolf clan boy for the ceremony."

A cold chill wafted over me. "What are you going to do?"

Horrible images danced through my head. Human sacrifice. Sadomasochistic sex. And those were just the ones I knew the names for.

"He has to draw the blood."

My mouth fell open. "That's it?"

Zee's lips twitched. "What did you think? That I'd screw him here in front of you and everyone? You did say he was good in bed, girl, but I'm too old for that shit."

My cheeks heated. How I could be embarrassed at a time like this I'll never understand.

"Time's a-wastin'. Don't make me send them to get you. I promise you won't like it."

Two of the wolves growled, the fur along their backs lifting. Zee was no doubt right. I wouldn't like it. But I'd like being a werewolf even less.

Will cleared his throat. I looked at him. He looked toward Zee. I frowned and followed his gaze.

The guns were in a pile near the edge of the forest, nearly out of sight. Zee didn't seem to know they were there. Goody.

Will and I joined Zee near the fire. She didn't waste any time. As the Indians continued to chant, then throw a little magic dirt into the fire, the flames turned from orange, to crimson, to neon blue—she put the machete into Will's hand. Holding on to his wrist, she grabbed mine.

Will and I both struggled, but it was no use. Zee had the strength of a werewolf, not a little old lady. One quick slice across my forearm and it was over.

Or maybe not. She dragged both of us nearer the fire, held my arm over the flames, squeezed the cut until a stream of red bathed the totem and dripped into the fire.

Whoosh.

The flames shot skyward. I shrieked and fell back, hitting the ground hard enough to make my teeth rattle. The machete clattered in one direction, Will in the other. But my gaze was riveted on Zee.

The moon shone in a bright silver stream through the trees, hitting her and her alone. The light bathed her face, turning her skin an ethereal white as if she glowed from within.

Zee plucked the totem from the fire, tossed the icon around her neck. The eyes of the stone wolf flared flame red. My blood stained her uniform shirt. It didn't matter. The shirt ripped open as she changed.

The Indians' chanting grew louder. The wolves began to howl. Mandenauer shouted something, but I couldn't hear him, and I couldn't take my eyes from Zee.

The change was unlike anything I'd seen before. She didn't become a wolf like Clyde—not completely. Instead, she remained upright, bipedal. White fur sprouted from her pores. Her feet became paws, but her hands stayed the same, as ears appeared on top of her head. Whiskers sprang from her lip; her nose and her mouth didn't change.

I blinked and she was a woman-beast.

As if a switch had been thrown in the sky, the silver light of the moon went under a cloud. The Indians stopped chanting. The wolves went silent. Zee turned to me.

Ugh, that just wasn't right.

Werewolves had human eyes. But Zee's eyes had gone wolf. With fur all over her face, and the canines she revealed when she smiled, the effect was pretty repulsive. That wasn't even taking into account the body of a human, covered with fur. She twirled for me, as if showing off a new dress.

"Uh, nice tail," I managed.

"Thanks."

Her voice was different—gravelly, more a growl than a smoker's grumble.

She didn't resemble the wolf god in the drawing, but I doubted the artist had ever seen one, either.

"Walking upright is good," Zee murmured. "And talking." She wiggled her fingers. "Opposable thumbs will come in handy."

"I bet."

There was a flash of movement behind her and a sudden snarl from one of the wolves. Zee turned, and Will plunged the machete into her chest.

All I could do was blink, shocked. Zee stared down at the hilt of the knife; then she lifted her gaze to Will. "You have got to be kidding me with this."

She grasped the machete and yanked it out, then tossed the thing into the bushes. A sickening slurping, sucking sound came from her chest. As I watched, the wound closed before it even had time to bleed.

"Told you they'd come in handy." She wiggled her thumbs. Then she backhanded Will so hard he flew into the forest in the wake of the knife.

I didn't realize I'd jumped to my feet and taken several steps after him until Zee grabbed me.

"Not so fast." She leaned closer. "How about a little nibble?"

I backed up; she let me go. The guns were still behind her. I wasn't going to get to them anytime soon. Will

was unconscious, maybe dead. Mandenauer was still surrounded by wolves, if they hadn't eaten him already.

We were, to put it in the usual vernacular, screwed.

"Join me, Jessie. I'll rule; you can be my right-hand
woman. We'll have so much fun."

"All I have to do is get furry."

"It's not so bad. You might even grow to like it." She
waved her hand at the werewolf army. "Most of them
do. Embrace your inner wolf, girl. Or die."

A movement from the forest caught my attention. I
cast my eyes toward the ground. "Let me think a minute."

"A minute, starting now."

I made a great show of rubbing my head. It still hurt,
but what I really wanted to do was see behind Zee without her following my gaze.

Will hovered in the sparse tree line at the edge of the
forest. Though his lip was bloody, his cheek already
swollen, he didn't hesitate. He grabbed my pistol from
the pile. Unfortunately, his hands were still bound and
he fumbled, unable to lift the thing or fire it.

His dismayed gaze met mine and I held out my hand.
He tossed me the pistol just as I kicked Zee in the chest.
Her wound might have healed, but from the way she
howled it still hurt like a bitch.

The gun connected with my palm as she gained her
feet. Would silver bullets work on the wolf god? Only
one way to find out. I shot her as she whispered my
name.

After the incident with the machete, I half-expected
Zee to laugh and kick my ass. Instead, flames shot from
the wound, so bright I had to shield my eyes. The wolves
howled mournfully.

When I lowered my hands, a great white wolf lay at
my feet. She was beautiful and she was dead.

Chapter 41

I sat next to Zee for quite awhile. No one bothered me. She'd been my best friend. My only friend. And I had loved her.

I didn't trust many people, but she had been one of them. Look where that had gotten me.

"Jessie?"

I glanced up. Mandenauer and Will hovered over me. There wasn't a wolf in sight.

"I've called my team," Mandenauer said. "They'll be here within the hour."

"Your team?"

"We have to do something about this, yes?" He indicated the empty clearing.

"What's *this*?"

He sighed. "Jessie, the wolves ran off when Zelda died."

"Won't they be cured now that she's dead?"

"There is no cure but the silver."

"Oh." I saw what he was getting at. "How are you going to figure out who's a werewolf?"

"A few of them I know. Miss Cherry, for instance. Karen Larson."

I shook my head. "I saw Karen get her brains blown out."

"With lead. She walked out of that morgue, and her principal, too."

"Clyde shot her," I insisted.

"Exactly. He knew better than to shoot one of his own with silver."

The conspiracies just kept on coming.

Mandenauer leaned over and removed the totem from Zee's neck. He held the thing aloft. The icon no longer glowed with evil, otherworldly light. It was a black stone, nothing more.

"Elise will want to study this." He pocketed the totem. Picking up Zee's torn trousers, he glanced at Will. "Take Jessie home."

"No, wait. I'm okay." I shoved away Will's helping hand. "I don't understand. Why did she die? She said she was invincible."

"That is what they all say, but I have never found it to be true."

Mandenauer withdrew a creased sheet of paper from Zee's pocket. His eyes moved back and forth rapidly as he read it. Then he lifted his head and held the paper out to me.

I crossed the short distance and took the missing page from Will's book of ceremonies. Quickly I scanned the contents. There was nothing there I didn't already know, except for one last thing.

"As the blood of the one who loves gives life to the wolf god, only by that person's hand can the god be destroyed."

I let the paper flutter to the ground. "She died because I shot her."

"Yes."

I wasn't sure how I felt about that.

"Go home, Jessie. Sleep. We will talk tomorrow."

"Won't you be halfway across Canada chasing wolves by then?"

"Not yet." He nodded to Will. This time when Cadotte put his arm around me I let him.

I awoke to the sunshine and my own bed. I didn't remember how I'd gotten there. Will's car had been nearby; Zee had made him drive. I'd climbed into the passenger seat, and I must have fallen asleep or passed out, because the last thing I did remember was driving through the darkened forest in the direction of the highway.

I was alone and wearing nothing but my underwear. Not only had Cadotte carried me upstairs; he'd undressed me. Again.

I took a shower, made some coffee. He'd left the note in the kitchen.

If you ever need me, you know where to find me.
                                                      Will.

What was that supposed to mean?

My mind tumbled back to last night. He'd been angry and hurt. I'd been a little preoccupied since. No time to discuss that anger.

What did he want from me? Could I give him what he needed?

I'd managed to *use* the L-word, but I didn't know if I was capable of actually *loving* someone.

Will still scared me more than the werewolves had. With him I had no control over myself. I gave him everything; I held nothing back. I wasn't sure if I liked that in me.

The doorbell rang. I didn't realize how hopeful I'd been until the sight of Mandenauer in the hallway made me sigh with disappointment.

"Come on in." I got him coffee. We sat at the kitchen table. "Any news?"

"We found a few."

I opened my mouth, then shut it again. I didn't want to know the details. At least not right now.

"The rest have scattered. My *Jäger-Suchers* will disperse. We will hunt them down."

"I'm sorry." I rubbed at the ache in my chest, the one that bore Zee's name and probably always would. "I froze last night. You could have gotten them all and none of this would be necessary."

"You think this is your fault?" He appeared genuinely surprised as he shook his head. "No. The fault is mine. I was more careless than usual. My age, perhaps. A certain arrogance." He sighed. "Which is why I am here this morning. I wish for you to become one of us."

"A *Jäger-Sucher*?"

"Yes. I must cut back on my field time. Not only because I appear to have lost my edge." His shoulders slumped. "But there is so much more administrative work to do now."

"Now?"

"The werewolf army Zelda created has increased the wolves a hundredfold. They will spread, as will the virus within them."

Hell. I hadn't thought of that. Mandenauer had been hunting and searching since WW II, and now there were more wolves instead of less. No wonder he was depressed.

"I have begun your training. With a little more work, you could do us proud. You would enjoy being a hunter-searcher. We make up our own rules as we go along."

I'd always liked rules, but in the last week and a half all I'd done was break them. Could I ever go back to the way things had been? Obviously Mandenauer didn't think so.

I got up and walked to the window. The sun was hot and strong. I couldn't believe how bright and cheery the world appeared. How could that be after all that had happened in Miniwa?

"Does everyone in town know what went on here?"

"Hardly."

I turned. "How can we explain Zee and Clyde being gone—just like that?"

"I have an entire division that deals with explaining disappearances. You need not trouble yourself over it."

I turned back to the sunshine. A secret society sanctioned by the government. Disappearances explained away by covert operatives. People who turned furry beneath the light of the moon. Little old ladies who wanted to be gods. And a whole host of other things I had yet to discover.

I had never liked woo-woo. If there was another world out there not rooted in a reality I understood, then the safe, rational universe I cherished crumbled. I liked things to make sense, because so little did. But refusing to believe in the unbelievable didn't make it disappear. Instead it only got stronger.

I didn't think I could stay here and continue to pretend Miniwa was safe. I couldn't write traffic tickets and break up bar fights when out there werewolves roamed free.

A flash at the edge of the woods caught my attention. Something white bobbing along, coming closer and closer. I slid the glass door open and stepped outside, but the movement was gone.

"It's Cadotte," Mandenauer said from right behind me.

Since I'd been thinking, hoping, the same thing, the

ache in my chest lightened as I leaned over the railing.

"If you decide to be a *Jäger-Sucher* you cannot have such an attachment."

It took me a moment to realize he hadn't been referring to the white flash in the woods but to Cadotte in general.

"*Jäger-Suchers* must hunt supernatural evil, things that kill horribly. We cannot allow anyone to be used against us. Or hurt because of us. Do you understand what I'm saying?"

I understood. I had to choose. Will or the job. In the past it would have been an easy decision. Today, not so much.

As strongly as I felt about chasing werewolves, I felt more strongly about Will. I didn't want to go back to the life I'd lived before he'd come into it. I didn't think that I could. I needed him to be whole. The woman I'd become once I knew William Cadotte was the woman I wanted to be.

I turned away from the woods. "Thanks for the offer, but I'll have to chose Cadotte."

He blinked. "You what?"

"You heard me."

"But . . . but, Jessie. The world is being overrun."

"And I'm real sorry about that. But I love him. I never thought I'd feel that way about someone or have someone feel the same about me. I'm not giving that up. Not even to save the world."

He scowled and heaved a long, aggrieved sigh. "It has been nice working with you. You would have made a stellar addition to my team."

He shook my hand, bowed over it with stiff formality, managed to refrain from clicking his heels; then with a final nod, Edward Mandenauer left the building.

"You tossed the world to the wolves for me?"

I shrieked and spun around. Cadotte stood on my balcony. "I hate it when you do that!"

"I should make more noise when I sneak up on you?"

"Damn straight," I grumbled, rubbing at my sternum, where my heart thudded and raced.

His ear had a Band-Aid; his arm was wrapped in gauze. One eye was nearly swollen shut. He'd never looked better to me.

Snaking his good arm around my waist, he yanked me against his body and kissed me—for a good long while.

When he lifted his head, my eyes were heavy, but my heart still raced. He nuzzled my temple, kissed my hair. "No one ever gave up anything for me before."

"Yeah? Well, don't let it go to your head, Slick."

"I doubt you'll let me."

We stood there in each other's arms. I held on tight. I didn't want to let him go—ever. "What are you doing here? Your note said I was supposed to come to you."

"I was afraid you wouldn't."

"You were wrong."

Will took my hand and led me into the apartment. I figured we'd head straight for the bedroom, but he surprised me by sitting on the couch and pulling me into his lap. "Tell me," he whispered.

I almost asked, "What?" except I knew. "I need you, Will. But—"

"No buts. Just let me wallow in that awhile, hmm?"

I shook my head. If we were going to do this, and it appeared as if we were, I wasn't going to start with a lie. He had to know.

"I've never loved anyone before," I admitted. "I'm not sure I know how."

"Me, neither. We can learn together." He was annoyingly cheerful. I didn't think he was taking my doubts very seriously.

"I don't know if I can be what you need."

"You already are."

My belly went all warm and mushy. God, he was good at this. "I—"

Will put his hand over my mouth and the doubts lay on my tongue unvoiced. "Jessie, I love you. I need you. I *chose* you. Do you feel the same way?"

I looked into my heart, my head, my past, then I looked at him, and I saw my future. I kissed his palm, and his hand fell away from my mouth. "Yes," I whispered.

"Then that's all I need."

Later, much later, as we lay in my bed and watched the sun dance on the ceiling, my phone rang. I ignored it, letting the machine pick up. Mandenauer's voice filled the room.

"Okay, Jessie, you can have Cadotte and the job. I suspect he can take care of himself anyway. In fact, ask him if he'd be interested in working with my research division. Then report to my cabin tomorrow morning."

The phone clicked off. I cuddled closer to Will's side. "Well?" I asked. "What do you think?"

"I *am* soon to be unemployed."

I twisted my head so I could see his face. "Why?"

"Summer school doesn't last forever."

"Interested in Mandenauer's offer?" I held my breath. I wanted that job, but I wanted Will more.

"Sure. What the hell?"

I couldn't believe my luck. I got to save the world and get the guy. Hey, not every girl finds a love that comes along once in a blue moon.

Read on for an excerpt from
Lori Handeland's

Hunter's Moon

Now available from St. Martin's Paperbacks!

Chapter 1

They say the hunter's moon was once called the blood moon, and I know why. A full moon shining through a crisp autumn night turns blood from crimson to black.

I much prefer its shade beneath the moon to that shade beneath the stark electric lights. But I digress.

I am a hunter. A *Jäger-Sucher* to those in the know—of which there are a select few. I hunt monsters, and in case you're thinking that's a euphemism for today's serial killers, it's not. When I say monster, I mean hell unleashed, tooth and claw, supernatural magic on the loose. The kind of thing that will give you nightmares forever. Just like me.

My specialty is werewolves. I must have killed a thousand and I'm only twenty-four. Sadly, my job security has never been in jeopardy. A fact I learned all too well when my boss, Edward Mandenauer, called me early one October morning.

"Leigh, I need you here."

"Where is here?" I mumbled.

I was not a bright and shiny morning person. This might have come from living most of my life in the dark. Werewolves emerged at night, beneath the moon. They were funny that way.

"I am in Crow Valley, Wisconsin."

"Never heard of it."

"Which gives you much in common with the rest of the world."

I sat up, awake, alert, senses humming. That had sounded suspiciously like dry humor. Edward didn't *do* humor.

"Who is this?" I demanded.

"Leigh." His long suffering sigh was as much a part of him as his heavy German accent. "What is the matter with you this morning?"

"It's morning. Isn't that enough?"

I did not greet each day with joy. My life was dedicated to one thing—ridding the earth of werewolves. Only then could I forget what had happened, perhaps forgive myself for living when everyone I'd ever loved had died.

"*Liebchen*," Mandenauer murmured. "What will I do with you?"

Edward had saved me on that long ago day filled with blood and death and despair. He had taken me in, taught me things, then set me free to use them. I was his most dedicated agent, and only Edward and I knew why.

"I'm all right," I reassured him.

I wasn't and probably never would be. But I'd accepted that. I'd moved on. Kind of.

"Of course you are," he soothed.

Neither one of us was fooled by my lie or his acceptance of it. Which was how we both kept ourselves focused on what was important. Killing them all.

"The town is in the northern part of the state," he continued. "You will have to fly to Minneapolis, rent a car, go . . . east, I think."

"I am not coming to Shit Heel, Wisconsin, Edward."

"Crow Valley."

"Whatever. I'm not done here."

I'd been working in Canada at Mandenauer's request. A few months back, hell had broken loose in a little burg called Miniwa. Something about a blue moon, a wolf god, I hadn't gotten the details. I didn't care. All I knew was that there were werewolves running north, plenty of them.

But as much as I might like to, I couldn't just blast every wolf I saw with silver. There were laws about such things, even in Canada.

The *Jäger-Suchers* were a secret branch of the government. We liked to envision ourselves as the Special Forces of monster hunting. Think *The X-Files* versus *Grimms' Fairy Tales* on steroids.

At any rate, we were supposed to work on the sly. A pile of dead wolves—threatened at the least, endangered yet in some places—would cause too many questions.

The *Jäger-Sucher* society had enough problems accounting for the disappearances of the people who had once been werewolves. Sad, but true—it was easier to explain missing humans than dead animals, but such was the way of the modern world.

My job, should I choose to accept it—and I had, long ago—was to catch the werewolves in the act. Of changing. Then I was well within my rights to put a silver bullet in their brains.

Bureaucracy at its finest.

Catching them wasn't as hard to do as you might think. Most werewolves ran in packs, just like real wolves. When they went to the forest to change, they often had a lair where they left their clothes, purses, car keys. Going from bipedal to quadrapedal had certain disadvantages, namely no pockets.

Once I found that lair . . . well, does the phrase, "like

shooting ducks in a pond," mean anything to you? It
was one of my favorites.

"You will never be done there." Edward's voice
pulled me from my thoughts. "Right now you are needed
here."

"Why?"

"The usual reason."

"You've got werewolves. Shoot them yourself."

"I need you to train a new *Jäger-Sucher*."

Since when? Edward had always done the training
and I . . .

"I work alone."

"It is time for that to change."

"No."

I was not a people person. Didn't want to be. I enjoyed being by myself. That way no one around me
could get killed—again.

"I am not asking you, Leigh, I am telling you. Be
here by tomorrow, or find another job."

He hung up.

Sitting on the edge of the bed in my underwear, I
held the phone against my ear until the line started to
buzz, then I replaced it in the cradle and stared into space
a while longer.

I couldn't believe this. I wasn't a teacher; I was a
killer. What right did Edward have to order me around?

All the right in the world. He was my boss, my men-
tor, the closest thing to a friend that I allowed myself.
Which meant he should know better than to ask me to
do something I'd given up along with my life.

I *had* been a teacher, once upon a time.

I flinched as the sound of children's voices lifted in
song drifted through my head. Miss Leigh Tyler, kindergarten teacher, was as dead as the man I'd once
planned to marry. And if she sometimes skipped through

my dreams, well what was I supposed to do, shoot her?

Though that might be my usual method for solving problems, it didn't work too well on the happy-go-lucky dream-Leigh. More's the pity.

I dragged myself off the bed and into the shower, then packed my things and headed for the airport.

No one in Elk Snout—or wherever the hell it was I'd been hunting—would notice I was gone. As I did in every area I visited, I'd rented an isolated cabin, telling anyone who asked, and it was shocking how few people did, that I was with the Department of Natural Resources, studying a new strain of rabies in the wolf population.

This excuse conveniently explained away my odd hours, my penchant for walking with a gun or three, as well as my cranky nature. The hunting and fishing police were not well-liked by the common folk. Which got me left alone—my favorite thing to be.

I arrived at the airport, where I was informed only one plane a day flew to Minneapolis. Luckily that single flight was scheduled late in the afternoon and there were plenty of seats.

I had ID from the J-S society, which established me as a warden and allowed me to ship my weapons—a standard issue 12-gauge Remington shotgun, my personal hunting rifle, and a Glock 40-caliber semiautomatic, also standard DNR issue. An hour after touching down, I hit the road to Crow Valley.

I didn't bother to call ahead and announce my arrival. Mandenauer had known all along that I would come. No matter what he asked of me, I would agree. Not because I respected him, though I did, more than anyone I'd ever known, but because he let me do what I had to do. Kill the animals, the monsters, the werewolves.

It was the only thing I had left to live for.

Chapter 2

By the time I reached the little town in the north woods, the moon was rising. Not that I could see more than a quarter.

But the orb was out there—waiting, breathing, growing. I knew it, and the werewolves knew it. Just because the sky wasn't glowing with a silver sheen didn't mean the monsters weren't changing and running and killing.

As I slowed my rental car, which I swear was the same four-cylinder piece of shit I'd turned in at the airport in Canada, a flicker of movement from an alleyway caught my attention. I coasted to a stop at the curb and got out.

The place had a deserted air that all small towns get after the supper hour. However, I wasn't sure if this was the usual "rolling up the sidewalks" tradition or if the populace had started to stay indoors after dark because of the wolves.

Edward had to have a more serious motive than the common werewolf outbreak for bringing me here. Even if I was training a new guy, there had to be a reason to do it in Shit Heel. I mean Crow Valley.

The shuffle of a shoe against concrete drifted to me from the alleyway.

"Better safe than sorry," I murmured, and reached into the car for my sidearm.

The rifle or the shotgun would have been better, but, as much as I might have liked to, I couldn't waltz along Main Street carrying a firearm as long as my leg. I might have had the necessary ID, but I wasn't in uniform. Someone would stop me, then there'd be questions, answers. I didn't have time. Nevertheless, if there was a wolf in that alley, he'd be close enough to pop with my Glock.

I crept to the opening and glanced down the alley. The single streetlight threw the silhouette of a man against the wall for just an instant before he disappeared at the far side of the building.

I'd have let it go, except for the howl that rose toward the waiting night. The hair on the back of my neck prickled and I shook my head. Once upon a time the thick braid that had reached to my waist would have waggled and rubbed away the itch. But I'd hacked off my hair long ago and now sported a near-military crew cut. Life was so much easier that way.

As I was slinking along the front of the structure in the general direction of the man I'd observed, a chorus of answering howls rose from the forest that surrounded the town.

I glanced around the corner just as a wolf padded toward the trees. I let out a sigh of relief. I wouldn't have to wait around. Only an amateur shot a werewolf mid-change. Then you were left with a half-man, half-wolf, which was a little hard to explain. Believe me. I've tried.

Though I always burned the body, I never knew who'd wander across my path while the bonfire was blazing. Always better to wait until it was a complete wolf to do the deed.

But dallying could be hazardous to the health. Lucky me, I'd come across a fast changer—either an over-achiever or a very old werewolf. This one wasn't as large as the usual male, but definitely a wolf and not a dog. Even huge dogs have smaller heads than wolves, one of the differences between *Canis familiaris* and *Canis lupus*.

The wolf loped toward the woods as the howls faded into the night. I let him get as far as the trees before I followed. The wind was in my favor, blowing across my face as I scuttled across the street. Still, wolves had ex-cellent hearing, werewolves even better, so I didn't want to get too close, too fast.

I didn't want to get too far behind either. I took three steps at a half-run and entered the cooler, darker arena of the forest.

Immediately, the lights from Crow Valley became muted; the air cooled. I'd been born in Kansas, land of very few trees, and to this day, whenever I entered the woodlands of the great white north, I got spooked.

The evergreens were gargantuan, as ancient as some of the things I hunted, and so thick it was hard to nav-igate through them. Which was probably why a majority of the wolves, as well as most of the werewolves, grav-itated north.

My eyes adjusted to the gloom quickly, and I hurried after the gray bushy tail ahead, my gun ready. I'd done this enough times to know better than to put my weapon away. I wasn't Wyatt Earp, and I didn't plan to draw down on a werewolf. They were quicker than spit and twice as nasty.

A sound to the left made me freeze and spin that way. I held my breath, listened, looked. Heard nothing but the wind and saw even less. I'd stopped in a small clearing—the shadowy sheen of the moon lightened the area just a bit.

I turned back, hurried forward, blinked. Where was that tail? Nothing lay ahead of me but trees.

"Son of a—"

A low growl was my only warning before something hit me in the back and drove my face into the dirt. My gun flew into the bushes. My heart was beating so fast I couldn't think.

Training kicked in as I grabbed the wolf by the scruff of the neck and flipped the animal over my shoulder before it could bite me. If there was one thing I'd hate more than being alive, it would be being alive and furry.

He hit the ground, yelped, twisted, and bounded to his feet. I used the few seconds I had to spring to a crouch and yank the knife from my boot. There was a reason I wore boots even in the heat of summer. Kind of hard to conceal a knife in a sneaker.

I'd yanked out tufts of gray fur when I flipped the wolf, and they fluttered in the breeze. The animal growled. Eyes, pale blue and far too human, narrowed. It was pissed, and because of that, didn't think before leaping.

The beast knocked me to the ground. As I fell, I shoved the weapon into the wolf's chest to the hilt, then twisted.

Flames burst from the wound. Silver did that to a werewolf; one of the reasons I preferred killing them from a distance.

The animal snarled in my face. I held on to the knife despite the heat, despite the blood, and as the thing died in my arms, I watched its eyes shift from human to wolf. It was an oddity I'd never get over, that change at the end.

Legend said that werewolves returned to their human

form at death, but that wasn't true. Not only did they remain wolves, but they lost their last remnant of humanity as they went straight to hell—or at least I hoped that was where they went.

When the fire was gone and the wolf stopped squirming, I shoved the body away and yanked out my knife. Then I saw something that disturbed me.

The wolf I'd killed was female.

I scanned the area, searching for the male I'd expected. I was certain the shadow I'd observed in the alley had been a man's. I'd followed the wolf that had come out on the other side. Hadn't I?

This one? Or had the male from town been following her as I had? If so, he would have attacked when she did. They couldn't help themselves. Another mystery. Why wasn't I surprised?

I retrieved the gun, cleaned off my knife in the grass, then stuck it back in my boot. I wiped my bloody hands on my jeans—they were already stained, as was my shirt, but at least the dark material of both, combined with the less than bright sky, helped disguise *what* was staining them.

My palms tingled. A quick examination proved they were sore, but not blistered, so I ignored them, following standard *Jäger-Sucher* procedure as I made a wolf bonfire to get rid of the evidence.

After sprinkling the body with a special accelerant—a new invention courtesy of the scientific division of the *Jäger-Sucher* society—I threw on a match. The flames shot past my head. Hot, strong, fiery red. Just what I needed to get my job done quickly.

Until recently, burning wolves took a long, long time. In order to remain secret and undetected, *Jäger-Suchers* needed to do their jobs and dispose of the evidence before anyone was the wiser. The new accelerant was a big help in that direction.

I thought to check in with Edward while I waited for the flames to abate. Unfortunately, I'd left my cell phone in the car. Oh well, if I woke him, it would be payback for his waking me. And I liked payback—almost as much as I liked killing things.

"Isn't that illegal?"

The voice, coming from behind me without warning, had me pulling my gun as I spun around. The man stared at my Glock without blinking.

I frowned. Most people flinched when you stuck a gun in their face. And mine was in his face. He'd gotten so close I had nearly clocked him in the nose with the barrel.

How had he snuck up on me like that?

Narrowing my eyes, I gave him the once-over. This was fairly easy since he wasn't wearing a shirt.

The veins in his arms stood out, as if he'd been lifting—reps for definition rather than weight for strength. His chest was smooth yet defined, with flat, brown nipples that only accentuated the pale perfection.

I'd never been much for beefcake. Hell, be honest, I'd never been much for men. Seeing your fiancé torn into bloody pieces in your dining room did that to a girl.

However, I found myself staring at this one, fascinated with the taut, ridged muscles at his abdomen. Even his shaggy brown hair was interesting, as were his oddly light-brown eyes, which shone almost yellow in the wavering light of the moon. I figured in the daytime they'd be plain old hazel.

His cheekbones were sharp, his face craggy. As if he hadn't been eating well or sleeping any better. And despite the pale shade of his eyes, there was a darkness to them that went deeper than the surface. Still, he was handsome in a way that went beyond pretty and stopped just short of stunning.

He had managed to pull on some black pants, though the button hung open, and his shoes must have been with his shirt. Which explained how he'd gotten so close without me hearing him.

Suspicious, I kept my Glock pointed at his left nostril. "Who are you?"

"Who are you?" he countered.

"I asked you first."

He raised a brow at my juvenile retort. He was awfully calm for a guy who had a gun staring him in the face. Maybe he didn't think I had silver bullets inside.

The thought made my hand tighten on the weapon. Was this the man I'd seen in the alley? The one I'd thought had become a wolf, then run into the woods.

"You mind?" he grabbed the barrel, shoving it out of his face, then twisting the gun from my hand in a single motion.

I tensed, expecting an attack. Instead, he handed it back to me, butt-first. I'd never seen anyone move that quickly. Anyone human, that is.

If he were a werewolf, he'd have shot me already, or attacked along with his girlfriend. I relaxed, but only a little. He was still a stranger, and Lord knows what he was up to in the woods, in the dark, without his shoes.

"Who are you?" I repeated.

"Damien Fitzgerald."

Damien? Wasn't that the name of a demon? Or at least it had been in some 1970s horror movie I'd refused to see. I'd never been much for gore, even before such unpleasantries entered my life on a daily basis.

The name Fitzgerald explained the pale skin and dark hair, even the auburn streaks placed there by the sun.

But the eyes were wrong. They should be blue as the Irish Sea.

Their hue bothered me almost as much as their soul-deep sadness, the flicker of guilt. I'd seen that expression a thousand times before.

In the mirror.

He folded his incredible arms across his smooth chest and stared down at me. He wasn't truly tall, maybe six feet if that, but I was five-four in my shoes.

I hated being short, petite, almost blonde. But I'd learned that guns were a great equalizer. It didn't matter if I weighed a hundred pounds, I could still pull a trigger. A few years of judo hadn't hurt either.

Back in my Miss Tyler days, I'd highlighted my hair, worn pink lipstick and high heels. I stifled my gagging reflex.

Look what that had gotten me. Scars both inside and out.

"What's with the dead wolf bonfire?" he asked.

I glanced at my handiwork. It was hard to tell what I'd been burning, but maybe he'd been hanging around longer than I realized. So I gave him the same song and dance I used with every civilian.

"I'm with the DNR."

He made a face, the usual reaction to the Department of Natural Resources, I'd discovered. But he didn't behave like most people did when I introduced myself—getting away as quickly as possible and never looking back. Instead he stared at me with a question in his eyes.

Finally I asked, "What?"

"Why are you burning a wolf? I thought they were endangered."

"Threatened."

His blank stare revealed he had no idea of the technicalities that surrounded the wolf population. "Threatened" meant wolves could be killed under certain circumstances by certain people. Namely me. As to the circumstances . . .

"There's an itsy-bitsy rabies problem in the wolves here," I lied.

One eyebrow shot up. "Really?"

He didn't believe me? That was new. I was a very, very good liar.

"Really."

My voice was firm. I didn't want any more questions. Especially questions I'd have a hard time answering. Like how did we know the difference between a rabid animal and a sick one?

In truth, we couldn't without testing at the Madison Health Lab. Standard DNR procedure was to contact the local Wildlife Manager, then APHIS—a federal agency that deals with nuisance animals.

Thankfully, the common man didn't know government procedure, so my lies usually worked. It helped that the word *rabies* freaked everyone out. Folks wanted the virus obliterated, preferably yesterday, and if someone with a uniform or an ID was willing to do that, they didn't ask too many questions. They just got out of my way.

Too bad Damien wasn't like everyone else. He tilted his head, and his unkempt brown hair slid across his cheek. "Rabies? How come I haven't heard about it?"

I'd fed this lie a hundred times before, and it tripped off my tongue without any thought at all.

"The news isn't for public consumption. We'd have a panic."

"Ah." He nodded. "That's why you aren't wearing your uniform."

"Right. No sense upsetting people. I'm taking care of things. So you can go back to . . . wherever it is you came from." I frowned. "Where did you come from?"

"New York."

"Just now?"

His lips twisted in what should have been a smile but wasn't. "No, originally."

Which explained the slight accent—the Bronx maybe, I wasn't sure. A Kansas girl who'd spent the last few years in the forest chasing werewolves didn't have too many opportunities to check out the accents of hot Irish men from New York City.

"Have you lived here long?" I turned away, using a hefty stick to poke up the fire.

"You never told me your name," he countered. "Do you have some kind of ID?"

I continued to stir the fire, considering what I should say. It wouldn't hurt to give him my name. I even had DNR ID in my back pocket. The resources of the *Jäger-Sucher* society were far-reaching, even downright amazing in some cases. But why was he so interested?

"What are you?" I countered. "A cop?"

"Actually, yes."

I let out a yelp and spun around. Damien Fitzgerald had disappeared as if he'd never even been.

The woman who stepped into the clearing wore a sheriff's uniform. She was both tall and voluptuous, which annoyed me on sight, and she walked with a confidence that bespoke someone who could take care of herself, even without the gun. Her dark hair had been cut short to frame an attractive, though not exactly pretty, face.

Her gaze took in the wolf pyre, then lifted to mine. "You must be the *Jäger-Sucher*."

Chapter 3

I winced and glanced around the clearing. "*Shh,*" I snapped.

Her eyebrows lifted. "Who do you think's going to hear me? The raccoons?"

"There was a man—" I frowned. "Didn't you see him?"

"No. You were talking to yourself when I got here."

"I was not. There was a man." I waved my hand. "He was wearing pants."

"Always a good choice."

"But nothing else."

"Even better. The last time I met a naked man in the forest it was the start of something big."

"He wasn't naked. Completely."

The woman shrugged. "Too bad. Where'd he go?"

"I don't know."

"You're sure there was a man?"

Was I? Yes. Definitely. I hadn't lost my mind since . . . I'd found it the last time.

"He said his name was Damien Fitzgerald. Don't you know him?"

"Can't say that I do. But then, Mandenauer and I just got here last week. From what you're telling me, he sounds like a prime candidate for the fanged and furry club."

Finally I heard what she'd said, what she'd been saying. She knew about the *Jäger-Suchers*, the werewolves, Edward. The guy I was supposed to train had just turned into a girl. "You're . . ."

"Jessie McQuade. And you must be Leigh, my trainer."

I scowled. We'd see about that. I could think of few things I'd like to do less than teach this spectacularly competent woman all my tricks.

"You *are* Leigh," she said.

I grunted.

She took that as a yes. "Mandenauer is waiting at my place. Follow me."

Without so much as a by-your-leave, she kicked apart the remnants of the fire and stomped on the cinders. Then she marched back in the direction I'd come.

My gaze scanned the clearing, but there was no sign of the half-naked man. I even hurried to the place I'd last seen him, crouching in the leaves to examine the ground for a footprint. But the earth was hard and he'd been wearing . . . hardly anything.

A wolf howled near enough to make me jump, far enough away so that I followed Jessie at a walk instead of a run. I wasn't going to let her, or them, know just how spooked I was.

Had there been a man named Damien? Probably.

Was he merely a man? Or had he been more? I might never know that for sure.

Jessie's place was an apartment located in a small complex adjacent to the sheriff's office. I parked beside the squad car and followed her up the flight of stairs to the second floor.

"Are you really a cop?" I asked. "Or is this just pretend?"

"I'm a cop."

She didn't elaborate, and irritation flared again. Jessie got to do her chosen job while she saved the world. I got to pretend I was a warden and earn the scorn of every community.

But I couldn't exactly be a werewolf hunter and a kindergarten teacher. The very thought was ludicrous.

The door sprang open before she could touch it, and a tall, emaciated silhouette spread across the hall floor.

"Edward," I murmured.

Jessie cast me a quick, surprised glance, and I realized I'd said his name aloud in a delighted voice that didn't belong to me. I couldn't afford attachments, not even to him, so I straightened my shoulders, cleared my throat, and stuck out my hand. "Good to see you, sir."

"Jeez, why don't you click your heels and salute?" Jessie muttered, pushing past him.

Edward Mandenauer was as unlikely a leader of an elite monster-hunting unit as could be imagined. Cadaverous-thin, he owned every one of his eighty-plus years. But he could still pull the trigger, and he'd killed more monsters than anyone, even me. I admired him. More than I would ever say.

"I told you to come directly to me, Leigh." Edward stepped back so I could enter the apartment.

"I'm here."

"You took a detour."

"How did you know?" I scowled. "How did *she* find me?"

"Your car was abandoned in town. Jessie ran the license plate, then tracked you into the woods."

My interest was piqued. Tracking had never been my strong suit. I wasn't patient enough. Jessie had to be very good to have found me as quickly as she had in the thickness of a forest that must be as strange to her as it was to me.

"From the look of the bonfire," Jessie tattled, "she's already started blasting away."

"That's my job," I snapped.

"This is *my* town."

"Girls, girls," Mandenauer admonished.

"Don't call me a girl," Jessie and I said at the same time.

We glanced at each other, scowled, and turned away. Mandenauer sighed. "You need to work together. There is something odd happening in Crow Valley."

That got my attention. "Odder than werewolves?"

"To be sure. Did you make note of the name of this fair city?"

Crow Valley. I hadn't thought about it. Stupid me.

For reasons unknown to science, wolves allowed crows to scavenge from their kills. Some naturalists believed that the birds flew ahead, located suitable prey, then circled back and led the wolves to it. In gratitude or perhaps as payment for services rendered, the wolves didn't chase the crows off the corpses.

Whether this was true or not was anyone's guess. But the fact remained that where there were a lot of one, there were a lot of the other. Wolves felt at home around crows. Werewolves appeared to as well.

"After the incident in Miniwa," Edward continued, "the wolves increased. Many of them came here."

"And you know this, how?"

He just gave me one of his stares. Edward knew everything.

"When the sheriff in this town left—"

"Left or was eaten?"

"Not eaten. Not this time. The odd occurrences with the wolves disturbed him. He called the authorities with his tall tales, and I was notified. I convinced him to take a leave of absence, then gave Jessie his job."

You thought there were a lot of conspiracies in the government? You wouldn't even know about the ones Edward was involved with. Any odd report—unexplained events, wolves run amok, monstrosities wandering over hill and dale—the information was forwarded to Edward, and he sent a *Jäger-Sucher* to determine what needed to be done, and then do it.

"What about Jessie's other job?" I asked.

"We had done all we could in Miniwa. The wolves ran from there. We waited, but they did not return."

"What's going on here?"

He glanced at Jessie. "Tell her what we know."

Jessie hesitated, but in the end she shrugged and flopped onto the couch, gesturing me into a chair nearby. The apartment was sparsely but adequately furnished, as if she'd only brought the essentials.

No pictures on the walls, no knick-knacks on the tables, though Jessie hardly seemed the knick-knack type. Instead, every spare surface was covered with books, papers, notebooks. She didn't seem the studious type either, but then, what did I know?

"Werewolves are being killed in Crow Valley," she began.

"Good for you."

You may have wondered how we knew the difference between a dead wolf and a dead werewolf. I'll let you in on a little secret. If you shoot them with silver, they explode. Live or dead, doesn't matter. I kind of liked putting a bullet into the dead ones. Call me sick. Everyone else does.

"They were being killed *before* we got here," Jessie continued. "From what I can tell, it started a little over two weeks ago."

I sat up straighter in my chair. A little over two weeks ago would have been the last full moon. That couldn't be good.

I glanced at Edward. "You've got no one working in Crow Valley?"

"No."

"Rogue agent?"

"Doubtful."

"Why?"

"Because the werewolves are not being killed with silver."

"Then how can they be dead?"

"There is only one other way to kill a werewolf," Edward said.

"How come I never heard of it?"

"Because it rarely happens."

"And why is that?"

"The only other way to kill a werewolf, besides the silver, is for a werewolf to kill one of its own."

"They never kill their own kind. It's against the werewolf rules of conduct."

"Apparently we have come across one who can't read."

Humor again. What was *wrong* with the man?

"Wolves and werewolves may appear the same," Jessie said, "but they're not."

"No shit," I muttered. I was already sick of Miss Know-It-All-Come-Lately.

She ignored me. Point for her.

"Though it's rare, wolves *will* kill another wolf, but werewolves won't. They'll fight, drive each other from their territory, but they won't kill. I'd say it was a remnant of their humanity shining through, but we all know that most humans aren't very humane."

How true.

"So what's going on?" I asked.

"That's what we're trying to find out."

"Why?"

She blinked. "I'm sorry."

"What difference does it make who kills them as long as they're dead?"

Jessie glanced at Edward and he took over.

"It does not matter who kills them. What matters is that there is a werewolf out there behaving unlike a werewolf. I do not like it."

"Because . . . ?"

"The last time one of them behaved oddly we met the wolf god."

"You think someone's trying to raise another wolf god?"

He shook his head. "A wolf god can only be brought forth under the blue moon. That time is past."

"Then what?"

"I do not know. But I have a very bad feeling."

I'd been around Edward long enough to know that when he had a very bad feeling, the shit was usually going to hit the fan real soon.

"What's the plan?" I asked.

"You teach Jessie all that she needs to know."

"Why?" I demanded. "You've always taught the new guys."

"I am not as young as I used to be."

"Yeah, join the club."

His lips twitched, almost as if he might laugh. Wonders never ceased these days.

"I have enlisted the help of an expert to search the pages of history. Perhaps we will find a mention of what they are up to this time before it is too late. Until then, I must go back to headquarters. Elise needs my help."

Elise was Dr. Hanover, head research scientist at the J-S Institute in Montana, and Edward's right hand. There was something else between them, too, though I'd never quite figured out what that something was. He was old enough to be her grandfather.

"You're not going to leave me alone with *her*?" I demanded.

"There are at least four hundred people in this town. You will not be alone."

"You know what?" Jessie stood and put her hands on her hips. "I don't need her help. I did just *fine* in Miniwa without any training at all."

"Yeah, I heard about that," I sneered. "Thanks to you, the werewolf population has doubled in this area, and there are fresh new recruits running all over Canada. I just spent the last three months thinning them out."

Jessie's fingers clenched into fists, and she took one step toward me before the apartment door opened.

I had only an instant to register that a man was running through the room, then he grabbed Jessie around the waist and lifted her off her feet.

I started forward, but Mandenauer's hand on my arm stopped me. Good thing, too, because the guy locked lips with Jessie, and the two of them shared the deepest, hottest, wettest kiss I'd ever witnessed outside of a pornographic movie.

I knew I should look away, but I couldn't tear my eyes from the sight. In my line of work, I didn't get a chance to see much affection. I didn't get a chance to see anything but death, and that was the way I wanted it. So why was I watching Jessie and whoever with misty, longing eyes?

He lifted his head, stared into her face, and very gently touched her cheek with his knuckle. She smiled and covered his hand with hers. It was as if Edward and I, maybe the whole world, didn't exist.

True love. Hell.

"She's going to get us killed," I muttered.